Previously published Worldwide Suspense titles by
LISSA MARIE REDMOND

THE SECRETS THEY LEFT BEHIND
A FULL COLD MOON

THE PARTING GLASS

LISSA MARIE REDMOND

W RLDWIDE

TORONTO • NEW YORK • LONDON
AMSTERDAM • PARIS • SYDNEY • HAMBURG
STOCKHOLM • ATHENS • TOKYO • MILAN
MADRID • WARSAW • BUDAPEST • AUCKLAND

W☒RLDWIDE™

Recycling programs
for this product may
not exist in your area.

ISBN-13: 978-1-335-01226-5

The Parting Glass

First published in 2021 by Severn House,
an imprint of Canongate Books Ltd.
This edition published in 2024.

Copyright © 2021 by Lissa Marie Redmond

Harlequin Enterprises ULC
22 Adelaide St. West, 41st Floor
Toronto, Ontario M5H 4E3, Canada
www.ReaderService.com

Printed in U.S.A.

THE PARTING GLASS

This one's for Dan

He had his faults!

ONE

EVEN THOUGH LAUREN RILEY knew what he was about to say, she still stiffened in expectation when Judge Mitchell read the piece of paper in front of him. 'Steven Henry Harrott, having pled guilty to the charge of murder in the second degree for the death of twelve-year-old William Munzert, I sentence you to twenty years in prison, the maximum I can sentence you to under the guidelines of 1978.' He slid his thin silver glasses off his nose and set them on the desk in front of him, leaning forward. 'Were it in my power, I would give you the maximum allowable now, life without parole. Were it in my power, I'd take back the last forty leisurely years of your life and bestow them on William Munzert and his family. While twenty years very likely is a life sentence for you, Mr Harrott, it seems hardly like justice for the suffering you've caused.'

In December of 1978 Billy Munzert rode his bike to the milk machine at the corner of his Kaisertown street with a fistful of quarters and never came back.

Buffalo Police Cold Case detective Lauren Riley liked Judge Mitchell, who she knew to be tough but fair. In New York State, defendants in cold cases had to be sentenced by the guidelines in place at the time of the crime. In 1978, the maximum sentence for second degree murder was twenty years. Lauren's eyes cut over to Billy's family—his mom and dad surrounded by their surviving children and grand-children. They were worn out, broken and devastated. Even if the judge could have sentenced Harrott to life without parole, it wouldn't have made much of a difference. Harrott gave them all a life sentence the day he abducted their son.

Five months earlier Lauren had been investigating a case in Iceland, of all places, when her partner Shane Reese called to tell her that the national DNA databank had come back with a hit. Steven Harrott's DNA had been matched to a sample taken from Billy Munzert's bike, recovered miles away from where he was last seen, caught in some branches on the bank of the Buffalo River. After Lauren came home, the two of them worked the case nonstop, culminating in a three-hour videotaped confession in which Harrott told them where to find Billy's remains.

Lauren had gone home that night and cried herself to sleep. Then she'd gotten up the next morning and super-vised the excavation to recover Billy's skeleton, biting the inside of her cheek the entire time, filling her mouth with blood. For her, physical pain was easier to deal with than the mental kind.

Watching what was left of that small body being un-earthed was the stuff of nightmares.

Today Steven Harrott sat in the front of the courtroom, staring straight ahead with a strange smirk on his face. Lauren dug her nails into her palms.

His thick frame was stuffed into an ill-fitting dark blue suit, probably supplied to him by his court-appointed at-torney. He was in his seventies, but Lauren had seen pic-tures of him from around the time of Billy's disappearance. He'd been tall and lean with thick black hair and a match-ing mustache. He'd driven a muscle car, the kind a twelve-year-old boy on a bike would be impressed by. Now he was almost totally bald with white wisps combed over the top of his head. A short, rough beard covered his face, like he hadn't shaved in a week. She could feel the bile start to rise in her throat. Her leg started to bob up and down until Reese pressed his hand on it, holding it in place.

'Good job, partner,' he whispered, pulling his hand away. 'You got him.'

'We got him,' she whispered back as the judge rattled off the standard speech about appeals.

Mrs Munzert turned toward them, tears streaming down her face while her husband sobbed in his oldest daughter's arms. She didn't smile, she didn't speak, but the profound look of gratitude threatened to bring Lauren to tears. Lauren had two daughters of her own and could barely imagine what it would be like to have one of them ripped away from her forever. And then have to face the monster who did it and listen to his hollow words of remorse read from a piece of yellow legal paper, probably written by his lawyer, saying how sorry he was, how he was a different person. Even though he'd victimized others over the years. It was sickening.

When Mrs Munzert looked away, Lauren tugged Reese's sleeve. 'Let's get out of here.' She gave an appreciative nod to Joan Skillaci, the prosecutor who'd worked her ass off weekends and holidays, putting the case against Harrott together. Still making notes, she caught it out of the corner of her eye and gave Reese and Riley the tiniest of waves on their way out. Lauren knew she still had a mound of paperwork to get through and no time to chitchat.

They had to pass through a gauntlet of news cameras and reporters parked outside the courtroom. Questions were shouted and microphones stuck in their faces. Everyone knew who Lauren Riley and Shane Reese were. The former blond bombshell was now a bespectacled, short-haired, middle-aged brunette. They wanted to get footage of Lauren with her younger, handsome biracial partner who'd survived being shot a year ago.

Lauren had on her usual court outfit—black pants and blazer over a white button-down shirt—while Reese was rocking a pair of dark-wash jeans and a golf shirt with the Buffalo Police emblem on the upper left chest. They were a handsome-looking pair. That made for great headlines.

Reese and Riley passed the district attorney, Carl Church, who was giving a statement about the case, praising the detectives both past and present as well as his prosecutors for bringing Harrott to justice. His deep voice booming as he answered questions, Carl never mentioned Lauren by name. He didn't even look in her direction as she walked by. Lauren and Church had been on opposite sides of a murder trial almost three years earlier. That had led to a series of events that culminated in him putting her in front of a grand jury last year that disappointed him by 'no billing' her—not the outcome Church had wanted. He would tell the press that they were on the same team, but Lauren knew they were anything but. She felt bad that she'd pulled Reese down with her. *Reese chose to be my partner*, she told herself, *and he still chooses to be my partner. That's what really pisses Church off.*

Reese had a much better bedside manner than Riley. He was the type of person other people naturally gravitated toward. He had a lot of buddies on and off the job, loved watching football, and played baseball in a summer league. Lauren had always been an introvert—only a few good friends, no hobbies. She'd concentrated on her daughters and her job. Now that the two girls were in college, she liked to believe she'd been successful in both those areas.

Still, it hurt sometimes when Reese got invited out for a beer and she didn't.

People respected Riley but they actually *liked* Reese.

Walking out of the State Supreme Court building, they headed over to the new police headquarters in Niagara Square. It was a beautiful spring day in Buffalo, the sun was shining, a breeze was blowing in from Lake Erie and everybody was out on the streets. In Buffalo, you took the good weather when you got it and made the most of every second, because it was so unpredictable. It wasn't unheard of to have a snowstorm in May after a string of almost eighty-degree days. Summer came around for good sometime in June, but right now, May was still a crapshoot.

People were everywhere downtown, many lounging around the obelisk in Niagara Square, sitting by the carved lion statues. Some were on their phones, while others were typing into laptops, taking advantage of the free Wi-Fi. Middle-aged ladies in dark business suits and white sneakers walked briskly by, trying to get their daily steps in during their lunch hour. The line at the hot dog vendor on the corner was four deep. Everyone was whiling away the afternoon of this unusually warm day in the shadow of City Hall.

'You OK?' Reese asked as he swiped them into headquarters on the Niagara Street side with his key card.

'It's never a done deal until the sentence is passed,' she replied as they entered the old Federal Courthouse building the city had converted into the police and fire department's main offices. 'I always think the defendant is going to yank his guilty plea at the last minute.'

'That's because you're always waiting for someone to pull the rug out from under you,' he said, holding the elevator door open for her so she could get in first.

'That's because someone usually does.'

He swiped his card again and hit the button for the fourth floor where the Homicide squad was located. As opposed to their cockroach-ridden former building, which had minimal security measures, their new offices were equipped with video surveillance and the need to swipe a key card to open every door. On their first day in the new building Reese had counted that it took eight different swipes to get into their office in the Homicide wing.

'Cry me a river, Riley. You just made the police commissioner, the mayor and the district attorney all look fantastic. That should buy you at least a month or two of goodwill, don't you think?'

She looked up at the climbing digital numbers and smiled. 'That's what I love about you, partner, always the optimist.'

TWO

'I'm in the middle of an autopsy, Captain.'

'You're in the middle of looking at autopsy photos from 1985.'

'I'd love to indulge you, sir.' Lauren's thick black-framed glasses slid down her nose as she looked up at her boss from her cluttered desk. She pushed them back up with her index finger. She'd gotten the exact same pair as the last ones she had, but for some reason these were constantly slipping down her face. 'But I'm very busy right now.'

'Today, Riley. I'm not asking you, I'm ordering you.' The day after Steven Harrott pled guilty, Captain Ansel Carey, a thin, nervous-looking man, leaned in the doorway of Riley's Cold Case office. Carey was referred to as Antsy whenever his back was turned, short for Antsy-and-Agitated, which is what he was ninety percent of the time. Today was no different. 'I heard you huffing into the Homicide office like a locomotive. You have a one o'clock appointment with Dr Grisanti. I made it myself.'

Normally, their detective sergeant would handle such things, but he was off on vacation for two weeks and had left specific instructions not to call him for any reason. 'Everything in the Homicide office is a matter of life and death,' he'd told them in his gravelly voice. 'And it still will be when I get back. Let the captain handle it. If my work phone rings, you're suspended.'

Reese snickered from behind a folder. Lauren balled up a piece of scrap paper and launched it at his bald head. Outside in the hallway she could hear Marilyn, their report technician, answering the Buffalo Police Homicide squad's main phone line. The mother hen of the office, Marilyn would have admonished them to cut it out and pay attention to the captain.

'Captain—' Lauren began.

He held up a hand, cutting her off mid-protest. 'You've been putting it off for two months now. I let it slide because I thought your sergeant was handling it.' It was no secret Antsy was afraid of Sergeant Connolly. And with good reason; the man had hands the size of a grizzly bear's. 'You know the departmental doctor has to clear you once a year. I don't make the rules, I just try to enforce them.'

'Next week. I promise. We have that trial coming up and I'll go after one of the pre-trial conferences. Kill two birds with one stone.'

The captain was not moved by her pleas. He glanced at the watch on his left wrist. 'You've got an hour to get over to his office on Main Street. And Reese, I'm ordering you to not let her be late.'

Reese dropped the manila folder on his desk, sending random papers scattering to the floor. 'Since when am I my partner's keeper?'

He jerked a thumb at Lauren. 'Since you joined forces with this unlikely superhero.'

Reese snickered again, covering his face with his hands in case she launched another projectile at him.

'That would make you my sidekick,' Lauren told him, needling him on purpose. A suspect had called him that once. Things hadn't ended well for that guy.

Ignoring Reese and Riley's childish behavior, the captain pointed straight at Lauren, in case she thought he was joking about the order. 'One o'clock. Don't be late.'

He spun on his heel, closing the door behind him.

'Thanks, partner,' Reese said, trying to tidy up his desk after the storm of papers he'd just caused, still pissed about the sidekick comment. 'Way to get me in trouble with Antsy.'

She glanced back down at the picture she'd been examining before Antsy had interrupted her. It was a color photo of a man sprawled face down on a sidewalk. Ice cream was melting in a puddle around the top of the cone the victim still grasped in his hand. A lone shell casing lay next to his left shoulder. He'd never seen it coming. The victim was a known associate of a long-time drug dealer from North Buffalo. Now, an inmate in a federal correctional facility was telling his lawyer he had information on the shooter, a rival drug dealer, and wanted to work out a plea deal in exchange for testifying. Lauren wasn't convinced the inmate was credible. He'd had since 1985 to come forward with his information, and so far he hadn't given them anything the original detectives hadn't heard from the streets at the time of the murder. Unless the inmate could give them something concrete, that case was staying cold. Better to leave it unsolved than to arrest a man on the word of an unreliable witness.

Carefully sliding the autopsy photos back into their white sleeve, Lauren shook her head. 'I don't know why I have to do this. We have cases to work.' She walked over to their mess table where they spread out the contents of old files. It was a technique they used to look for clues other detectives might have missed. By spreading out the reports, pictures and statements, they could stand back and visualize the case in its entirety. As her eyes skipped over the paperwork in front of her she made a quick mental checklist: pull up the evidence, reinterview witnesses, double-check that the DNA recovered from the scene had been retested with the latest technology and revisit the original crime scene.

'The same reason I had to do it two months ago. Because you got injured on duty.'

Lauren had been more than just injured on duty. She'd been stabbed a year and a half ago in the old headquarters building one night after Reese had gone home. If he hadn't come back to get his cap, she would've died on that filthy carpet in their former office. Vince Schultz, the cop who'd stabbed her, was now sitting in Attica while she still bore the scars of his attack. Just like Reese wore his crisscross scars on his scalp. The city allowed him to wear an official Buffalo Police baseball cap to cover them. It was the least they could do since he had also got them in the line of duty.

'Look, I'll drive you over. It's a beautiful May day. Get it? May day? It rhymes.' Reese was met with a stony glare. 'We'll get some lunch afterwards. How long could it possibly take to examine your skeleton-like body?' Lauren was tall and naturally thin, but getting stabbed had caused her to lose an unhealthy amount of weight which she'd never been able to gain back. Reese thought by teasing her, he could motivate her to eat more. That was his excuse, anyway.

'Considering it took him over two hours to inspect that planet-sized melon you call a head, probably not too long.' She didn't need an excuse to insult him; she just did it whenever she saw an opening.

Reaching over to the coat rack, he plucked up his cap and plunked it down on his head. 'Touché, my friend. Touché. But let's get going because I'm starving.'

They exited their office into the main Homicide wing. Marilyn put a hand over the mouthpiece of the landline she was talking on. 'The father from the Henderson case called. You need to call him back. He wants an update.'

Marilyn ran the Homicide squad like the conductor of a train that never stopped. No matter how many homicides they solved, another one came in to take its place. Some days it was two more or, worse, three. She singlehandedly managed to juggle all the cases for the entire squad: scheduling appointments, keeping track of court appearances, entering the payroll information. She was an attractive, short-haired woman in her early sixties who wore the required navy polyester pants and white shirt that was the uniform of report technicians across the department. Today she had a little brooch of pink sparkling flowers pinned to her shirt.

'I tried calling him yesterday,' Lauren told her, 'but he was at work.'

'Try him again,' was all she said and went back to her call.

Lauren made a mental note to call Mr Henderson as soon as they got back. If he had to call the office again, she and Reese would surely feel the wrath of Marilyn.

Lauren Riley and Shane Reese were unlikely partners. She had just turned forty-one, was the divorced mom of two college-aged daughters and had very little life to speak of, other than the job, even though they were both away at school. Reese, on the other hand, was a biracial bachelor, almost six years younger than her, who had an active social life outside the police department. Somehow their worlds had not only collided since they'd started working together, they'd actually meshed. A year ago Reese had gotten shot and Lauren had almost lost him. He'd moved in with her after he had gotten out of the hospital, and she'd taken care of him the way he'd taken care of her after she had been stabbed during a previous case. Their nonromantic relationship was the cause of many whispers in the department. But even the gossipers couldn't deny they were a great team, solving one cold case after another.

Lauren had struggled around Christmas time with her mounting mix of feelings for him. Were they more than partners? Yes, that was clear. They may have been involved in constant verbal jabs but they valued and respected each other, like all long-time partners did. She'd finally given up trying to figure out a label for the two of them after her solo trip to Iceland for a case. Maybe there was no label for their relationship, no way to tie it up neatly with a bow. It was nice to ride to work with him in the morning, not eat dinner alone, and he liked to do yard work. Why did it have to be more than that? Lauren slept upstairs and he had his own bedroom and bath on the first floor. Her two daughters approved, relieved she wasn't living by herself anymore. They were both convinced that Lauren having too much time on her hands was a recipe for disaster.

That part she'd proven right time and again.

What she and Reese had was solid and steady and comfortable. And after a string of failed relationships, that was more than enough for her. At least, that's what she told herself.

Right then she didn't want to think about her unusual living arrangement, she just wanted to get her stupid examination over. They exited headquarters, crossing the street to the lot where the police vehicles were kept. Reese tossed the car keys in the air and caught them as he walked, one of his nervous habits.

'Remind me to call the father from the Henderson case,' she told him, not trusting her mental note. He hit the unlock button on his key fob and the lights on one of the old unmarked cars they used blinked.

'I'll call him while the doctor is checking you over,' he said, opening the driver's side door. 'I have his number in my work phone. He's a good guy, works a lot. I'd really like to put that case together. So don't screw around at your physical.'

I'm perfectly fine, she thought as she got into the passenger side. *And I've got more autopsy photos to go over after lunch.*

THREE

'I CAN'T SIGN off on you going back to work, Detective Riley.'

Lauren nearly fell off the edge of the exam table, the paper runner bunching under her as she slid down a good four inches before she gripped the sides, catching herself. 'Excuse me, Doctor. What was that?'

Dr Grisanti, the Buffalo Police Department's physician, snapped off a latex glove, popped the top of the trash can with the toe of his shoe and dropped it in. 'It's your lungs. I let you talk me into letting you go back to full duty because I was hopeful your lungs would fully recover over time. It just hasn't happened.'

'What does that mean?' Lauren resisted the urge to pull off the flimsy gray gown she was wearing and toss it in the garbage with the used glove. It wasn't like it was covering much to begin with. He might have to add pneumonia to her list of maladies if he didn't hurry up with the examination.

'It means I'm recommending they put you on paid Injured on Duty status until we revisit your lungs and you've shown some progress.'

Lauren's head was spinning. Antsy had forced her in for an annual physical. It was supposed to be routine, a formality, not career-ending. She and Reese had literally just been joking about it. Now the doctor wanted to put her on Injured on Duty leave a year and a half after the initial assault. Granted, she did have some issues with shortness of breath, but getting stabbed in the side and collapsing a lung will do that to a person. *I'm also over forty and an ex-smoker*, she thought. *Is he taking that into consideration?* Then it dawned on her that he actually might be, and that those were compounding factors. Better to leave that argument alone for now.

'And when will that be?'

The salt-and-pepper-haired doctor turned away from his patient and sat down on a metal stool. Beside the prerequisite cautionary posters listing the warning signs for a heart attack, the exam room had one of those tables that jutted out from the wall. He pulled himself up to it and began to peck at the screen of his computer tablet. 'I'd like to see you back in six months. Let's hope with rest and physical therapy—'

'Six months! And I already did physical therapy. Obviously, it didn't help.'

He pushed his wire-rimmed glasses up his thin nose. 'You think I don't get reports? You only went when you felt like it. And rest? You got stabbed and within a couple of weeks you were in a shootout on the Skyway. Then, a few months later, you had a showdown with a homicidal maniac in the middle of a snowstorm. Should I even mention jet-setting off to Iceland for a murder case? In the last eighteen months, I think you've spent maybe three weeks recovering. Your body needed more time than that, even if you didn't.'

She held up a hand. 'I appreciate your concern, but I'm fine. If I wasn't, I wouldn't have been able to do those things in the first place. You really need to clear me, Doc.' She was a cold case homicide detective. Her job was constant and dangerous, there was no way around it. Surely he wouldn't sideline her because she couldn't make the ball go above the red line on the breathing test he'd made her take.

Now he swiveled around to face her. 'And you need to rest. Actually do nothing. Except perhaps go on a vacation.'

'For six months?'

He shrugged and turned back to his screen. 'It's better than the alternative.'

'What's the alternative?'

'I mark your file Unfit for Duty and they pension you out.'

Lauren ran a hand through her short, choppy brown hair. 'You'd rather have them give me a disability pension than let me go back to work?'

'It's not that I'd rather do it, it's that I have to do it. I want you alive.'

'My partner got shot in the head and you cleared him at his physical two months ago.'

'Your partner got his head *grazed* by a bullet,' he clarified. 'You're a homicide detective, you of all people should know it's not the same thing.'

It had sure looked like the same thing to Lauren when Shane Reese was lying in the ICU with his brain trying to climb out of his skull, but she bit that comment back. She was trying to persuade the doctor, not piss him off. 'Why six months? How about two?' she negotiated.

'I'll see you in six months, Detective Riley. Take up gardening, learn to paint, join a health club, but no police work.' Turning back to his computer, he used his finger to scroll through her medical records. 'Apparently, it's very bad for your health.'

FOUR

'WELL? WHAT'D HE SAY?' Reese asked as Lauren slammed the passenger door closed. His green eyes narrowed. He thought he could read Lauren after being partners with her for the last few years, but he always seemed to be proven wrong. She was more unpredictable than Buffalo's weather.

Lauren pulled the seatbelt out and snapped it in place. 'Six months.'

'Six months for what?' Reese was confused. She made it sound like she'd just received a prison sentence.

'The doctor is putting me on Injured on Duty status for the next six months and if my lungs don't start getting with the program, I'm off the job.'

Slumping back in his seat, Reese let out a low whistle. 'Are you kidding me?'

'Does it look like I'm kidding?'

'I don't know.' He shrugged. 'You always have that scowl on your face.'

Lauren bent forward, catching her forehead in her hand. 'This is serious, Reese. They're going to kick me off the force.'

'They can't do that.'

Lauren lifted her fingers, staring at him sidelong.

'OK, so they can do it,' he conceded. 'They won't though. The commissioner loves you. After everything you've done for the city—'

She cut him off. 'You mean done *to* the city. And even Commissioner Bennett answers to someone. This is the excuse City Hall and Carl Church have been looking for. I've been more trouble than I'm worth.'

District Attorney Carl Church had been the one to send her off to Iceland on a homicide investigation, fully expecting her to fail. No one was more shocked than he was when she actually managed to solve the case. She never found out what he'd had in store for her if she'd come home empty-handed. At the time she was thinking she would have gotten demoted. Now she couldn't help thinking that he was behind this sudden change of duty status. Getting her booted off the job was better than a demotion, after all.

Reese shifted the car into drive and eased out of the parking space in front of the building the city doctor's office was housed in. 'Once again I have to remind you that the world does not revolve around Lauren Riley. You take six months off, you get better, and you continue on your merry way toward a normal retirement. End of story.'

She ignored that. He was just trying to make her feel better. They both knew that if the doctor didn't clear her, she was off the force. 'I better call the captain and let him know, if Doctor Grisanti's secretary hasn't notified the department already.'

'Why don't you wait until after lunch? Calm down a little. You don't want to say something you might regret.'

Regret was a way of life for her, why should today be any different? She crossed her arms over her chest. 'I am not sitting on my ass for six months.'

'Good. Because sitting on that bony thing would hurt like hell.' A rusty white Chevy sedan cut in front of them and Reese laid on the horn. The pickup behind them laid on theirs, causing Reese to slow to a crawl out of spite. Now the truck was riding Reese's bumper, not realizing it was an unmarked police car. Finally, the driver got fed up and turned down the next side street. Reese waited for Riley to call him a child, but she just sat silently looking out of the window. After a minute it started to unnerve him and he began humming to himself to fill in the silence.

After three rounds of 'Row, Row, Row Your Boat', Lauren told him, 'Head over to the County Office building.'

'I'm starving.' The tone of his voice always got an edge to it when he was hungry. 'You must be too. You didn't eat this morning. I want to go over to Bullrick's Tavern. What could possibly take precedence over a nice roast beef on weck?'

Beef on weck was a Buffalo specialty sandwich that consisted of thinly sliced roast beef on a salted Kimmelweck roll dipped in au jus. It was a holdover from the days of the steel plants, when hungry workers would stop at their local bar on their lunch hour for a hot sandwich and a beer. Some of the older taverns in town kept a crock pot behind the bar simmering with roast beef, and a plate of rolls next to it. It was one of Reese's favorite lunches because one was just enough to tide him over until dinnertime. Two filled him up and three put him in a food coma on the couch.

A thin smirk of a smile curled the corner of her lip. 'I'm getting my private investigator license renewed.'

FIVE

THEY NEVER WENT back to police headquarters. Reese called in a half-day and Lauren made him take her to the State Office building under protest. She waited in line while Reese sulked in the corner, waiting. After she'd filed forms, paid licensing fees and collected more paperwork to be filled out at home, they finally stopped at Bullrick's and got food. Reese's stomach had complained loudly the entire way. He'd wanted to go in and sit down at the restaurant, but Lauren was hyper-focused on getting the paperwork done, so he'd gotten their meals to go. He'd driven one-handed, dripping au jus down the front of his shirt as he steered and ate at the same time.

She'd called their captain on the way home, but he'd already heard from the doctor's secretary, just as she'd predicted. Antsy had sounded pissed when he told her to come in the next day to fill out all the paperwork. The last thing he wanted to do was approve overtime because one of his detectives was off for six months. One of the things she'd learned early on the job was that everyone was replaceable, and the brass was more worried about budgets and saving money than solving cases. They left the caring part to the detectives.

Now, in the comfort of the five-bedroom colonial she'd acquired mortgage-free in her divorce, Lauren had all the licensing papers fanned out in front of her on the kitchen table while Watson, Reese's West Highland Terrier, squeaked his favorite toy on her foot.

'You're really going through with this?' Reese asked as he leaned against the kitchen wall, his half-eaten beef on weck poised in front of his mouth, ready to take another bite. 'I thought you said that the private investigation business was more trouble than it was worth.'

'I need to make money, Reese.' She motioned around the room with her hand. 'How else am I going to keep a roof over your and Watson's heads?'

'You don't have a mortgage and you drive a Ford Escape you paid cash for,' he pointed out. Lauren's second husband had been a very wealthy real-estate attorney who'd been more than generous in their divorce proceedings. She'd lost a spouse but gained a sprawling residence in an exclusive gated community no mere city employee could afford. Hence the room for Reese and Watson to move in. 'You're on paid leave. You probably have so much money stuffed in your mattress you can't roll over. Just do what the doctor tells you and he'll let you come back to work.'

'My ex doesn't pay for my daughters' college tuition anymore.' She'd put a stop to that this year. It wasn't worth putting herself in his debt. It had been another way for him to keep some control over her. But it was just her luck they'd both decided on private, pricey, out-of-state schools. 'And not having a mortgage doesn't mean you don't pay taxes.'

'I get that, but do you hear what I'm saying?' Frustration crept into his voice.

'I have every intention of following his instructions.' She was trying to placate him now. 'I'll go to physical therapy three times a week. I'll walk every morning. I'll

do breathing treatments. But I can't just sit around the rest
of the time. It's not in my nature.'

'I'm aware of that.' Reese rolled his eyes. 'No one is
more aware of that than me. So you'd rather follow some
cheating husband around or watch some lady scamming
her job for disability as she's gardening?'

'There's more to it than that. And did you call the dad
on the Henderson case?'

'You know I did. I gave him an update and he's coming in to the office next week.' His green eyes narrowed;
he knew what she was trying to do. 'Don't change the subject. The doctor doesn't want you to work. He wants you to
rest. Period.'

'I've worked since I was fifteen years old—'

'—fifteen years old.' Reese overlapped, mimicking her.
Watson jumped up on his legs, tail wagging. Reese slipped
him a tiny piece of his sandwich. 'I'm not going to argue
with you. I'm going to eat my food and enjoy the rest of
my day off. You know what? If you want to run around
playing private investigator, go ahead. I'm not your father.'

'Thank you,' she said, returning to the paperwork. She'd
let her private investigator's license run out last year but
had the good sense to take the exam to renew it four months
ago, just in case. Now all she had to do was refile all the
proper forms.

'I wasn't serious, you know that, right?'

'I know,' she said without looking up. 'But I'm going to
pretend you were.'

SIX

LAUREN'S ABRUPT DEPARTURE from the police department did cause a bit of a stir when local news outlets somehow got hold of the story. It boggled her mind that being put on administrative leave for an old injury could even be considered newsworthy. A lot of her victims' families were upset and making waves. Lauren's clearance rate proved she was a hard worker, but it was her and Reese together who had solved a lot of high-profile cases. The families didn't want half the team. She felt bad that they were fighting for her when she should have been fighting for them.

The only silver lining was that the news outlets liked to use old photographs of her, when she had long blond hair. It was shorter now, and darker, and she'd taken to wearing her glasses most of the time. It was a great disguise from the general public, who still expected her to look like a model, instead of the middle-aged lady she actually was. And truth be told she liked the way she looked now. She was still attractive, but it was more about the way she held herself. There was something about being over forty that had finally made her comfortable in her own skin. She'd always been a confident person, but now it was for the right reasons and it showed.

While waiting for her renewed license to be mailed to her, Lauren spent the first few days of her forced relaxation period making lists of projects she wanted to accomplish around the house. She then started calling contractors, who all told her they were booked until August. Contractors in Buffalo had only a short window to work in the warm weather, so you had to plan ahead and expect delays. If they were telling her August, it was more likely they'd start work at the end of September.

When the home improvements didn't pan out, she thought maybe she'd take a trip to see her parents in Florida. She called them on the phone, talked to her mother for fifteen minutes, then scratched that off her list. They were going to visit her sister out west for a month, and Jill's house was much smaller than Lauren's.

She talked and FaceTimed with both of her daughters almost every night. She'd taken Watson for so many walks that he actually ran away from her when he saw his harness and leash in her hand. She tried to read a book her neighbor, Dayla, had lent her. It was a paranormal romance. She made it three chapters in before giving it back. Falling in love with a ghost just didn't appeal to her; she already had too many ghosts in her life.

After a week of having to watch Reese go to the Homicide squad without her every morning, Lauren was bored out of her mind. Physical therapy only ate away an hour a day, three days a week. There was no way she could entertain herself at home for six months. She'd grill Reese on their cases as soon as he walked in the door after work. He was good about it, bringing home files for her to go over and calling to run things by her, but it wasn't the same.

She did find one case interesting, the murder of a man inside his comic book store in 1989. From the look of the crime scene photos, there'd been a hell of a fight before he was shot to death. If Reese could find the evidence, they might be able to get DNA from any number of things. Not the cash register though, that had remained untouched. It was intriguing. Lauren made Reese put a request in to locate the evidence. Now that the department had moved all the archived evidence to a storage facility in North Buffalo, instead of storing it at headquarters where it was readily available, their CSI would probably find it by the time she was back in six months. Hopefully.

She hired a cop's son to design a website for her private investigator business, but refused to put her picture on it. There was a contact button that sent questions right to her email, which was so much better than putting a phone number out there. Sifting through ten emails from people who wanted her to follow their spouse around was better than wasting twenty minutes listening to someone complain about how they were being wronged, only to have them hang up when they heard her hourly fee for doing surveillance.

She'd gotten forty email enquiries since her website went live and hadn't taken a single case. That was one of the perks of being your own boss, you got to pick and choose which cases you wanted to pursue. After a little nagging from Reese, Lauren had agreed not to take on any cases likely to result in car chases, shootouts or knife fights. But that being said, unless something really interested her, she wasn't going to be bothered with cheaters or insurance fraud scammers either. She passed those along to a retired cop she knew, whose private investigator business specialized in those types of cases. They were the kinds of clients on which most firms made the bulk of their money. Lauren wanted to make a profit, of course, but she didn't want to be bored. She was too good at what she did to be bored. A middle ground was what she needed.

Two weeks into her paid leave and five days after she officially received her renewed private investigator license in the mail, Lauren's phone vibrated on the nightstand next to her head, waking her out of a dead sleep.

She felt around until she managed to snag it before she opened her eyes. Picking it up a second too late, the phone vibrated in her hand again, signaling she had a voicemail. She checked the source: an unknown local number. The time at the top said it was almost nine o'clock in the morning. 'Ugh,' she exhaled, disgusted with herself for sleeping in so late again. On a normal working day, she was awake by six, so being on leave did have its perks. And she was getting more rest, just like the doctor ordered, but at the rate she was going she'd be getting up at noon by her third month off.

Pausing for a second, she listened for Watson downstairs. Nothing. It was Reese's day off. He must have taken him out for his morning walk or else Watson would have been in her room, begging to be under the covers with her.

She hit play and listened to the gracefully composed voice of an older, educated, and very self-assured woman.

'Hello, Detective Riley. My name is Sharon Whitney and I'd like to sit down with you this afternoon if you're available and talk about a matter that I'm dealing with. I think it may necessitate me hiring a private investigator. Please call me back as soon as you can as I fear time may be of the essence. Thank you very much.' Instead of rattling off a call-back number the woman practically sang the digits into the phone.

Time might have been of the essence, but Lauren had to get up, brush her teeth and grab some coffee before she even thought about it. She waited until she was sitting at her kitchen table with her favorite oversized coffee mug practically overflowing before she looked at her phone again. She wondered how this Whitney woman had gotten hold of her personal cell number.

Strangely enough, a man answered when she called back. 'Mrs Whitney said you might try to reach her. If it's convenient for you, she'd like to meet you today at noon here in her home.'

'I'd like to speak to Mrs Whitney, please.'

'She had to step out. She told me to inform you that even if you don't decide to take her on as a client, she'll still pay your fee for your time today. And your discretion.'

Lauren's curiosity was piqued. Clients usually tried to pay for as little as possible. 'I always conduct myself in a professional manner,' she replied. 'And my discretion comes with the fee.'

'Very good. Should I say you'll be joining her then?'

She caught a flash of Watson's white fur out of the corner of her eye. He and Reese were playing a round of fetch in the backyard. Reese would wind up, making Watson jump around in anticipation, and then would let a green ball fly across the yard. Watson zoomed after it, snatching it off the ground and running right back to drop it at Reese's feet. She glanced at the calendar next to the fridge. She'd forgotten what it was like to enjoy a day off. When every day was a day off, time lost all meaning. She could now understand why the retired guys always said you needed to have a plan for when you left the job. It was easy to let the weeks slip by.

Watson jumped up on Reese's jeans, scattering blades of fresh-cut grass across them. Reese laughed and threw the ball again before brushing them off.

'Hello? Are you still there?' The man's voice snapped her back to the phone call.

'Yes,' she said, reaching for a pen lying on the kitchen table. 'Let me write down the address.'

SEVEN

THE HOUSE WAS located on Nottingham Terrace, not too far from her own home. Stately turn-of-the-twentieth-century mansions lined one side of the street. The other side bordered Delaware Park and offered a terrific view of the tennis courts. These houses didn't come up for sale often. They were mostly kept within wealthy families, passed down from generation to generation. They were some of the most expensive residential real estate in Buffalo.

She parked her car in the circular driveway and went up the walkway to the ornate front entrance. Painted red with shining brass hardware, the doorbell made a faint *bong* somewhere within when she pressed it. Etched glass in the shape of a lotus blossom bloomed across the door. *This probably cost as much as my car*, she thought. Lauren suppressed the urge to reach out and touch it. From somewhere inside she heard footsteps approaching. The last thing she wanted was for the potential client to see her fondling the woodwork.

A well-appointed blond in her sixties opened the door. 'Hello.' She gave Lauren a wide, toothy smile, stepping back to let her in. 'I'm Sharon Whitney.'

'Lauren Riley,' she replied, walking into the foyer. 'But I assume you knew that or you wouldn't have let me in.'

Sharon motioned to a panel on the wall. A small split

screen showed the front walk and the view on the other side of the door. 'It's all very state-of-the-art. I have my security systems updated regularly. Unfortunately, I learned the hard way. This way, please.'

Lauren followed her under a beautiful crystal chandelier in the foyer, past a grand double staircase. The house was so quiet you could hear their footsteps echoing on the shiny hardwood floors as they walked. The scent of freshly cut flowers filled Lauren's nose, although she couldn't see the source. Somewhere in the house there was a huge, extravagant floral arrangement, she was sure.

Just like a funeral home, she thought.

'Please, have a seat,' Sharon Whitney said as she ushered Lauren into her great room. A silver tea service was set out on the coffee table in front of the tastefully elegant beige sofa. Perching on the edge, Lauren expected the guy from the phone call, who she pictured as a white-gloved butler, to show up at any moment to pour her a cup. When no one appeared and Sharon sat in the floral wing chair across from her, she picked up the pot and served herself.

'Do you like tea?' Sharon asked, lifting her own delicate china cup and saucer from the side table next to her.

'I'm more of a coffee person,' Lauren admitted. 'But this is fine. Thank you.'

'You're very welcome.' Sharon bent to meet the cup with her lips. She was in no hurry to get to the point, despite what she'd said on the phone. She savored the sip, dramatically closing her eyes and breathing out with a smile. Lauren sensed that Sharon Whitney did everything slowly, theatrically, and with purpose. Everything about her seemed scripted to fit a role she was playing—from the blond updo with strategically placed gray streaks, to the dark pink pantsuit with its white collared shirt underneath, to her nude shoes with just a hint of a wedge heel. She was the perfect blend of money and experience, with a trace of leftover sixties flower child thrown in to spice things up.

Lauren's eyes scanned the room. 'You have an eye for art. These paintings are lovely.'

'Thank you.' Sharon was pleased that Lauren had noticed. 'I try to rotate my collection every season so that I get to view all my paintings at least once a year. It's a little quirk of mine.'

'It must be quite a collection.' At least twenty paintings were spread out over the walls; some were the size of a postcard, while the one over the fireplace reached nearly to the ceiling.

'I meant in every room of the house, dear. These are just my favorites. For now.' There was a twinkle in her eye as she set the saucer down. *It's time to get down to business*, Lauren thought.

'It's funny you brought up my art collection, since that's the reason you're here.'

Bingo. Lauren sipped her tea. Like her coffee, she took it black. 'Really? I don't do much business in the art world. None at all, actually. If you're looking for information on a painting or artist or buyer, I might be able to point you in the right direction.'

'That's not the kind of private investigator I need.' She leaned back in her chair, each hand gripping an armrest. 'How familiar are you with my ex-husband, Howard Whitney?'

Lauren shrugged. 'A little. He and his family are fixtures here in Buffalo. The Whitney family is old money, dating back to the grain barons at the turn of the twentieth century. They were instrumental in establishing Buffalo as a shipping hub on the Great Lakes.'

Sharon seemed impressed at Lauren's knowledge of the

city's history. 'And you used to be married to old money as well, correct?'

The lady had done her homework, Lauren could respect that. 'I was married briefly to Mark Hathaway, yes.' Lauren herself came from no money. Her dad was a retired autoworker. She'd been a single mom of two while working full time in the department when she met Mark. It should have been a Cinderella story with a happily ever after ending, only he'd decided to let other women try on his glass slipper.

'I'm in a book club with Mark's mother. She speaks very highly of you. She's the one who gave me your number. Every time you make the paper or are on another true crime show, she tells us how smart you are, how diligent and trustworthy.'

I bet she does, Lauren sniffed into her teacup, *now that we're divorced.* The irony of Mark's mother having good things to say about Lauren now was not lost on her. Mrs Hathaway had been convinced Lauren had only married Mark for his trust fund money and had spent their entire brief marriage in a constant state of passive-aggressive uptight politeness toward her. 'How is Mrs Hathaway?'

'Still battling her arthritis, I'm afraid. But I didn't bring you here to catch up on the latest society gossip. I'm involved in a matter that's been going on for over forty years and I need someone I can trust.'

'Forty years is a long time,' Lauren commented.

'You're a cold case detective,' she replied, rubbing her thumb absently over the rim of her cup, erasing the red lipstick she'd just deposited there. 'It doesn't get much colder than this.' She took a deep breath and went on. 'Forty years ago, I met Howard Whitney. I was twenty-five and a bit naive and he was forty-five and divorced. I had just graduated with my master's degree in fine arts and was working in a very exclusive New York City art gallery. I'm originally from Long Island. The Hamptons, actually.'

When Lauren didn't react to that revelation one way or another, she went on. 'He was a friend of the gallery owner and an art collector who spent a ridiculous amount on pieces. He did have excellent taste, I've got to give him that. The attraction between us was immediate. And so was the friction, I suppose.' She smiled faintly at the memory. 'We got married three months after we met. There was no prenuptial agreement. I came from money, he had money, there didn't seem to be a need. A few days before we wed, he bought a small Picasso the gallery's owner had managed to get his hands on. I absolutely loved it, and he gave it to me as a wedding gift.'

Lauren let out a sigh. 'I think I know where this is going.'

'We were married for twenty tumultuous years,' she went on as if Lauren hadn't spoken. 'We finally decided to divorce each other. Neither one of us would give an inch about anything. He refused to move out of our home. I refused to move out of our home. I wanted the painting and he didn't want to give it to me.'

'The famous Whitney break-in,' Lauren interrupted.

If that flustered her, she didn't show it. 'There was no break-in. My husband was home alone. I had gone out to dinner and drinks with some friends. When I came back, around one in the morning, I found him on the floor of our living room beaten almost to death and the painting was gone.'

'Wasn't a handyman thought to be involved?' Lauren had been a young mother when the crime happened. It had been all over the news for days: a bitter divorce, both parties still living together in their city mansion, a brutal assault, missing art, and a trusted household employee under suspicion. It had all the makings of a Lifetime Movie before Lifetime Movies were a thing.

'I'm convinced my ex-husband set the entire affair up with James Patrick Breen, our employee, to make it look like a robbery gone bad. Our security system hadn't been breached. It was definitely an inside job, as they say.' She leaned forward now, arms crossed over her knees. 'Ms Riley, that painting is still out there, and I want it back.'

The crime had topped the headlines for weeks at the time, but Lauren was still foggy on the details. Though it had taken place in Buffalo, the Cold Case squad only worked homicides. It would have been handled by the precinct detectives at the time, probably with the help of the FBI. However, Lauren knew that the statute of limitations on an assault and robbery would have long since passed. The file would have been closed and sent to the police department's archives years ago. She didn't know how the FBI managed their cold cases but she imagined a similar scenario.

'Mister Breen was investigated and cleared, wasn't he?' she asked.

Sharon took another sip of her tea and nodded. 'The authorities searched him and his apartment on our property right after the crime, but the painting was never located. There wasn't enough evidence to charge him with anything. He said he was watching television alone when it happened. My ex-husband claimed he didn't remember anything but getting hit from behind as he walked into our living room. James moved out immediately, and then went back to his native Ireland less than a year later. *Fled* back to Ireland is more like it.'

'Did he suddenly become a millionaire?'

Sharon Whitney shook her head and gave Lauren a

knowing smile. 'Wouldn't that have been convenient? No. Sadly, he's been living in the same ramshackle cottage for the last twenty years.'

It was time for Lauren to get to the huge, looming elephant in the room. 'Didn't your husband accuse *you* of hiring someone to steal the painting?'

'He only tossed around that allegation so I wouldn't get my half of the insurance money. But it's not about money. It never was. Look around you.' She gestured at the artwork hanging on the walls. As little as Lauren knew about art, she knew a beautiful painting when she saw one. Right now, she was literally surrounded by them. 'I loved that painting and now I feel like there's a real chance I might get it back.'

'Why now?' Lauren asked. 'What's changed all of a sudden?'

Sharon Whitney's mouth set in a grim line. 'James Breen died four days ago. I received a phone call in the middle of the night.' She put her hand over her heart. 'When it rang, it nearly scared me out of my wits. It was the authorities in Ireland. Said he collapsed. Illness had gotten the better of him. He was only a year older than me.'

'That's young,' Lauren agreed neutrally, not wanting to speculate on her age. 'What did you do when you found out?'

'I got in touch with my lawyer immediately and had him make Mr Breen's sister in Ireland an offer for his cottage that she couldn't refuse.' There was a hint of steel in her voice. 'The sale is pending but the important thing was to lock down the premises so Howard couldn't get in there first.'

'You make it sound like a race to the finish,' Lauren said.

'I'm sixty-five, Howard is eighty-five. If he dies now, the secret of what happened to the painting dies with him.

I think there may be some clue in the cottage as to where
Jimmy stashed the painting. Maybe the proof that Howard has had it all this time is somewhere inside. Or maybe
someone he knew has some information. Jimmy liked to
drink and say he was involved with the IRA. Maybe that
was who he stole the painting for.'

'Isn't the IRA in Northern Ireland?'

Sharon frowned slightly, remembering her former employee. 'He used to brag he was involved with them somehow. Mostly when he had whiskey on his breath. Maybe
he ran a safehouse, I don't know. I need you to go over to
County Kerry and find out.'

Lauren poured another cup of tea and wished she had
some of the Jameson she kept in her kitchen. 'That would
come with a steep price tag.'

'Give me a number. I'm feeling generous.' Sharon's smile
reappeared as she studied Lauren's face with the practiced
eye of a veteran gambler. Lauren wasn't stupid, she didn't
know the going price for a small Picasso, but she knew it
was in the millions. Maybe this wasn't all about the money,
but it was definitely partly about the money.

'*If* I agree to do this'—Lauren emphasized *if*—'there's
a lot of legwork I'll have to do before I go over. I'll need to
file Freedom of Information Act requests with the FBI and
the Buffalo Police Department immediately—'

'Done and done.' Sharon reached down and pulled open
a drawer in the table next to her. She retrieved two folders
and held them up. 'I needed these when we took the insurance company to court to pay up. They paid the three
million it was insured for and I had to split it with my ex.'
Now she laughed out loud, polite and practiced, like the
tinkling of bells. 'That was the last time my husband and
I were on the same side of anything.'

'Even if I find the painting, won't its ownership still be in dispute?'

That knowing smile played across her lips again and she began to fan herself with the files ever so slightly. 'I'm not asking you to do anything illegal. At this point the painting is still as much mine as his. He's eighty-five years old. It took over seven years to finalize our divorce. I'm willing to hold on to the painting while he sues me.'

'That's a pleasant thought,' Lauren commented. 'You waiting out your ex-husband's death.'

She leaned forward again, arm draped over her crossed knees. 'I'm sure that if he got the news tomorrow that I was hit by a bus, he wouldn't shed a single tear.'

What a loving marriage they must have had, Lauren mused to herself. 'Won't your ex have people looking for the painting as well?'

'That's why I need you to get over there as fast as possible. Tonight, ideally, but no later than tomorrow. Once Howard finds out Jimmy died, he'll have his people combing the Irish landscape for it as well.'

Taking a deep breath, Lauren stood up. Sharon Whitney held out the paperwork to her as she crossed the room. Lauren took the files from her and said, 'I'll look these over. Give me a couple of hours to think on this.'

'You have until six this evening, then I'm going to have to make a call to the next person on my list.'

When Sharon made a move to stand, Lauren held out her free hand. 'Don't get up. I'll show myself out.'

'Very good. There's an envelope attached to that first file with a check in it.' Sitting back, she picked up her teacup from its saucer and took a sip. Sharon Whitney's rocking back and forth in her chair was making Lauren seasick. 'Thank you for your time.'

Lauren turned, knowing she'd been dismissed, and headed for the foyer. Just as she was about to exit the room she paused, turning back to look at Sharon Whitney. 'What's the name of this painting anyway?'

Sharon's face practically glowed as she answered. 'Technically, it doesn't have a name. It was a small piece on scrap canvas he did for a friend during his Rose Period. It only measured fourteen by nine inches roughly.'

That was no answer. 'What was the subject matter?' Lauren pressed.

'A harlequin standing next to a horse.' That smirk came dancing back over her face. 'My ex-husband and I nicknamed it *The Fool*.'

EIGHT

INSTEAD OF DRIVING HOME, Lauren headed south toward downtown. 'Call Matt Lawton,' she instructed out loud once her phone was plugged into the car's USB port. The sound of ringing filled the interior and then the familiar voice of FBI special agent Matt Lawton came through her speakers. 'Hey, Lauren,' he said. 'Long time, no see.'

It was good to hear his voice again. 'Let's change that right now. Can you meet me?'

'Give me ten minutes and I'll be free. How about at the statue of Shark Girl down at Canalside? I'm just finishing up a lunch meeting down there.'

'I'll see you in ten. Don't take a selfie without me.'

Lauren and Matt had been thrown together five months ago to investigate the murder of an Icelandic citizen. Reese had still been off with his head injury, so the two of them ended up in Iceland together. They hadn't kept in contact much since getting back—they were both busy with cases at their respective agencies—but Matt had genuinely sounded happy to hear from her.

Canalside was the name given to the excavated terminus of the Erie Canal. Buried for decades and forgotten, the city had decided to dig up the area near the Naval and Military Park in the early 2000s. The result was a mixed-use park/entertainment venue/outdoor history museum. It had turned an unused, abandoned property and its parking lot around the remains of the old Memorial Auditorium, the home of the Buffalo Sabres hockey team until it was replaced with the new arena, into a thriving destination for locals and tourists alike. One of the coolest things that resided at Canalside was the statue of Shark Girl. Literally a young girl's body sitting on a rock, hands demurely clasped in her lap, complete with a fancy blue dress and topped with a shark's head. The irony that there were no sharks in Lake Erie just made it all the more fun and bizarre. It had become a local tradition to take a selfie with Shark Girl.

As Lauren walked up to where it was displayed, she could see the line of people waiting patiently for their turn. Tired-looking moms held the hands of squirming kids, while teenagers made duck faces into their phones. Leaning against the railing of the raised walkway, away from the crowd, Matt Lawton waved when he saw Lauren approaching.

'Want to get in line?' she asked, jerking a thumb in the direction of the statue. Matt looked just the same as when she last saw him: same dark hair, same crooked smile. The biggest difference was that he was finally dressed appropriately for the weather. His trench coat was just the right weight for a mid-May afternoon in Buffalo. Originally from Arizona, this past winter had been his first with snow and ice and it'd been pretty miserable for him, especially with a baby at home. Matt had walked around freezing with light jackets and shiny leather shoes that didn't grip the ice. Lauren understood it took time to learn to navigate the wild fluctuations of Western New York's weather and was glad to see he seemed to be getting it down at last.

'I already have a hundred pictures with Cara and Drew,

including one framed on my desk, but I will if you insist.' Drew was his son and Cara his wife. Matt was over the moon about the both of them. Lauren could picture him here with them on a sunny day, Cara trying to balance Drew on her lap while Matt tried to get him to smile.

'No, I'm good. I was only kidding,' she laughed. 'Come walk with me. I want to talk to you about something.'

As Lauren and Matt walked along the path down to the water, she asked him what he knew about the Whitney break-in.

'Oh man, that's one of those cases the older agents tell you about when you first get assigned to a place, sort of infamous, you know?' He rubbed his chin with his hand, scratching at nonexistent stubble on his baby face. 'The agent originally assigned to it worked it to death and just couldn't catch a break. He retired years ago. It's not closed, per se, but it's not actively assigned to anyone right now. Why? You got a lead?'

'Actually, no. I got hired by an interested party to look into it, that's all I can really say.'

'If you're worried about stepping on anyone's toes, don't. It's one of those cases new agents get handed to look over so they're familiar with it, but there's nothing to be done about it. No one's done any work on the missing Whitney Picasso in years.'

'I just wanted to check and make sure. The last thing I want to do is stick my nose into an active investigation.'

'Art stolen from a private residence is treated differently from art stolen from a museum. Museum heists get the full FBI Art Theft squad treatment. Paintings stolen from someone's home get our cooperation, obviously, but it's handled on more of a local level unless we think it's part of a wider ring.' A teacher leading a group of grammar school kids toward the excavated canal walls trooped past them. Matt waited for the last straggler to catch up with his class before he went on. 'The painting is listed in the National Stolen Art File. That's about as active as the case is right now. I think you're safe if you want to poke around. The case originated with the Buffalo Police Department, so the FBI would defer to you anyway.'

'Maybe I wasn't crystal clear. I got my private investigator's license renewed. I got hired by a civilian to look into it. I'm not investigating it for the department. They put me off duty because of old work-related injuries.'

'Oh, right. I think I saw something about that on the news.' His voice took on a grave tone. 'Just be careful. That painting is literally worth millions.'

Lauren was touched by his genuine concern. 'I'll be fine. I think it's a snipe hunt but I'm not going to turn down the amount this client is willing to pay,' she said. 'You know me, I only manage to get my partners *almost* killed.'

Matt rubbed his collarbone with his good hand. A homicidal scorned wife had run him down in the street when they were in Iceland. Unlike her previous injuries, his had healed amazingly fast. 'Just watch yourself and don't go it alone. You've been rumored to take matters into your own hands in the past.'

'That's not a rumor. You know firsthand it's one hundred percent true.'

'That's not funny,' he said, frowning. Lauren hadn't gone lone wolf when Matt had gotten injured in Iceland. She'd had their Icelandic police counterpart with her, but Matt had still been sidelined in the hospital while she continued with the investigation. He'd tried to stay in the game from his hospital bed, relaying information to them as they tracked down a killer.

'I'm not going alone,' Lauren assured him, giving him a playful swipe on his good arm. 'In fact, I'm about to hire the first employee for my newly rebooted PI agency.'

NINE

'WHAT DO YOU have going on the rest of this week?'

Lauren found Reese in his favorite spot—laying on her couch with Watson sprawled on top of him watching a baseball game he'd DVR'd on TV. It was his habit to watch his favorite old games in the offseason. A huge bowl of chips sat on the floor next to him. Every other play he'd pluck two chips out, eat one, then feed the other to the dog. Watson licked his fingers, so he'd do it again.

'Me? Nothing.' His hand stopped, poised over the chip bowl, about to pluck two more out. 'Our trial got postponed, did I tell you that? The assistant DA called today. Harris fired his lawyer so that's on hold. I blocked off ten working days for nothing.'

'No, you didn't tell me.' She flopped down into her chair. Somehow after Reese had moved in, the couch had become 'his' and the armchair 'hers'. If Watson wanted to lay on one of them, then they both capitulated to the dog. 'That's a lucky break for us though, because we have a job.'

His voice raised a notch. 'What do you mean by "us" and "we"?'

'I have a very rich lady who wants to hire me for a ridiculous amount of money to try to find a painting.'

Reese looked over from the screen, cocking an eyebrow. 'What's the catch?'

'She thinks it's in Ireland. I'm going to tell her I won't do it unless you can come with me.' Lauren grinned her first genuine smile in weeks. 'I believe I need an assistant.'

'I'm not your assistant.' He turned back to the game. 'I want no part of your private investigating act.'

'Do you want to make double your salary just to look around a cottage in Ireland and ask a few questions?' Lauren held up the check Mrs Whitney had written with the payment proposal paperclipped to it. Reese wiped his fingers on his jeans and took it from her.

His green eyes widened when he saw the numbers. 'Is this lady batty? Why does she think her painting is in Ireland?'

Lauren tossed the two folders over to him, hitting him in the chest and startling Watson, who sat up and barked at her. 'You were only a teenager when the Whitney break-in happened. Read up on it. It's a real whodunit. I have to let her know in a couple of hours if we're going to take the case.'

'Why do I have to go?' he complained, sounding like one of her daughters when it was time to go to their Great-Aunt Judith's house at Easter. Still, he opened the flap on one of the files and started leafing through the pages. 'You love to go off by yourself and get into bizarre trouble. Why change your MO now?'

'Because the doctor said I needed a vacation. And with the money she's willing to pay, we might as well both get one.'

'This is not what the police doctor meant when he told you to go on vacation.'

'You should be proud of me. I found a case that's not too boring and not particularly exciting. I finally found a happy medium.'

He sighed as he looked at the photographs of the Whitney's mansion. 'Why do only rich people hire you to solve their problems?'

'Because poor people can't afford to hire private investigators. They have to rely on the police.' Lauren had done
her fair share of pro bono work over the years, mostly for
family and friends, but the reality was that you had to have
disposable income to employ a private detective. Conse-
quently, she ended up getting paid to nose round in the business of the local one-percenters most of the time.

'Still, it must be one hell of a painting,' he muttered to
himself, scanning an old report.

'It's a Picasso that's the center of a custody battle. Read
the files. That's a picture of it right there.' She pointed to
the photograph on top of the stack of papers he was holding.

He pulled it out of the pile, holding it almost to his nose
as he examined it. 'It's a funky-looking clown standing
next to a funky-looking horse. Or donkey.'

'It's a horse. And the funky clown is called a harlequin.'

He shuffled it back into the folder. 'It's not really my
taste.'

'Your taste is a framed Buffalo Bills jersey.'

'Hey!' he protested. 'Only if it's autographed.'

Lauren fought the urge to roll her eyes at him. 'You'll
be able to buy twenty signed Bills jerseys with what she's
paying us. Just start packing. I have to make some calls.'

'I still haven't said I was going to go with you. And what
about Watson? We can't just abandon our child.'

Lauren waved him off as she got up. 'I already called
Dayla. She's going to take great care of him while we're gone.'

'Dayla? You want to entrust Watson to Dayla?'

'She's a mom,' Lauren pointed out. Reese and Dayla Oli-
ver, her neighbor from down the street, had a very compli-
cated relationship. He thought she was flighty, and she tried
to do everything in her power to convince him it was true.
Still, she was a great friend to Lauren and had been there

for her and her daughters over the years. Lauren trusted her to take care of Watson and her house while they were gone. She knew Reese did too, he was just being difficult. 'And a grandmother. Stop being a baby. I know for a fact you have almost a month's worth of vacation time banked. If you don't use it, you'll lose it. You might as well come to Ireland with me.'

He tossed the files onto the coffee table in front of him. 'I think the real reason you want me to go with you is because between the two of us I'm the only one who knows how to drive a stick shift *and* I drove on the opposite side of the road when I was stationed overseas in the army.'

'That was certainly a consideration when I thought about hiring you as an associate for this case.' *Damn him for knowing me so well*, she thought. 'Besides, you're the one who's been saying I need to get out of the house and do things.'

'I meant going to a cooking class, not flying off to Dublin.'

'It's not Dublin,' she tossed over her shoulder. 'It's Keelnamara.'

'Keena what?'

'Keelnamara. It means *Church by the Sea* in the Irish.'

'I can't even spell that!' he called as she walked up the stairs. She didn't bother to respond. She knew he was going with her.

Once she was in her bedroom with the door closed, she called Frank Violanti, attorney extraordinaire. He'd represented her a year ago when the district attorney's office had put her in front of a grand jury after her showdown, as the departmental doctor put it, with a young sociopath in a waterfront warehouse and only she had walked out alive.

She got 'no billed'. The department lifted her suspension and she went back to work in the Homicide office.

'What did you do now, Detective?' he asked without saying hello first.

'Very funny, Counselor,' she shot back as she sat on the edge of her bed. 'I actually have some questions on marital assets.'

'You taking the ex back to court? Hasn't the poor man suffered enough?'

'Oh, Frank, if I wasn't in such a good mood I'd drive over to your office and throat punch you.' She'd never throat punched anyone in her life, but Frank didn't know that.

'I think I like you better when you're in a bad mood. What's up?'

She gave him the run down on Sharon Whitney's request without naming names. The case was so well known he figured it out immediately, but she would neither confirm nor deny who her client was.

'There's no statute of limitations on marital property. If it was stolen or misplaced, the item still has to be sorted out by the court when it resurfaces,' he told her, then asked, 'No prenuptial agreement?'

'Nope.'

'Poor bastard,' he sighed into the phone. 'Always get it in writing.'

'So if I find the painting I can lawfully return it to my client?' she asked, just to be perfectly clear.

'Until a court says otherwise, it's as much hers as it is his. Possession is nine-tenths of the law.'

'Thanks, Frank. Just wanted to make sure everything was above board.'

'Hold up, I didn't say that. If you do find the painting, which I think you won't, but if you do, you'll be opening a can of worms that can wriggle around for decades.'

'He's eighty-five years old.'

'You'll be opening a can of worms that can wriggle around for months.'

'What they do about it in court is their problem. I just want to make sure my ass is covered.'

'Hold on.' She heard him try to muffle his phone. 'Vera. Vera. Ve-ra! I need the Tompkins file. Please.'

'Frank?'

'I'm here. My new executive assistant doesn't know where anything is in my office. I haven't even shown her the room I designated just for you yet.'

She ignored that comment. Usually she loved to spar verbally with Frank but she was on a deadline. 'Thanks for the information. If you need me for anything I'll be out of the country for a week or two.'

'Keep my number on speed dial.'

'Will do.' She clicked off and scrolled through her phone log until she found Sharon Whitney's number.

'Hello?' Sharon answered the phone herself this time. Lauren wondered where her manservant who'd run interference for her earlier was.

'Mrs Whitney? I'll take the job, but I have an associate that needs to come with me. I hope that won't be a problem.'

'No problem at all. Of course, you'll pay him yourself out of your own fee,' that same cool, assured voice told her. 'I'll text you the number of my travel agent. Just give him the details of the extra traveler. He's already started to make all the arrangements for you to catch a red eye tomorrow.'

'You were that sure I'd take it?'

'My dear, you must be tired of blood and murderers and death. Wouldn't it be nice to recover something beautiful and reintroduce it to the world for once?'

'Yes, actually,' Lauren smiled into the phone, 'it would.'

TEN

'WHAT ARE YOU DOING? Our flight leaves in six hours.'

The day after Lauren met Sharon Whitney, she stood in her living room watching Reese pack. She unbuckled her belt, pulled it out of two loops of her jeans, then slid her off-duty gun holster over her hip. 'I want to talk to the husband,' she said, slipping on a black blazer that concealed the weapon. She knew exactly how to wear it so not even a bulge showed, even on her pencil-thin frame. She topped the ensemble off with a mid-weight waist-length coat, left unbuttoned.

'What are you going to tell him without giving up your client?' Reese had his army duffel bag open in front of him on the living room floor. In his left hand he held three baseball caps. A fourth sat on top of his clothes. 'Should I bring the Bisons, the Bills or the Sabres hat?'

'I like the Yankees cap,' she said. 'And I don't have to tell him anything. I can say I'm a private investigator. Maybe he'll assume I'm with the insurance company. Maybe he'll know it's the wife. Maybe he'll think it's about something else. I don't care. I just want to feel the guy out.'

Reese plucked the Yankees hat from atop the pile of clothes and tossed it on the couch. 'Seems unnecessary, if you ask me.' Watson jumped on the couch and tried to snag the cap. Reese grabbed it just in time.

'I didn't ask you, and why did you just take out the cap that I told you to keep?'

'Your fashion sense is notoriously lacking. Whatever you recommend must go.' He put the Bisons hat in its place. 'It's a shame because that's one of my favorite ball caps.'

Lauren pushed her glasses up on her nose. The thick black frames were another fashion choice Reese often derided her for. 'You coming with me, Diva?'

He stood staring down into his bag. 'Nope.' He shook his head and replaced the Bisons hat with the Bills. 'I've got a lot of packing to do.'

'Oh, I heard your voicemail kick in when you were in the shower,' she said, snapping her fingers. 'Charlotte left a message. I thought you were done with her months ago.'

'I am,' he told her. 'We are.'

Lauren had only met Charlotte once when they'd double dated with a UPS driver Lauren was seeing. Charlotte was a bigwig with one of the local banks, investment funds or some such thing. That night was the last time Lauren saw Charlotte or the UPS driver.

'If you'd just make a clean break, you wouldn't have this problem,' Lauren admonished for the hundredth time. Reese was notorious for stringing women along, simply because he had a hard time breaking up with them. He always felt guilty for not reciprocating their feelings and kept giving in and coming back, just to break their hearts all over again.

'Hey, when a woman gets a piece of this,' he motioned from his head to his feet, 'they just keep coming back for more.'

'Disgusting.' Lauren wrinkled her nose as she started for the door. 'I'll see you later.'

'You're wasting precious time,' he shot back at her. 'I

need help deciding which pair of sneakers to bring. And I have to take Watson and all of his accoutrements over to Dayla's house. He'll be heartbroken if you don't say good-bye. You don't need to talk to Whitney.'

Lauren didn't bother to argue. He was right. It really wasn't necessary for her to speak to Howard Whitney. Sharon had hired her to do a very specific job that for her purposes didn't involve him at all.

She left Reese juggling headgear, hopped in her car and headed for the thruway anyway. She'd walk down and see Watson before they left. Lauren didn't intend on making this a prolonged visit.

Mr Whitney no longer lived in the city of Buffalo. He now resided in an enormous estate forty minutes south of the city that overlooked Lake Erie. The view of the city was just a thin band of man-made structures that curved around the easternmost tip of the Great Lake.

The Whitney family had made its fortune shipping grain at the turn of the last century. Until the 1950s they'd dominated the Great Lakes, with freighters stopping at all the rust-belt cities, filling the grain elevators and moving on. Howard Whitney had seen the writing on the wall and moved his money into trucking companies, abandoning the silos that now stood derelict along the lake. Too expensive to tear down and too obsolete to be of use for anything else, his family's legacy stood as a constant reminder of what Buffalo had once been. There'd been rumors around the police department that Whitney was involved with the mob, which had long had a foothold in the city. There was even talk he'd been involved in a couple of hits on the West Side in the seventies—before most of La Cosa Nostra had left the city to go south to Florida, or gone into legitimate businesses with less physical risk involved. The allegations against him of illegal activity had never been proven, but Lauren knew she'd be stupid to dismiss them. A retired mobster was still a dangerous mobster. Although it was hard to picture an old-school gangster living in the suburban landscape she was now driving through.

Unlike the concrete and blacktopped urban neighborhoods she was used to, the houses along the lake were spaced out on vast lots that backed right up to the beach. That was something Lauren had to explain to people she met when she traveled. Lake Erie had beautiful sand beaches and rolling waves with white caps, just like an ocean. Buffalo was situated at the lake's narrowest point, with only a river separating the city and Canada. There was always a discussion in the police academy about a person shooting a gun from the American shore and killing someone on the Canadian shore—whose homicide would it be? The short answer was no one really knew, although armchair experts loved giving their dissertations on why it would be one country or the other or both.

All Lauren knew was that anything that dealt with multiple jurisdictions on an international level was a red tape nightmare. She was glad she was going to Ireland as a private citizen and not an agent of the state.

Lauren got off the thruway and headed over to Route 5, which could take you along the lake all the way into Erie, Pennsylvania and beyond. She wasn't going quite that far, but the city was getting smaller and smaller in her rearview the further south she drove. Canada became a faint line on the horizon to her right before disappearing completely.

She turned up her music and rolled down her window a crack to let the fresh air in. The week before, the temperature had dipped into the forties during the day. Now it was almost seventy out. The warmth of the sun on her face made her feel like a flower blooming after the long dreary winter they'd had.

Lauren's GPS warned her to take the next right in 1,000 feet, causing her to hit the brakes. It was easy to let the speed gauge creep up on that particular stretch of road. Thankfully, at noon on a Tuesday, no one was riding her bumper.

The entrance to the driveway was no more than a break in the hedges that surrounded the property. There was no gate, but Lauren did notice a security camera mounted on a pole as she turned in.

The driveway ran straight toward the main house, where it curved in front. It led to a massive multi-car garage with a circular pad in front of it. Lauren parked in front of the third set of doors and got out. The columned white mansion looked like a movie set with the sparkling lake behind it. She could smell the freshly raked black mulch in the spring flowerbeds as she came up a paved walkway toward the front entrance. Inhaling the scent deeply, she ignored the stitch in her side that was popping up more frequently. *Hell, it's less than a hundred yards to the house.* Her hand wrapped around to her scar. *I should be able to sprint to it without any problems.*

A young woman came out, meeting Lauren before she got to the first step of the porch. 'Can I help you?' she asked. About thirty years old, with long, sleek black hair, she wore an expensive-looking white cardigan over a pretty pink top.

Lauren stopped, hand on the porch railing. 'My name is Lauren Riley and I'm looking for Mister Whitney. Is he in?'

In a polite but firm voice she replied, 'I'm sorry, do you have an appointment? He wasn't expecting anyone.'

'No, but I was hoping to be able to speak with him. I'm a private investigator.'

Her eyes narrowed. 'I know you. You look different but

you're the police officer that's always on the news. The one who killed that boy who was finding women on dating sites and murdering them.'

Lauren's gut clenched. David Spencer had been a twenty-year-old serial killer. She doubted if he had ever been a boy. Still, the fact she'd had to take his life was something she wrestled with almost daily. She stuffed her scarred hands in her pants pockets at the thought of it. 'Yes, but I'm also a licensed private investigator. I'm not here in my capacity as a police officer. I just have a few questions I'd like to ask your—'

'Grandfather,' she finished before Lauren could say employer. 'Howard Whitney is my grandfather. I'm Kelsey Whitney.'

'It's nice to meet you, Kelsey,' Lauren replied. 'You must be his son Archer's daughter.' Archer was Whitney's son with his first wife, before he met Sharon.

'You really know our family tree.'

Lauren smiled and shrugged it off. 'It's nothing a simple Google Search wouldn't turn up.' If Kelsey was freaked out that Lauren knew her lineage, she didn't show it. She actually swept her arm back, gesturing toward the far side of the house. 'Grandpa's on the back porch. Let's take a walk around the house and see if he wants to speak with you.'

That was the upside of being on TV all the time. Kelsey Whitney let a total stranger onto her grandfather's property without even asking Lauren for ID. For some reason, people inherently trusted the people they saw on the television. It made her private investigator job so much easier.

Trailing behind Kelsey, Lauren started to have second thoughts about coming out to see Howard Whitney. She told herself it was to gauge the type of person he was. Was Howard Whitney the man Sharon claimed he was? Would he stage his own assault and robbery just to keep the painting out of her hands? Truth be told, it was more to quell her curiosity than anything else. She'd already taken the case. Unless she wanted to give the money back, she was getting on that plane in a couple of hours, no matter what he was like. Still, it was always better to know exactly who you were dealing with when you dove into something like this. He had just as much riding on the outcome of her investigation as her client.

The neatly trimmed grass was soft under her shoes as they hugged the house until they emerged in the backyard. A perfectly mowed lawn continued right to the edge of a small cliff. Wooden steps led down to the beach twenty feet below. Lauren looked out across the water. The estate was a perfect island of isolation.

'Hello, dear!' Lauren heard behind her. 'Who might this be?'

Lauren spun to her left to see a porch that extended the entire length of the mansion. To the right of a set of double doors an elderly but spry-looking man in blue sweater and tan pants was standing next to a wicker chair. He sported an impressive head of white hair, cut neatly and parted perfectly down one side. A laptop was set up on a matching coffee table in front of him.

'This is Lauren Riley, Grandpa,' Kelsey said, starting up the porch steps. 'She's a private investigator.'

He squinted against the afternoon sunlight, shading his pale blue eyes with a blue-veined hand. 'I know you from somewhere,' he said.

'She's that Buffalo cop who caught the serial killer,' his granddaughter chimed in.

'The police lady from TV!' He snapped his fingers in

recognition. Sometimes her dark hair and glasses didn't disguise her, just delayed the inevitable.

Lauren followed Kelsey over to her grandfather, biting back the urge to correct him and say 'officer'. At eighty-five, she doubted she was likely to change his way of addressing women. 'I'm not here as a police officer, Mister Whitney,' she said, coming to a stop in front of him. 'I'm here as a private investigator. You're under no obligation to talk to me.'

'I'm never under obligation to talk to anyone,' he said. The breeze off the lake ruffled his white hair. 'Come join me. I was just checking the markets.' He had an easy, pleasant manner about him. Whitney was what her mother would have called 'an old-time gentleman', meaning he still held the door open for ladies and helped you with your coat.

Lauren took a seat across from Kelsey, who beamed at her grandfather in adoration.

'I just meant this isn't official police business,' Lauren said. 'Do you have any idea why I'm here? Why someone would hire me to talk to you?' she fished.

Sitting down, he shut the laptop with a snap. 'I can think of three separate matters off the top of my head. But you're not going to tell me which one, and I'm not going to guess and give away all my secrets.'

'That's a lot of issues you have.' Lauren couldn't help but smile at him. She'd tried to game him and he'd clapped right back at her.

'You don't get to be my age, with my money, and not make an enemy or two.' His eyes practically twinkled. He was enjoying this. 'If you do, you're doing it wrong.'

'I must be doing it wrong because I have a lot of enemies and no money.'

That made him chuckle. 'What do you want to know? If nothing else, I'm intrigued.'

She made a show of looking around the stately porch. 'How long have you lived in this house? It's beautiful.'

'I moved here after I divorced my fourth wife, Judith. Did she hire you? That seems like something she might do.'

'How many times have you been married?' Lauren asked, though she already knew the answer.

'Including my current wife Beverly, five times. I think it's safe to assume at my age there won't be a sixth wedding. But you never know.' He gave an innocent shrug. 'Beverly didn't hire you, I hope. I haven't finished paying my divorce attorney for the last one.'

He hadn't really answered her first question and she hadn't answered his about who hired her. It was like they were in a very carefully choreographed dance-off.

'I'm sorry I can't disclose who hired me. I can tell you that you're not the target of the investigation.'

He studied her face thoughtfully. 'Then I think I know why you're here. I believe my second ex-wife, Sharon, might have hired you to do some dirty work for her.'

'What makes you think that?' Lauren asked, neither confirming nor denying she was her client.

'There's been some developments overseas that we both have an interest in.'

'What sort of developments?'

He leaned forward, elbows on his knees, smile never faltering. 'You tell Sharon I'll always be one step ahead of her.' When Lauren didn't say anything, he sank back in his chair, still smiling pleasantly. 'Whatever that may mean.' He locked eyes with her, waiting for her next question.

'I don't think I'm going to get the answers I need today,' she admitted, standing up. Lauren knew when she'd hit a brick wall. 'I'm sorry I've wasted your time.'

He rose along with her, gentleman that he was. 'I'm

afraid it's me who's wasted yours. I've been a cat too long to get licked by a kitten,' he said, and gave her a wink. 'It's been a pleasure, Miss Riley. Tell Sharon I said hello.'

'Bye, Detective Riley,' Kelsey said, not unpleasantly.

Lauren didn't reply so as not to officially out her client, just gave a polite smile and nod. She could feel his and his granddaughter's eyes on her back as she turned to leave.

He definitely could have staged the art heist, she thought as she made her way around the house again to get to her car. *He's been playing chess with Sharon Whitney for twenty years. The only question now is, where's the knight?*

ELEVEN

'ARE YOU SURE you remember how to drive a stick?' Lauren asked as Reese popped open the trunk of their rented sedan in the Dublin Airport lot. Their red-eye flight from New York City had got them into Ireland at five in the morning. After retrieving Lauren's luggage, going through customs and finding the car rental stall, it was after six a.m. and the sun had just broken over the horizon.

Lauren set the cup of coffee she'd bought at one of the kiosks on the roof of the car. Her neighbor, Dayla, had warned her that it would only be in the fifties temperature-wise in Ireland in May. She unzipped her suitcase, pulled her fleece jacket out and slipped it on.

'It's like riding a bike, you never forget.' He took Lauren's suitcase, squished the telescoping handle down into the bag, then hefted it into the trunk. He slung his own duffel bag in next and slammed it shut. 'It's the remembering to stay on the other side of the road that's hard.'

'I'll navigate,' Lauren assured him, picking up her coffee cup. That was the one thing she could not leave behind.

Reese paused at the driver's side door and took a long look at the tiny car. 'Both of our knees are going to be under our chins.'

'I didn't make the reservations. And you're short anyway.'

'I'm five-eleven,' he reminded her, opening his door.

'Practically one of the wee folk,' she said, and slid into the passenger side.

'Enough with the short jokes unless you want to drive, Big Bird.' That insult had lost its sting since she'd cut her hair short and let it darken. It was amazing how much she didn't miss being blond. It was too much upkeep the older she got; she just couldn't be bothered to run out once a month to get her roots done. She was finding middle age to be a wonderfully freeing time.

'Look, I'm putting in the address to the bed and breakfast.' Her finger hovered over the GPS built into the dashboard. 'I'm doing my share.' Glancing from the address on her phone to the touch screen, she punched in the numbers.

'Don't talk, OK?' Reese adjusted the rearview mirror. 'I need to concentrate. It's been a while.'

A pleasant-sounding British lady's voice took them out of Dublin Airport and into the outskirts of the city. Lauren sipped her coffee as the Irish countryside rolled by and didn't say a word. It was a four-hour drive to their destination of Keelnamara, a village just south of Killorglin. Their contact person was a Mrs Theresa Fitzgerald. According to the paperwork Sharon Whitney had forwarded to Lauren, not only was Mrs Fitzgerald the proprietor of the bed and breakfast they were staying in, she was also the real estate agent handling the sale of Jimmy Breen's cottage.

Lauren wasn't about to make the same mistake in Ireland as she had in Iceland. She'd been so awestruck by the landscape that she got sidetracked. And when she got sidetracked bad things happened. *This is no vacation*, she told herself. *I'm here to do a job, not sightsee.* And part of that job was to familiarize herself with the painting she was looking for and Picasso's work in general.

She'd printed out everything she could manage in the

short time she had after getting back from Howard Whitney's house. It was all basic Google Search stuff, but she needed to study it. She extracted a folder from the oversized tote she'd used as a carry-on and started reading all about Picasso's Rose Period. Interestingly enough, the article said Picasso was so poor during this time that he burned a lot of his paintings for heat. The untitled piece owned by the Whitneys was given to a friend as a gift and had remained in France until the start of World War One, when it was sold to a private collector in the States. It remained in that family until Sharon Whitney's gallery arranged its sale to her future husband in 1980. It then disappeared from their Middlesex Road mansion on 12 August 2000. Its sale price in 1980 was two million dollars. It had been insured for three million. Lauren sucked in her breath when she read its last estimated value: upwards of twenty million dollars, if put up for auction.

'Reese,' Lauren said, breaking the silence. 'Listen to this.' She gave him the Cliffs Notes version of what she'd just read, with an emphasis on the monetary value. He let out a low whistle.

'Why was that thing in a house in Buffalo and not in a museum somewhere with massive security and guards?' he asked.

'It's a lesser known, smaller piece that's never been on public display. In 1980, when Howard Whitney bought it, there wasn't the crazy demand for Picassos there is now. It's caused his works to appreciate in value considerably. I know two million dollars is a lot of money, but twenty million dollars is a shit-ton of money.'

'It's the kind of money people get killed over,' he agreed.

'I wonder if James Breen knew how much it was worth in today's market?' Lauren wondered aloud. She didn't know how computer savvy the handyman had been, but it wasn't hard to Google the information. He must have known the painting would increase in value over the years if he'd been the one to go to the trouble of stealing it in the first place.

Reese paused for a moment, mulling over the information she'd just rained on him, then asked, 'How did he die again?'

'Sharon Whitney told me he had been sick.'

'Shouldn't the FBI be handling this?'

'They did at first. I talked to Matt Lawton about it. Remember, I told you in the kitchen when you were having breakfast?' She got a blank look in response. When Reese was concentrating on eating, sometimes things went in one ear and out the other as he chewed. 'The Buffalo Police Department called them in immediately. But because it was a private residence and not a museum, the feds have different rules.'

'Oh yeah, now I remember,' Reese replied.

Lauren could tell when he was lying, so she went on. 'I read the rest in the file. The FBI helped search James Breen's apartment in Buffalo with the BPD the night of the theft and had surveillance on him for weeks afterwards. When nothing turned up, and James left the States ten months later, that was it. He was out of both agencies' jurisdictions. The local agent who picked up the case did what he could with the Buffalo detectives for a while. Both Sharon and her husband Howard hired private detectives back then who looked for money transactions, watched his house in Ireland, asked questions. I have their reports here.' She rattled the papers in Reese's direction. 'But he never made any big purchases and lived a law-abiding life. Basically, the case got ice-cold. Before the year was over law enforcement moved on to the next big case.'

'And the Whitneys' PIs turned up squat, so they took their toys and went home too.'

'Right,' Riley said. 'The more I read these files the more I think James was involved with the theft of that painting. None of the security alarms were tripped. The house was locked up when Sharon got home and found her husband, and there was no sign of forced entry. Nothing else was taken, even though there were valuables in the same room as the Picasso that would have been much easier to fence at the time.'

Reese spun the wheel and eased the small car around the curve of a roundabout. 'You really think a sixty-six-year-old handyman in Ireland kept a twenty-million-dollar painting hanging on his bathroom wall all these years so he could look at it every time he took a dump?'

'No, but maybe there's something in his cottage that can tell us where the painting is now.'

'What do we do if we locate this precious piece of artwork? Roll it up and stick it in your carry-on?'

Lauren had been thinking about that since she took the job. 'We secure it and call Sharon Whitney. Then keep securing it until she makes arrangements to take it off our hands.'

'It's a twenty-million-dollar painting and we don't even have guns.' Reese's eyebrow raised with the level of doubt that filled his voice. 'I have to believe whoever has it isn't going to give it up willingly.'

Lauren sighed and turned her eyes back to the passenger side window. The multiple shades of green that made up the landscape reminded her of why it was called the Emerald Isle. 'I'm well aware of that fact.'

'You want to hear another fact?' Reese asked, the corners of his mouth turning down into a grim frown.

'No,' she answered.

'I think we're in way over our heads.'

The story of my life, she thought bitterly. *And probably my death too.*

TWELVE

THE VILLAGE OF Keelnamara was nestled in the valley between Dingle Bay and MacGillycuddy's Reeks, Ireland's highest mountain range. According to Google Maps, there was no real village to speak of, just a collection of houses scattered on the slopes leading down to the water with exactly one pub, one small grocery store, a church, one petrol station and a post office. Fishing and collecting mussels were the main industries in the area and had been since time immemorial, although oyster farms had been introduced in the last thirty years. Even though it was in the Ring of Kerry, it was off the beaten tourist path. There were no shops in Keelnamara touting Aran sweaters, no jewelers selling Connemara marble bracelets. As they passed the little white clapboard Catholic church overlooking the sea, that had probably stood for generations, it occurred to Lauren that this was rural Ireland at its purest, and she wasn't sure if they'd be met with welcome, scorn, suspicion, or a mix of all three.

Lauren texted the owner of the bed and breakfast, Mrs Fitzgerald, when they were five minutes out. She called Lauren back on her cell right away. 'I'll be waiting for you,' she told her in a beautiful lilting Irish accent. *I'm the one with the accent*, she reminded herself as they crested a small hill. In front of her was Dingle Bay. If she twisted

around, she'd see the peaks of MacGillycuddy's Reeks. She
was surrounded by mountains, sky and the sea.

They came over another hill and immediately saw an ornate wooden sign proclaiming 'Fitzgerald's Bed and Breakfast'. It was situated on a small hill and Lauren could see
that it sloped gently all the way to a beach, less than a quarter mile down the road. Thick hedges ringed the property
along the sides, with a low stone wall boxing in the front.
It had a black wrought iron gate, which now stood open,
waiting for them.

They pulled into the driveway of a large, red-brick cottage, complete with green painted shutters. It was so post-
card-perfect, Lauren could picture the smoke curling from
the stone chimney on cold nights. A woman in her late sixties who Lauren assumed was Mrs Fitzgerald was waiting
for them in the doorway. She waved the car forward until
they were parked next to a red Honda in front of the garage.
She was a tiny woman, no more than five feet tall, with
short-cropped silver hair and round glasses on a beaded
chain around her neck. A fuzzy cream-colored wool sweater
topped a long brown skirt that swished around her legs as
she walked toward them. Instead of shoes, she wore ankle-
high rain boots. With the sky a dark, cloudy gray, Lauren
thought that didn't bode well for the weather. She was glad
she'd brought her heavy tan trench coat. Not only did it have
a lot of pockets, it was also water-resistant.

'Hello and welcome to Keelnamara!' the woman called
as they climbed out of the car and stretched. It'd been a
long four hours without stopping. 'I'm Mrs Fitzgerald, and
you'd be Miss Riley and Mister Reese then?'

'Hello,' Lauren called back. Reese gave her a friendly
wave then popped the trunk and removed their bags.

She stopped at the end of the driveway. 'Come inside,

the both of you. I've got tea and biscuits for weary travel-
ers. I'll apologize in advance for the weather. It's supposed
to be rainy all week, I'm afraid.'

'It's better than snow,' Lauren replied, thinking back to
the snowstorm last year that started at the end of March
and lasted for four days. She'd spent most of that storm in
police headquarters with her lawyer, Frank Violanti, at her
side, explaining how she'd ended up in an abandoned warehouse with a dead serial killer.

Opening the front door, their host herded Lauren and
Reese through a large, neat living room, then led them into
a bright, airy kitchen. While the outside of the house looked
antique and quaint, the inside had been remodeled with all
the latest amenities. A floral teapot sat on a marble-topped
kitchen island. Three cups had been set out along with a
matching china sugar bowl and creamer. A plate of brown
cookies, just out of the oven, was waiting for them.

'This is wonderful,' Lauren told her, sitting on one of the
stools. 'You didn't have to go to all this trouble.'

Mrs Fitzgerald waved Lauren off. 'It's no trouble at all.'
She moved past Reese and pulled his seat out for him.
'You're a handsome one, aren't you?'

Reese sat down as she poured a steaming cup of tea for
him. Rewarding her compliment with one of his 1,000-watt
smiles, he said, 'Thank you.'

Lauren loved watching Reese soak up the attention.
Sometimes she forgot how young he was, almost six years
her junior, still in his mid-thirties and boyishly good-look-
ing even with his shaved head. Before he'd sustained his
head injury, he'd had flawless caramel-brown skin. Still,
with his clear green eyes and perfect smile, women turned
to puddles when he switched on the charm.

Mrs Fitzgerald patted his hand and took a seat next

to Lauren, across from him. 'You're here about Jimmy's place,' she said.

Lauren liked a woman who got right down to business. 'It says in the paperwork I received that you're the real estate agent who sold Jimmy's cottage to Sharon Whitney.'

She chuckled, gripping her teacup with both hands. 'Real estate agent, innkeeper, church secretary and local historian. Keelnamara has one hundred and seventy-five residents. One hundred and seventy-six when Kelly Shanahan has her baby. In a townland this small you learn to wear many hats.'

Lauren made a mental note to stop referring to Keelnamara as a village. She'd never heard the word townland used to describe a place before. It seemed fitting now that she'd heard it from Mrs Fitzgerald's lips. 'It's lovely here,' Lauren said, eyes wandering to the window. A huge brown rabbit lopped around the side yard, stopping to chew, then straightening up to listen before hopping again.

'That's a hare,' Mrs Fitzgerald told her. 'A resident pest, but they won't bother you. Now where was I? Oh, Keelnamara. It's not a big town like Killorglin. The families have been here for hundreds of years. The children tend to leave but they always come back. There's something about the call of the mountains and ocean you can't escape. My own two sons live in Dublin now, but they want to come back. There's not much work around here if you're not a fisherman, like my husband.' Her voice got a little wistful when she spoke about her sons being gone, and Lauren could tell that if it were up to her, they'd be home in Keelnamara already.

'Does your husband fish right here in the bay?' Lauren asked.

'Well dear, it's not the kind of fishing you're thinking about,' she laughed. 'He and a few friends raise oysters. They import the seed oysters from France and raise them in bags. You'll see the raised oyster trestles out in the water. They get collected around Christmastime. Then mussel season starts and ends in April. Mussels you have to dredge for. County Kerry is renowned for its shellfish. You should try them if you get the chance. They're grand.'

'Now that mussel season is over, what do they do?' Lauren asked.

'Fish for salmon. But it's a tricky business. You have to leave the net out in the bay, and when it catches a salmon the fishermen have to race out to the net before a seal gets there first.'

'It sounds like hard work,' Reese commented.

''Tis.' Mrs Fitzgerald reached over and took his hand in hers, turning it over and looking at his smooth palm. 'Your hands tell tales, you know. Yours don't tell the tale of the ocean.'

Lauren instinctively closed her hands into fists at her sides, hiding the angry raised scars on her palm. They told the tale of a desperate fight to survive, of glass cutting deep and the surgeries afterward. The image of David Spencer bleeding out on a dirty concrete floor with a shard of window glass she'd jammed into his neck filled her mind. *Maybe the damage to my lungs wasn't my worst injury*, she thought.

'I'm a city dweller through and through. I haven't done much in the way of manual labor,' Reese admitted, pulling his hand away gently, trying to get their host back on track. He'd caught Lauren clenching her hands out of the corner of his eye. He knew when it was time to change the subject. 'Tell us some tales about Jimmy Breen.'

'Jimmy was a good man.' She gave a sad sort of sigh at the thought of him. 'Odd in his ways. When you go to his place, you'll know why I say it. He could never throw anything away. He was a fixer, you see. He always thought an item would be of use someday if he held onto it long enough.'

'Is that how he made his money? Fixing things?' Lauren asked, relaxing her hands a little.

'He did,' she replied. 'He could repair anything with a motor. Worked on patching up the engines and riggings of the fishing boats.'

'Nothing steady?' Reese asked.

'He wasn't one to tie himself down to a regular job. He fixed whatever needed fixing and moved on. He did do quite a bit for Michael Shea, down at the pub.' She shook her head. 'What a week. First, he drops dead on the walking path by the pub, then your American employer offers more money than his sister has ever seen in her life for his cottage, and now you two show up.'

Lauren was sure Sharon Whitney had told her that Jimmy had been sick. 'He died from a fall?'

'That's the look of it, they say. A heart attack maybe. Jimmy didn't take very good care of himself.' Lowering her voice conspiratorially, she said, 'The local undertaker in Glenbeigh took his body to the university hospital in Tralee at the county coroner's request. He wanted an autopsy. So did his sister, Sheila.' She shook her head. 'Poor thing is grief-stricken.'

'You know Jimmy Breen's sister as well?' Lauren asked, still puzzling over why Sharon Whitney would think he had been ill. If he'd had a heart attack, maybe he'd been getting treated for high blood pressure or cholesterol when he lived with the Whitneys twenty years ago in the States. He would have been in his forties back then, old enough to start having heart problems.

Mrs Fitzgerald nodded. 'I know the whole family. Sheila Breen married Daniel McGrath. The woman was widowed when their son Martin was just a wee lad. She's had a tough go of it. It's a tragedy Jimmy died, God rest his soul, but Sheila getting that windfall couldn't have come at a better time. Jimmy was an odd one, but he helped her out all he could.' She lifted her teacup and took a sip. 'Even in death, it seems. More than I can say for her son.'

'I take it you don't approve of Sheila's son?' Reese asked.

A scowl crept across Mrs Fitzgerald's smooth, pale face. 'Sheila's boy, Martin, came back to Keelnamara two months ago. He's been nothing but a misery to her. He went about stealing fishing equipment ten years ago. The Garda caught him and sent him to prison for a spell. When he got out, he moved to Dublin, where he fell in with some more bad actors. He returned to prison in short order. Now he's out and back living in her house, no job, covered in obscene tattoos, and drinking in the pub all day.' She added a little milk to her tea. Lauren's was sitting untouched before her so she picked it up and sipped it to be polite. Between Mrs Whitney and Mrs Fitzgerald, she'd had more tea in the last week than the last year.

'Poor Sheila believes that if his father was still alive, he'd straighten up,' Mrs Fitzgerald continued. 'Jimmy tried to take him under his wing when Martin returned home. The two of them ended up on the stool next to each other at Robber O'Shea's.' Her voice lowered in disapproval. 'That's the name of the local pub.'

'Good to know,' Reese teased.

'The Guinness is good there,' she admitted, echoing a saying Lauren's grandfather was fond of. 'Just ask Mister Fitzgerald when he gets home. He enjoys a pint or two there himself quite often.'

Lauren fished around in her tote bag. 'Have you ever

seen this painting?' she asked, handing the photograph to Mrs Fitzgerald. 'In Jimmy's possession or otherwise?'

Picking up the glasses from around her neck and setting them on her nose, Mrs Fitzgerald examined the picture. 'I have not,' she said, handing it back to Lauren. 'There were rumors when he came home all those years ago that he was mixed up in something criminal back in the States involving a fancy painting. I didn't believe the gossip. I never saw him with a painting of any kind. When you see his place, you'll understand.'

'Could he have given the painting to his sister, Sheila?' Reese asked, biting into a biscuit. In deference to their host, he chewed with his mouth shut.

'If he did, I never saw it and she never mentioned it.' Her smile shifted into a slight frown. 'I visit her two or three times a week. She's been in dire straits financially since she lost her husband. Mr Fitzgerald and I try to help out where we can, but she's a proud woman. Doesn't like to take charity.'

She motioned back toward the living room. Over the stone fireplace was an enormous copy of 'Starry Night' by Vincent van Gogh. The swirling blues and yellows perfectly complemented the décor in the room. 'That's about as artsy as we get in these parts. I think they have a picture of the dogs playing the cards in Robber's pub next to the big Guinness mirror. That'd be the closest thing we have to a museum.'

'Thank you for the tea and cookies,' Lauren said, standing up and slinging her tote over her shoulder. 'I think I'd like to go to my room and rest a bit before we head over to Jimmy's cottage.'

Reese waited until Mrs Fitzgerald stood and then rose. 'I'm a little jet-lagged myself. Sounds like we've got our work cut out for us.'

'It does sound like it,' she agreed. 'Just one piece of advice for you both, if you don't mind.'

Lauren grabbed the handle of her rolling luggage. 'Please,' she said. 'We could use all the help we can get.'

Mrs Fitzgerald's voice took on a low, serious tone and her eyes narrowed. 'If that painting is here, find it and get it as far and away from Keelnamara as quickly as you can. If Jimmy really did have it, it brought him nothing but bad luck.'

THIRTEEN

'THIS IS WHERE you'll both be staying,' Mrs Fitzgerald said, sweeping the door open with her arm, her mood lightened since giving the cryptic message about the painting being bad luck.

The guest cottage, which looked so tiny from the outside, was deceptively spacious and airy on the inside. Only one-story, long and narrow, the word *ranch* didn't seem an appropriate way to describe it. You could tell the cottage was much newer than the main house, even though it had obviously been built to match its general style. Same paint job, same brick chimney, same doors and windows. It was the cute little sister to the grand lady up front.

Reese and Riley filed into the kitchen where the white wood table was set with four light blue placemats centered around a stoneware jug filled with wildflowers. White fabric blinds hung from the window, which looked out across the back lawn to a path that led to another gate. 'If you go out that way,' Mrs Fitzgerald followed Lauren's gaze, 'that leads right down to the beach. But be careful, it's a rock beach, not the sand type most visitors are used to.'

Lauren rolled her luggage near to the stove, standing up straight so she could have a look. The hedges and up and down roll of the hills obscured the beach itself, but not the green-gray water, which looked angry under the overcast sky. She was relieved to see a coffee maker on the marble kitchen countertop.

'The Wi-Fi password is here on the fridge.' Mrs Fitzgerald tapped a piece of paper stuck to the stainless-steel door.

'Great.' Reese stopped, whipped out his phone and punched the code in. 'I'll text it to you,' he told Lauren.

'This is lovely,' Lauren said, moving from the kitchen into the living room. Whoever had designed the guesthouse had laid it out so that you entered into the kitchen, which led into the living room, where a long hallway branched off with the bedrooms and the bathroom. It gave every room in the cottage, except one bedroom, a water view.

'Me and the Mister built this guesthouse when B and Bs were going up everywhere across Ireland. The majority of our guests are relatives of the people who live in Keelnamara. They stay here when they come for a visit.' She shrugged her thin shoulders. 'Most of the tourists want to be closer to Killarney.'

'They don't know what they're missing,' Reese said, looking around.

'The smart TV has cable and streaming services available,' she said, motioning to the flat screen mounted on the wall above the fireplace. 'The remote is on the coffee table.'

'I have to admit I wasn't expecting everything to be so modern,' Lauren told her. She'd pictured a stereotypical rustic but charming Irish cottage like her grandmother Healy used to talk about. But Lauren's grandmother had been talking about her own parents' ancestral home she'd visited in the 1960s, with no indoor plumbing and a single bedroom for a family of seven. Grandma had never seen this present-day, contemporary Ireland.

'I think people believe we still live under thatched roofs and draw water from wells,' Mrs Fitzgerald chuckled. 'My husband and I make sure our guesthouse has all the latest amenities.'

She's right, Lauren thought, eyes traveling around the room. *It rivals any Airbnb I ever rented in the States.*

Dingle Bay filled the view of the front window. Lauren drifted over to it, looking out over the water.

'Breathtaking, isn't it?' Mrs Fitzgerald came and stood next to her. 'We have the sea in front of us and the mountains at our back. It's a little slice of heaven nestled here.'

'Just pick any bedroom?' Reese asked. He'd traveled enough when he was in the army to not get sucked in by a pretty view.

Their host pointed. 'The bathroom and bedrooms are just down that hall there. Take any one you wish.'

Reese lugged his duffle bag down the darkened hallway. 'The light switch is on the left!' Mrs Fitzgerald called after him. He felt around on the wall and flicked the light on.

'I'm taking this one,' he said, stepping halfway into the door on the right.

'Thank you,' Lauren told the tiny silver-haired lady. 'We should be all set.'

'If you need anything, me and the Mister are right up front. Well,' she jokingly frowned, 'Himself is at the pub just now. I'll be right up front.'

Lauren watched as she let herself out, then went and grabbed her luggage from next to the stove. Even with all the modern amenities, the guesthouse was warm and inviting, with its stone fireplace and pictures of John F. Kennedy and the Pope on the wall, mixed in with family photographs, all grouped together with matching frames, just like Lauren had seen in the latest home décor magazines she loved to pore over, but never had time to implement in her own house. Mrs Fitzgerald had invested a lot of time and money into her rental property and it showed.

She rolled her suitcase over the dark green carpet to her bedroom. Reese had shut his door and she could hear him banging around in his new room.

A pale blue duvet covered a queen-sized bed that dominated the middle of the room. An old-fashioned landline sat on the nightstand next to a digital alarm clock. The room itself was very bare bones and utilitarian: bed, nightstand and dresser with attached mirror. Mrs Fitzgerald seemed to favor a more minimalistic décor style for the bedroom. Lauren was willing to bet Reese's room across the hall was almost an exact match. *When visiting Ireland*, Lauren supposed, *most people didn't spend much time in their rooms. Too busy seeing the sights or visiting relatives.*

From across the hall, she heard the familiar sound of Reese snoring. He could fall asleep anywhere as soon as his head hit the pillow. Putting her cell on the nightstand, she lay across the duvet cover on her bed without changing out of her clothes. She let the jet lag wash over her and was out before she could start counting sheep.

FOURTEEN

COTTAGE WOULDN'T HAVE been the word Lauren used to describe Jimmy Breen's place. *Shack* was more like it. A one-story weathered structure set high up on a rocky patch of land, the only positive thing it had going for it was its view of Dingle Bay. It sat alone, on top of a hill with no immediate neighbors, beaten down by the elements. The only other structure nearby was a huge half-finished complex of some sort right on the water, about a half-mile south, that they'd passed on the road. She imagined someone had had big plans for it that had fizzled.

They almost missed their sharp left turn, obscured by some sad-looking bushes. The grade was steep as Reese pulled up the gravel driveway to a cracked concrete pad at the top. *For a handyman, James Breen didn't take too much pride in his own home*, Lauren thought as she took in the drooping gutters and missing roof tiles.

'We know he didn't sell the painting and invest in real estate,' Reese said. They parked behind an ancient Fiat Tempra with a sagging bumper. Mrs Fitzgerald had given them the keys to the cottage after their much-needed two-hour nap. Reese had accepted and devoured the strawberry jam sandwich she'd offered him, but it was now after noon and Lauren still hadn't eaten. She made a mental note to stop at the little grocery store they'd passed on the way into Keelnamara. Hopefully, it carried coffee as well as food. She could survive without eating, coffee not so much.

Now that she was at the top of the hill, she could make out houses and structures further up the shore, past the unfinished building, going north toward the church, which sat like a white beacon against the rocky coast and gray surf. The word *solitary* popped into her head.

Dull blue curtains covered the dirty windows of Jimmy's cottage. The lawn looked like it hadn't been cut in months, maybe years, with weeds growing up between the rocks. There were no trees to speak of, just more thick overgrown bushes that seemed to frame the house. Crudely cut, flat stepping stones led from the driveway to a concrete slab in front of the door. Lauren imagined Jimmy salvaging the stones from a job he'd worked on, asking for them and dropping them one by one on his front lawn.

Lauren and Reese exited their car, both stopping to look inside the decrepit vehicle. 'Think it runs?' Lauren asked, touching the cracked sideview mirror.

He tried the handle. It was locked. 'Probably. Our friend was a fix-it man after all. It's held together with duct tape and bungee cords. I bet it purrs like a kitten.'

'Or rumbles like a pride of lions.'

'Always so negative,' Reese admonished. 'Don't judge a car by its paint job. Or lack thereof.'

Walking up the stepping stones, he motioned to the front door. A piece of paper was stuck to it with red tape. Written on it in black block letters, possibly by the late Jimmy Breen himself, was 'NO TRESSPASSING'.

Lauren trailed behind Reese a little, trying to fish the keys out of her pants pocket. 'I don't think you're going to need those,' Reese said, coming to a stop so fast on the concrete stoop that Lauren almost ran into the back of him.

The door had been kicked in. Splinters of wood stuck out from the frame, littering the concrete below. Lauren automatically went left as Reese went right, flanking either side of the entrance. Her hand went to her hip for the gun that should have been there but wasn't. 'Son of a bitch,' she whispered.

Reese held up his index finger and mouthed the count-down: *three, two, one.*

She shoved the door wide open and they both hugged the sides, waiting to see or hear movement from inside. The last thing they wanted to do was rush unarmed into a burglary in progress.

Reese bobbed his head in and out, making sure the living room was clear, then stepped inside. 'I'm not sure how much damage the burglar did. He might have come over to clean up.'

The first thing that hit her was the smell wafting out, even before she walked in behind Reese. It turned out to be a good thing she hadn't eaten.

Jimmy Breen had been a hoarder. Old newspapers were stacked to the ceiling along with case after case of empty beer bottles. Trash, broken electronics, pots and pans, fast-food ketchup packets and filthy clothes littered the floor. The couch against the far wall had been stacked with all types of debris, but whoever had broken in had tossed it on the ground and slit each cushion open, spilling yellow foam stuffing. A television cabinet sat across from it with both of its doors ripped off. An old-fashioned VCR had been yanked out of it, wires still attached to the TV whose screen had been smashed. The wood-burning stove in the corner was black with soot and ash, blocks of peat moss stacked up next to it. Lauren couldn't imagine Jimmy Breen lighting a fire in this place. One stray ember and the whole thing would go up like a bonfire.

'I'm going to assume that all this garbage was here when Sheila McGrath and Mrs Fitzgerald locked the place up, but the damage wasn't,' Lauren said, covering her mouth and nose with her hand. From her vantage point she could see a small kitchen, plates piled high in the sink. A bedroom door was open to their left, the thin mattress pulled off the bed and similarly slashed open. Another door to their right was closed and Lauren presumed it was the bathroom. There wasn't space for it to be anything else. She stepped over a trash bag and tried the handle. 'Ugh,' she wheezed, looking around the closet-like bathroom. The medicine cabinet had been ripped from the wall and lay in the moldy bathtub. 'Now we know where the smell is coming from.'

Reese picked up a slashed throw pillow and tossed it across the room. 'The house was a disaster before the break-in. We won't know what's what unless we bring the sister here.'

'Let's secure the door as best we can and call the Garda.' Lauren bent over, picked up the mandatory picture of JFK off the ground and rehung it on its hook. 'Mrs Fitzgerald said the coroner asked for an autopsy. I think that was a smart move.'

'Give me your hand,' Reese reached out, helping her over what looked like a lawnmower engine, 'this place is a death trap.'

FIFTEEN

'JIMMY WAS A pack rat, to be sure,' Scannell, the barrel-chested officer of the Garda, told them as they stood on the overgrown front lawn. Lauren had called Mrs Fitzgerald, who'd contacted local Garda Scannell, who met them at the house. He'd pulled in behind their rental car and come ambling up the mismatched paving stones in his navy uniform pants and yellow and black reflective jacket. He was friendly enough but guarded. He wasn't quite sure what to make of Reese and Riley. 'I wouldn't be surprised if some of the local teenagers came for a visit. They're good kids around here but they get a bit bored.'

'This looks like someone was looking for something,' Reese pointed out.

'The alleged painting,' he replied knowingly. 'The same thing you two are looking for. I came over here as a courtesy to Mrs Fitzgerald when Jimmy's sister sold the house. Sheila was in a bad way. I locked the place up myself after they did the walk-through and there was no painting inside and nothing was damaged. Cluttered, but undamaged. Sheila sold the house contents and all, said she wanted none of it except a milk jug that belonged to their mother. Everything else was to go with the house.'

'Did Mrs Fitzgerald fill you in on the particulars of why we're here?' Lauren asked.

'Myself and the wife and four kids live a stone's throw from the Fitzgerald place.' He hitched his thumbs in his belt loops. 'There's nothing that happens in Keelnamara that doesn't reach my ears. I just don't know what you intend to accomplish. No one's ever seen the painting. I'll extend all the professional courtesy I'm able because Mrs Fitz says you're regular police back in the States as well as private detectives.' He waved a hand at the cottage. 'But you've seen Jimmy's place. I don't know who else you'd investigate except for Sheila McGrath, and that's laughable.'

'We don't want to cause any trouble,' Lauren threw in quickly. 'We just need to talk to a few people, see if anyone can point us to where the painting might be if it isn't here.'

He rubbed his chin absently. 'You can try Sheila, although I don't think she'll be much help. If she had the bloody painting, she wouldn't have had to sell the cottage, would she?'

Now that Lauren had his tacit approval to ask questions around the townland, she took advantage of the opportunity to get some information out of him.

'What about Sheila's son, Martin? Would he talk to us?'

Scannell snorted. 'Good luck with that gobshite. He raised holy hell when he found out Sheila was selling.'

'Was Sheila's son with her when she and Mrs Fitzgerald did the walk-through?' Reese asked.

'He was. And he wasn't happy. That's why Mrs Fitz wanted me to be here when Sheila turned the keys over. He didn't agree with the selling of the contents. He wanted to go in and rifle through Jimmy's belongings. Got kind of heated with me. And with his poor mother standing here crying.' He shook his head. 'A real shame to be acting like that.'

'Did he leave with his mother?' Lauren crossed her arms over her chest as a wind blew up from the bay. It ruffled the mop of dark hair that topped the Garda's round face. He was wide in the chest, not too tall and what she would have described as solid. Scannell was the kind of guy they tied the rope around to be the anchor in a game of tug-of-war at family picnics.

'He did. She managed to get him in the car and they drove off. I should have known this would happen.'

'Mrs Fitzgerald said the coroner wanted an autopsy. What do you think about that?' Lauren asked. Now that the door was open, she was going to walk in as far as Scannell would allow her.

He scratched his chin again, debating on how much he should reveal to these two strangers standing in front of Jimmy Breen's trashed cottage. 'I think it wasn't a bad idea. Jacky Foley, a local fisherman, found Jimmy as he was trying to get his skiff into the water at the boat launch. Jacky and his family live in the apartments across the street from the walking path. I was in bed when I got the call. Jimmy was face down on the pavement.' Scannell gave a shudder at the memory. 'Horrible, it was. I didn't know if all the trauma to the head was from the fall or foul play, so I called the station house in Killorglin and they sent Detective Quill down, but it took some time for him to get here. We're a centralized department, but detectives only work out of the main Garda stations.'

'Any signs of a robbery?'

'Hard to say. He still had money in his pocket. Jimmy was a scrapper, though. If someone approached him, he'd surely try to defend himself.'

Lauren filed that piece of information away. 'Did the sister see his body?'

'Thankfully, she did not. She rushed down to the walking path, hysterical, when she heard the news. Word travels

fast in these parts. Some of the local boys held her back.'
He ran a hand through his thick hair. He and Reese had
the same habit; they both had to be doing something with
their hands constantly. 'No one should see their loved one
like that. Detective Quill managed to calm her down. He's
a good man and a good detective.'

'Was Sheila McGrath's son at the scene?' Reese asked.

'Martin showed up a bit later, after Detective Quill had
got there. Smelled to high heaven like whiskey. I made him
get in the back of my patrol vehicle and I drove both him
and Sheila home.'

'He was on foot?'

'He was. I thought that was odd myself. He and Sheila
live a good ways from that part of the bay.'

*Why don't you question him about that too while you're
talking to him about the break-in?* Lauren was tempted to
suggest, but bit her lip. The last thing she wanted to do was
tell an officer in another country how to run his investigations. Especially Scannell, who even though he was answering their questions, seemed dangerously close to cutting
off the conversation. She got the feeling that if they hadn't
been staying with the Fitzgeralds he wouldn't have given
up any of this information. She and Reese would have to
do their own homework.

Now he tucked his hands in his pockets and sighed. 'I'll
check around the back of the house, make sure all the windows and rear doors are secure. I'll have to call the Crime
Scenes Unit over. Thankfully, they're in Cromane right
now. My colleague, Garda Lalley, was the first to respond
to a bad domestic dispute. Annie Brennan hit her husband
with a shovel early this morning. Almost cut two fingers
off. He's at the hospital getting sewn up right now.' He
looked down at the watch on his left wrist. 'They should

be about finished. I'll have them dust for prints then I'll go find Martin to ask him if he came back for a visit.'

Lauren knew from Google Maps that Cromane was the next town over. 'Will we be able to get back in the house? Maybe tomorrow morning?'

'I'll only hold the scene until they're done dusting for prints. Then you can go back inside.'

'Do you think it'd be possible for us to get in touch with Detective Quill? I'd like to ask him a few questions,' Lauren said.

'If you've got a card with your mobile number on it, I'll text him at his work number.' *That's Scannell's way of saying, 'Don't call us, we'll call you,'* Lauren thought.

'I do,' she replied.

'Good. Give it to me and I'll call the Crime Scenes Unit over to process this scene. Where are you headed to now?' he asked. The tone of his voice warned Lauren that this was his townland and he wasn't about to let them run amuck in it. He wanted to know what they were up to.

'I think we'll try to talk to Jimmy's sister. Maybe we'll get lucky and Martin will be home.'

'Martin McGrath is over at Robber O'Shea's pub. I saw his car parked in the lot as I drove over here. I want to speak with him first.' Scannell wasn't asking, he was telling them. 'If he's decided to head home and join his mum for tea, excuse yourselves.'

'Not a problem. If he's there, we'll back off until tomorrow. Here's my number.' Lauren produced one of her business cards from her back pocket. 'Please, if there's anything else you can think of that might help us find the painting, give me a call.'

He took it and looked it over. 'I watch a lot of American television shows about private investigators,' he said, tucking it away in his uniform shirt pocket. 'How true to life are they?'

Reese shrugged. 'I would have said they were extremely exaggerated in terms of the sheer number of dangerous situations they're always facing.' He jerked a thumb at Lauren. 'Then I met her.'

'Don't say it,' Lauren whispered under her breath as she watched Garda Scannell smirk and start to head toward his patrol vehicle. 'Please, don't say it.'

'Well, you're in luck,' Scannell called over his shoulder, 'because nothing ever happens here in Keelnamara.'

SIXTEEN

'ISN'T THERE ONE McDonald's in this entire country?' Lauren complained as they turned around and headed for the address that Mrs Fitzgerald had texted them. It wasn't an address really, just directions on how to find the street from Jimmy's cottage and the note that it was just after Sullivan's sheep farm. She watched the coast grow smaller in the rearview mirror; Sheila and Martin McGrath lived further inland.

'I saw one when we were by the airport. You were busy chugging your coffee and didn't say anything.'

'Thank goodness for the TripAdvisor app,' Lauren said, ignoring the comment. She held up her phone. 'The pub has food. The menu is posted on the website.'

'We'll get dinner there after we talk to Sheila McGrath. Didn't Mrs Fitzgerald say Jimmy was close to the owner?'

Lauren tucked her phone away. 'I think she did. I hope Sheila is in the mood to talk.'

Even with Mrs Fitzgerald's directions, they still managed to get lost. When they reached the bridge to head into Glenbeigh, they stopped, called Mrs Fitzgerald and she talked them step by step to Jimmy's sister's house. While it was true you could basically only go right or left in Keelnamara, driving on the wrong side of the road got them both twisted.

'Look for the sheep!' Mrs Fitzgerald told Lauren as

Reese turned down the road she claimed was Sheila Mc-Grath's.

'There's sheep in the fields every hundred yards,' Reese complained. 'I swear there's more sheep than people here.'

While that might have been true, Sheila McGrath's house was located next to an actual sheep farm, not just one of the locals who kept a small flock. Hundreds of the beasts stuck their black noses through the fence that lined the road as their car passed. When they reached the end of the fenced-in area, a large hedge divided the farm property from a robin's-egg-blue house that was a larger, tidier version of Jimmy Breen's. Only one-story, it had no garage, just the same concrete pad as Jimmy's at the end of the driveway. Lauren wondered if he'd poured them both himself. Flowerbeds on either side of the front door were freshly overturned, waiting for planting, unlike the unruly, scraggly bushes that choked the front of Jimmy's cottage. Rows of plastic trays containing plants sat on the lawn. It looked like Sheila McGrath had been gardening and had gotten interrupted.

Reese pulled over on the side of the narrow two-lane road so as not to block her car in. 'I hope she's home,' he said, turning the engine off.

'I doubt she'd leave her flowers unplanted out in the sun.'

'You call this sun?' Reese asked, motioning to the cloudy, overcast sky. Lauren opened the door and got out. From the fence line she heard a chorus of bleating animals. A woman in her late forties appeared in the front door. The sheep weren't the only ones who'd heard them pull up.

'Can I help you with something?' she called to them as they made their way up her front walk.

They stopped on the path in unison. 'Mrs McGrath? We're employees of Mrs Whitney, the woman who bought your brother's house. My name is Lauren Riley and this is Shane Reese.'

Reese nodded a greeting. 'Hello, Ma'am.'

Her eyes narrowed just a bit. 'Can I see some identification?' she asked, pulling her sweater tighter around her midsection. Lauren could tell she was a woman who had dealt negatively with the police before. She wondered how much trouble her son had gotten into since he'd returned to Keelnamara.

Lauren produced her private investigator's license and a business card from her pocket and passed them over. Sheila McGrath took them, squinting to read the print. 'Private investigators from New York here in Keelnamara. Who would've thunk it?' She had a fast way of speaking and her accent was thicker than Mrs Fitzgerald's.

'We were just over at Jimmy's property and there's been a break-in. We were wondering if we could come inside and speak to you,' Lauren said.

'Did you call Garda Scannell?'

'We did,' Lauren replied. 'He's already been up to the cottage and secured it. He's waiting on the Crime Scenes Unit.'

'He's a good man,' Sheila McGrath said, stepping off to the side and holding the door open for them. 'Come in then. Theresa Fitzgerald told me people from the States were coming over. I didn't expect you'd be here so quickly.' Word did travel fast in this townland.

'Mrs Whitney is anxious to finalize the details,' Lauren said, walking past her into the neat little house, the complete opposite of the garbage dump her brother lived in.

'Mrs Whitney,' Sheila McGrath sniffed. 'Didn't even have the decency to wait until my brother was buried before she swooped in.' She closed the door behind Reese.

'If I hadn't needed the money to give him a proper funeral, I'd have told her to pound salt.'

The living room was perfectly square, with a beige couch against the back wall, a fireplace to the right and an entertainment center to the left, next to an archway that led into the kitchen. A vase of wildflowers sat in the middle of her coffee table, giving the room a pop of color. Lauren and Reese both sat on the couch, while Sheila McGrath sat in a floral upholstered easy chair that faced the TV.

Sheila McGrath had pale reddish hair twisted in a knot at the nape of her thin neck. A long navy blue cardigan reached halfway to the muddy knees of her worn jeans, proof that she'd been gardening. Her face was an odd combination of blazing red cheeks set against deeply lined, creamy white skin. She didn't offer them any tea, nor did Lauren think any such offer was forthcoming. 'What's this about a break-in, now?' she asked, crossing her arms over her chest.

'The door to your brother's house was kicked in. Someone has ransacked it. Cut open the mattress and all the cushions,' Reese explained.

She put an elbow on the armrest, then a hand to her forehead. 'Isn't it bad enough they killed him?'

Lauren sat back against the couch, resisting the urge to pull out her notebook and start writing. She wanted this to be a conversation, not an interrogation. 'Who killed who?'

'The men who killed Jimmy, of course. Over a stupid fecking painting he doesn't have.'

'You know about the painting?' Reese asked.

'Everybody in Keelnamara knows the rumor about the damn painting,' she replied, her mouth turned down in a frown of disgust. 'Trouble is, he doesn't have it and he never did. If a man had a painting such as that, would he be living the way Jimmy did? I'm asking you. Would he?'

'I didn't know your brother, but I'm sorry for your loss.' Lauren tried to bring Sheila down a few notches. She could see the tears welling in the woman's eyes, about to spill over. 'I know all this must be a terrible shock.'

'A shock, she says.' Sheila's hand dropped from her face, and with it some of her anger seemed to dissipate. 'What's shocking is it didn't happen sooner. Why anyone would steal a Picasso in the first place is beyond me. Once you took it, what would you do with it? It's not like you could hang it over the hearth. But tongues around here have been wagging since he got back from New York over twenty years ago, about this secret treasure he was supposed to have. Men get to drinking and they get notions.' She tapped her temple with her index finger. 'Crazy notions and delusions of grandeur.'

'So you think someone from the area killed your brother because they thought he had the painting?'

'Isn't that what I just said? Only he didn't have it and he never had it. Now I just want Detective Quill to find out who killed Jimmy and let justice be done.'

'Is the cottage on the hill the only home he owned?' Reese asked.

'No, he had a villa on the French Riviera and a chalet in the Swiss Alps,' Sheila snapped. 'We could barely keep the lights on between the two of us without having to go on the dole.'

'What about a storage locker?'

'Even if he had the money, he wouldn't have spent it on something like that.' Lauren could see the truth in that; his whole cottage was a storage locker.

'Did he ever mention any problems with anyone? A spurned ex, maybe?' Lauren asked, pushing a stray strand of brown hair out of her eyes with the heel of her hand. She imagined it looked like she'd combed it with a fork, but Sheila McGrath didn't seem the type to care much about other women's grooming habits.

'Jimmy was engaged to a girl from County Clare. A dark-haired beauty named Anna. He met her when he was traveling around, working on roofs the summer after he turned eighteen. He lived with her for a few years, until she died in a horse-riding accident. That's why he left for America.' Sheila shook her head. 'There was no one after that. His heart never mended.'

'He never mentioned feeling threatened, did he?' Lauren asked.

'No. Jimmy was such a trusting soul. He thought everyone was his friend. That was his downfall, I tell you.' She took a deep breath, trying to control her emotions. 'My son is devastated. Jimmy was like a father to Martin.'

'Is that your son?' Reese pointed to one of the framed pictures in the middle of the mantle over the fireplace. Lauren got up and walked over, picking it up before Sheila could protest.

The photo was of a young man, maybe sixteen years old, with the same dull red hair as Sheila, smiling into the camera. Freckles dotted his nose and face as he held up an enormous fish he must have caught. Two older men stood in the background with their arms crossed and amused looks on their faces.

'That's my boy, Martin. He's had a rough go of it, but he's been doing fine since he got home, and now this.' Her lip began to quiver and a tear spilled over, tracing a line down her cheek. 'He deserved to have Jimmy in his life, since his Da was taken from him so young. That's Jimmy in the photograph behind him on the left.' Now the tears flowed freely and she buried her face in her hands.

Sure enough, when Lauren focused on the man in the picture, she could see the resemblance to both Martin and Sheila. He had the same pale red hair and anemic face. Compared to the large man next to him, he was on the short side, with a slim but muscular build.

Lauren and Reese knew from years of working in the Homicide office to just let her cry. Any words from them wouldn't be of much comfort. She was feeling cheated and angry and wanted someone to blame for her loss. While the rest of Keelnamara believed Jimmy had died of natural causes, somehow, in Sheila's mind, it was easier to think someone had killed him than that he'd just gotten drunk and fallen down or had a heart attack.

Lauren set the picture in its place and quietly sat back down next to Reese.

After a good minute had passed, Sheila sat up, wiped her nose on the back of her hand and turned her red-rimmed eyes on Lauren and Reese. 'Is that all you'll be needing?' she asked, mustering up as much dignity as she could.

'I know this is an imposition and I'm sorry to have to ask,' Lauren said, 'but would you be able to find time to come over to Jimmy's house with us tomorrow? We'd like you to take a look around and see if anything is missing.'

She nodded, sniffling. 'I can do that. I don't have to be at the hospital in Killorglin until nine. I'm a custodian on the night shift. Only two days a week now. Budget cutbacks. I barely get enough hours to keep the lights on. Jimmy was such a help. If I hadn't sold his cottage straight away, I don't know what I would have done. No one will hire my son, having a criminal record and all.'

'Hopefully, Mrs Whitney will get things expedited and you'll get your money quickly,' Lauren said, trying to sound reassuring. The poor woman looked like she was about to go to pieces right in front of them.

'Do you think she'd mind if I took my mother's milk jug out of the kitchen? I know the deal was house and contents, but I can't see what she'd want with that.'

'I'm sure that would be fine,' Lauren told her, making a mental note to text Sharon Whitney and let her know. She'd be sure to double-check the jug to make sure the painting wasn't hidden in it somehow.

Lauren and Reese stood up from the couch. Lauren took a step forward. 'Thank you, Mrs McGrath. We'll come by in the morning around ten, if that's OK.'

'Aye,' she agreed. 'Will Detective Quill be with you tomorrow?'

'We're hoping to get in contact with him today,' Lauren said.

Sheila crossed the room and opened the door for them. 'Maybe if the three of you put your heads together, you can figure out what happened to Jimmy.'

'Goodbye, now. See you in the morning.' The last thing Lauren wanted to do was make any promises about investigating Jimmy's death. She and Reese were there for the painting and the painting only. The local cops could handle a routine DOA.

The door had barely shut behind them when an old SUV came tearing into the driveway, yanking to a stop behind Mrs McGrath's car. A man popped out of the driver's side and stormed over the lawn to cut them off.

'Who the hell are ya and what are ya doing at my house?' he demanded. The handsome young man in the picture had been replaced with a thirty-something brute, barrel-chested with prison muscles, and half of his left front tooth missing. His red hair was buzzed so close to his head it was hard to make out the color, while a patchy five o'clock shadow covered his angular jaw.

Sheila had heard the car and came running outside. 'Martin! These are the private investigators the lady who bought Jimmy's house sent over. They just wanted to talk. Someone broke in!'

'Go back in the house, Ma,' he said through gritted teeth, eyes never leaving Reese. His chest was heaving, his hands clenched together in fists.

'Martin—'

'Go back in the house!'

Lauren heard the door slam behind them as his mother retreated.

'You think you can come here from America and intimidate my family?' Martin demanded, taking a step toward Lauren.

'We're not trying to intimidate anyone.' Lauren stood her ground, shooting an arm out to stop Reese from trying to defend her. She was a big girl and worse men than this had tried to push her around. Some had even succeeded, but not anymore. And not today. Bullies like him didn't scare her. She lifted her chin. 'We're just trying to recover some property for our employer that went missing when Mr Breen worked for her.'

'Whatever my uncle had belongs to me and my mum now. And you,' he stabbed a finger at her face to drive his point home, 'ya take one thing out of that house and you'll be answering ta me.'

'The house and its contents belong to my employer now,' Lauren said, keeping her voice even. She could feel Reese's heart thumping under her palm. 'Unless you go in with us or the Garda, I'll have you arrested.'

His lip curled in a sneer, showing off his jagged tooth.

'I'll do what I like, when I like. If you want ta try ta sic the Garda on me, you'd better be quick about it. And you better pray they get ta me before I get ta you.'

The blare of a horn made all three of them jump as Garda Scannell came careening to a halt behind Martin's car, boxing him in.

'Is that quick enough for you?' Reese asked with a wicked grin.

Martin's eyes jumped from them to the Garda and back. 'Remember what I just told ya,' he warned.

'Martin McGrath, stay right where you are,' Scannell commanded, coming around the front of his vehicle. 'I just missed you at Robber O'Shea's.'

'That sounds like a threat,' Lauren said, eyes locked with Martin's.

'It surely is, love,' he said in a low voice, slowly raising his hands above his head. 'One that I would take very seriously, if I were you. I'm just trying ta protect what's left of my family.'

'Don't be so dramatic, Martin.' Scannell walked up, breaking McGrath's glare. He was talking about Martin putting his hands in the air; Scannell hadn't heard him threaten Lauren. 'Get over here. I want a quick word. And behave yourself or you'll be hearing that cell door slamming again.'

Reese and Riley retreated to their rental while Martin and Scannell went over to his patrol vehicle. Martin leaned against the passenger side door, arms crossed, watching them get into their car.

SEVENTEEN

LAUREN SAW SHEILA MCGRATH peeking out from behind the curtain in her front window before they pulled away. Turning away from her scowling son, Scannell called something to her that Lauren couldn't hear. Martin yelled something as well but didn't take his eyes off Reese and Riley's car, like he was memorizing it.

Sheila's only response was to let the curtain fall back into place. Lauren didn't know what that meant for their scheduled meeting tomorrow. She had a feeling it was now cancelled. What she did know for sure was that Sheila McGrath was a woman who was used to her son's brushes with the law.

'What were the odds of him leaving the bar while we were at his mom's house?' Reese said, still pumped with adrenaline from the confrontation with Martin.

'The odds for us?' she asked, watching Reese's hands clenching and unclenching the steering wheel. 'One hundred percent.'

'The Crime Scenes Unit must have gotten over to the cottage pretty fast,' Reese remarked.

Lauren shrugged. 'It's not like New York here. I can't imagine it's a hotbed of crime in County Kerry.'

'I think it's time we hit Robber O'Shea's,' Reese said, glancing in the rearview to try to catch what was going on at the McGrath home. Lauren twisted around for a look.

Garda Scannell's vehicle was still parked behind Martin's, exhaust fumes coming from the tailpipe but no movement.

Turning forward, she said, 'I already put the address in Google Maps. Just keep going back the way we came. It's near the walking path where Jimmy's body was found. Why don't we stop at the path and check it out? Then maybe when we get to the pub some of the locals will be able to fill us in on what Jimmy was doing out there.'

EIGHTEEN

THE KEELNAMARA WALKING path ran for exactly one kilometer along the rocky shore from the foot of the abandoned resort to just before Robber O'Shea's pub. According to Mrs Fitzgerald, it was supposed to be part of the townland's attempt to draw in some of the Ring of Kerry tourists. Much like the half-finished resort, the money had run out when the economy had taken a downturn and it was never finished. Lauren admired the view from one of the parking lots that had been strategically placed along the road that ran perpendicular to it. The idea was to park and walk the beach made up of smooth round rocks ranging in size from boulders to pebbles. She could see the reasoning behind the walking path; it'd be hard to stroll along the beach, having to climb over a giant rock every couple of dozen yards or so, or risk breaking an ankle on smooth wet stones if you weren't sure-footed.

Even though it was a gray, overcast day she could still see across the bay to the opposite shore. Small boats bobbed in the water, further out than she would have thought safe, but what did she know? She'd grown up on one of the Great Lakes but had zero sailing experience. Just like Buffalo was known for its snowfall, and yet she'd never once gone skiing.

Well-taken-care-of wooden stairs led down to an asphalt

path lined with a wood and cable railing that curved along with the shape of the shore. It was elevated above the beach and strangely modern, given the architecture of the rest of the area. Lauren slid her hand down the smooth railing as she descended the stairs to the path, waiting for Reese at the bottom. She scanned around for video cameras. Lauren had heard that England had cameras everywhere, but she hadn't noticed one since she'd gotten to Ireland. She was sure they must have them in the bigger towns and cities, but out in the rural coastal townlands of County Kerry they seemed to be a rarity. All she could see were the Plexiglas information boards posted at intervals along the path, filled with information on the history of Keelnamara, coupled with old photographs and maps. There wasn't a single camera to record Jimmy Breen's last moments.

'Hold on,' Lauren said, studying one of the boards directly across from the mouth of the stairs. 'Keelnamara was originally into salmon fishing until it turned to mussels and oyster farming. It says the oysters grow in bags on raised trestles where they're harvested by hand. Just like Mrs Fitzgerald told us.' To the left of the path she could see what looked like long tables set in rows, sticking up out of the water. Row after row stretched into the bay. Further up the shoreline she could see the sorting building, partially obscured by a bend in the landscape. She scanned the water, saw the men in the boats bobbing, probably waiting for a salmon to get caught in their nets, ready to race a seal for it. She wondered if Mr Fitzgerald was out there right now.

She also questioned how the half-finished resort was planning to handle a working shellfish farm practically right next to it. The beds were interesting, but not something a tourist would want to look at from their high-priced hotel window every morning. Maybe that was one of the reasons it was never completed.

'Fascinating,' Reese replied. 'Does that sign give any indication of where Jimmy Breen's body might have been found?'

Lauren ignored the snark in his voice. 'Scannell said by Robber's pub. This is the closest car park to Robber's, not counting the one for the boat launch.'

Reese looked from one end of the beach to the other. There was no access to it from the path itself unless you crawled over the railing and dropped down about five feet onto the rocky shore. Lauren wondered how they'd even managed to build the small portion of path they'd completed. The money, manpower and resources must have been overwhelming for such a tiny townland. She was amazed they'd been able to build and maintain any of it at all.

'What the hell was Jimmy doing down here in the middle of the night?' Reese said, thinking out loud.

'The sign says the boat launch is that way,' Lauren pointed north, in the direction of Robber O'Shea's. 'Let's walk down there.'

In the bay in front of them they could see fishermen sitting in their boats with their yellow oil suits on, faces turned toward the horizon. There were other boats on the water that had no one manning them. They bobbed alone, moored, their owners gone for the day.

Reese and Riley walked side by side in the direction of the launch. Birds swooped in as they walked, landing on the ground in front of them, then scattering and landing behind them, hoping Reese and Riley were fishermen who might drop something tasty to eat.

Reese started humming an AC/DC song, hands in his pockets, face to the wind. A slight smile played on his lips, like he was remembering something special, something close to his heart. Maybe it was the smell of the beach, or the sound of the waves or the brisk breeze on his face. Lauren caught herself staring at him and quickly looked away before he noticed.

They strolled around a corner and could just make out the back parking lot of a pub. 'That must be Robber O'Shea's up ahead,' Lauren said. *It's funny*, she thought, looking up at the back of the brick building, *pubs in Ireland have such a distinctive look to them.* There was no mistaking it for another squat apartment building like the one across the road from where they'd just parked, or the neat little cottages they'd passed on the way to get there from Sheila's place.

The footpath changed as they got closer to the boat launch. Yellow caution signs reminded people strolling to watch for vehicles backing up. A ramp led from another car park off the main road, cutting across the path, right to the beach. It was wide enough and long enough for a truck to back a boat onto the rocky beach, or right into the water if it was high tide. The railings closest to the ramp's edges were wrapped in reflective tape, but there were still black scuff marks on them.

'There's nothing here,' Reese said, looking around. 'There's absolutely no reason Jimmy would've been down here at that time of night unless he was helping someone who was having trouble with their boat.'

'The walking path is shielded from the road,' Lauren pointed out, covering her eyes with her hand and squinting up to the top of the ramp. 'We can't even see if there are any cars parked in the lot. They cut this path right into the side of a hill overlooking the beach.'

'Let's head back to our car and go over to the pub,' Reese said, checking out the back of the establishment. 'It must have a hell of a view.'

'Not of the path at night.' Lauren turned and started walking back toward their rental car. 'There's a lamp post by the stairs we came down and two here by the launch but not a single one along the beach.'

'I suppose they were counting on the resort getting finished and tourists showing up, instead of driving by on the Ring of Kerry. In a place this size, without something to draw people here, you end up with a half-finished resort and matching walking path. Except for the boat launch, how much do you think the locals really use this?'

Reese had a point. The path was so short, you were better off walking on the obstacle course of a beach if you wanted a workout.

They climbed back up the steps as the seagulls swarmed to a spot on the beach. Lauren vaguely wondered what they'd come across just now that wasn't there five minutes ago. *I guess there's no telling where there's buried treasure*, she thought.

NINETEEN

ROBBER O'SHEA'S PUB was dark: dark wood paneling, heavy velvet curtains, a polished mahogany bar. Lauren had to blink a few times until her eyes adjusted after they walked in. The curtains were drawn, so there was no natural light coming in, just the dim glow from the overhead fixtures.

Bellied up to the bar at varying intervals were six men. Three were over seventy, one was Lauren's age and the others looked barely legal. It took a second for Lauren to remember the drinking age was only eighteen in Ireland. All six swiveled around on their stools when Lauren and Reese entered. It seemed highly unlikely that strangers wandered into the pub often, from the questioning looks on the patrons' faces. A bartender, wearing a navy blue sweater vest over a white button-down shirt with the sleeves rolled up, turned from the glasses he was stacking on a rack behind the bar and watched them approach.

'What can I do for you today, folks?' he asked in his lilting Irish accent.

'Are you Michael O'Shea?' Lauren asked.

'I am,' he replied with a smile that crinkled up the corners of his eyes and wagged his finger at them. 'But they call me Robber. And here in this part of Ireland, while O'Shea may be my official name, we drop the O', you see? Because it means "descent of" or "grandson of". Everyone knows who my people are. So if you're asking around about me, I'm Michael Shea.'

'Why leave the O in the pub name then?' Reese asked.

'For the tourists, of course!' he laughed. 'The ones that never came. My Da had the sign made when Keelnamara was going to be the next hotspot on the Ring of Kerry with the big, grand resort. It never got finished and I'm too cheap and lazy to change the sign.'

'That's a great explanation,' Lauren told him.

'I'm full of great explanations, love.' He gave Lauren a wink, which felt different to the wink Howard Whitney had given her. Howard had done it to get under her skin. Robber Shea was so openly charming it was hard to get mad. 'And you two must be the Americans that are staying at the Fitzgerald place. Mister Fitz told us all about it. You just missed him.'

Him and Martin McGrath both, Lauren thought. *And Garda Scannell. This is the Grand Central Station of Keelnamara.*

'I'm Lauren Riley.' She motioned to her partner, cognizant that all the men bellied up to the bar were listening to every word she said. 'And this is Shane Reese. I was wondering if you had time to answer a few questions for us.'

'I would, love, but it's just me and the cook until six.' The namesake of the pub had an easy going way about him and a smile to rival Reese's. Though Robber was in his early fifties, he sported a full head of curly brown hair that he kept so long it bounced when he walked. Lauren had to resist the crazy idea of pulling on a curl just to see it snap back into place. 'I can't leave these gentlemen parched.'

'I'm as dry as the desert,' the man her age said and took a loud slurp of his thick, foamy beer. From the smell of his dirty overalls, Lauren assumed he was one of the local fishermen.

'We could grab some food if the kitchen's open and wait,' Reese suggested.

'Now that sounds like a plan, my friend.' He motioned to the dining area off to the left of the bar. Just four small round tables were set with white place mats and cutlery. But sure enough, there was the framed print of dogs playing poker on the wall next to the biggest Guinness mirror Lauren had ever seen, just like Mrs Fitzgerald had told them. Two men threw metal-tipped darts at a board in the corner, recording their scores between throws on a chalkboard mounted next to it, the white chalk swinging from a piece of red yarn. 'Have a seat anywhere you like. The menus are on the table. I'll be by in a minute to get your order.'

'What're you drinking?' one of the older men asked Reese. 'The Guinness is good here.'

'I've heard that.' Reese smiled at the white-haired gentleman and held up two fingers to the bartender. 'Bring us two pints and leave one for my friend here.' He then gestured down the length of the bar. 'And another round for these fellows too.'

The men offered up a medley of 'cheers'. The oldest man grabbed Reese by the arm and pulled him in to talk with him. Lauren didn't want to seem rude, but she was starving so she left Reese with the locals, wandered over to one of the tables and took a seat. She watched him make the rounds of his new-found friends as Robber poured the black beers.

'It's good craic at the end of the day!' one of the older men exclaimed and slapped a hand on Reese's back while lifting a pint glass to him with the other. 'Cheers!'

'Your husband makes friends fast,' Robber said as he put her beer down in front of her a few minutes later.

'He's not my husband, he's my partner,' she practically sputtered, color rising to her cheeks, then realized in a lot of places partner meant almost the equivalent. 'I mean business partner. We're looking into a matter in Keelnamara for a client.'

'You're here about Jimmy,' he grinned. 'There are few secrets in a townland this size. Some, but not many. I knew who you were the minute you walked through the door. Mister Fitz's tongue gets loose when he has a few pints.'

His smile was infectious, and she couldn't help returning it as she took hold of the black beer. One of the perks of private investigating was that there were no rules about drinking on the job. *In fact*, she thought, bringing the pint glass to her lips, *in this situation it was encouraged*. 'Thanks for the warning.'

He gave the table a tap. 'Just give me a whistle when you're ready to order.'

She perused the menu while Reese and his new drinking buddies got louder and louder at the bar. When she couldn't wait any longer, she signaled the bartender back over and ordered them both the crispy-skinned salmon. 'Good choice,' he told her. 'Caught here in County Kerry. Possibly by Gregory "Mooch" McMahon, right there.'

Mooch lifted his glass to her with a shaky hand and she lifted hers in kind. He didn't appear to be bothered by his nickname. He still had on his yellow oil suit pants and boots. Lauren's father had been a recreational fisherman on Lake Erie and owned one of those rubbery get-ups. As soon as he got off the water and on dry land, he'd peel off the jacket, then the pants, saying how hot they were. If Mooch was sweating in his now, he didn't show any signs of it.

'Lauren!' Reese called over, his arm around the man who looked closest in age to her. 'This is my friend, Jacky Foley!'

'G'day to you, Miss!' Jacky raised his glass to Lauren. She gave him a wave and marveled at Reese. Just when she thought he was goofing off, he was questioning a witness. Even though it was no stretch to look for a local fisherman in the only pub in the townland, she still had to hand it to him. He was extracting information and having fun at the same time.

Reese finally wandered over to the table two Guinnesses later, after his food was nice and cold. He dug into it anyway, grunting as he shoveled it into his mouth.

'Did I ever tell you you're a disgusting eater?' Lauren asked.

'Only every time I eat something,' he replied with his mouth full.

The door swung open and a man walked in. He was a little more nicely dressed than the other men in the bar, with clean blue jeans and a pressed collared shirt. He did a double take when he noticed Reese and Riley before making his way to the bar. She didn't take offense; Keelnamara didn't seem to be the kind of town that had many strangers wandering its streets, let alone a biracial man and a tall, painfully thin woman who were obviously not traditional tourists. He must have been a regular because he settled on a stool away from the others and gestured to Robber, who automatically set a whiskey on the rocks in front of him without asking what he wanted.

Lauren shouldn't have mocked Reese for his appetite. She'd torn through her dinner, barely stopping to sip her glass of water between swallows, she was so hungry.

A few minutes later a younger man in his mid-twenties walked in and another round of hollers came up from the drinkers. 'Thank you, gentlemen.' He gave a slight bow before he ambled to the corner of the bar and lifted the rail.

'And you too, Mooch. Everyone seems in fine spirits to-night.'

'Ah, bollocks!' Mooch laughed, waving him off.

'Good evening, Declan. I'd stay and have a chat with you,' Robber nodded toward Lauren and Reese, 'but she was here first.' Robber handed him a white bar towel, which young Declan slung over his shoulder. He immediately began pouring pints for the patrons, making a point to set Mooch's down in front of him first.

'So what are you folks wanting to know?' Robber asked, pulling up a chair with a pint in his hand now that his relief had shown up. 'Besides how I got the name Robber, which is always the first question you folks from the States ask.'

'We wanted to talk to you about James Breen,' Lauren said.

A look of sadness clouded Robber's face. 'Terrible business. He was in here almost every night. Sometimes all day as well. May he rest in peace.'

'We're handling some business for the woman who bought Mister Breen's house. We were just over there and it's been ransacked.'

'Someone looking for that damned painting,' Robber muttered in disgust.

'Did he tell you he had it?' Lauren pressed. 'Did you ever see it?'

'He did not and I did not. I don't think it existed.' A note of anger crept into Robber's voice. 'People would needle him all the time and he'd play it up, call it his insurance policy but never actually tell what it was, you know what I'm saying? Jacky'd ask "Why ain't ye buying the next round on your priceless painting?" and he'd grin and answer back, "That's my insurance policy, Jacky-boy!" I never once heard him say he actually had it. Not one time.'

'Did he do work for you?' Reese asked.

'When I needed the gutters cleaned or a window replaced, he'd be the one to do it. He was good with his hands, drunk or sober.'

'Was that enough to live on?' Lauren asked. 'Working odd jobs, I mean.'

He shrugged. 'Jimmy didn't need much. He liked to pick things out of the trash, tinker with them. He'd go in the back storeroom and hold up something with wires sticking out of it and ask if he could have it. I never saw him buy anything expensive or fancy. And he never paid anyone to do a job that he could figure out how to do himself.'

'We saw the evidence of that at his cottage,' Reese said.

'He fancied himself as a master mechanic and a world-class crooner. He'd sing a line or two from "The Parting Glass" for me every night before he left the pub.'

'"The Parting Glass"?'

'You don't know it? Some people claim it's a Scottish song, but we Irish sing it best, in my own humble opinion.' Robber straightened up, tugged at his collar and crooned, '*Of all the money that e'er I had, I spent it with good company. And all the harm I've ever done, alas it was to none but me…*'

'Sounds like you were fond of him,' Lauren noted. As soon as he'd started to sing it she'd recognized it as the song her Irish grandmother used to sing to her as a kid on New Year's Eve as they watched the ball drop on TV.

He nodded, sending a couple of stray curls bouncing. 'I was. He was a dear friend to me. I'm hoping that Detective Quill comes back quickly and tells us all that Jimmy had a heart attack. The idea that someone from this town would hurt him is ridiculous.'

'Not even for a painting worth a lot of money?' Reese asked.

'Breaking into his place and looking for it is one thing. Hurting a man's another. It was probably just some of the local kids looking for some excitement.' Robber leaned forward on his arm, index finger pointed out from his pint glass. 'Jimmy and his nephew both liked to pretend they were bigger than they were, if you get what I'm saying. I half-believed Jimmy made up the story of the missing painting himself when he got back from the States. Just like Martin likes to say he has connections to the IRA from his time in prison. A lot of tall tales get told around a pub, you know.'

'So you don't believe Jimmy was attacked?' Lauren asked.

'I don't. Jimmy was harmless. Martin, I'm not so sure about, but these folks in Keelnamara aren't the violent types. I think it's likely he had one too many pints and tripped over his own foot.'

'Was he drinking in here the night he died?' Reese asked with a mouth full of food.

'He was, but we close at half past eleven on weeknights, unless it's slow. Which it was that night. He must have been having a taste somewhere else.'

'Maybe with his nephew, Martin?' Reese asked.

Robber shook his head. 'That I don't know. They were both in that day, but so was just about every able-bodied man in Keelnamara at some point. The gents like to stop in, swap fishing stories and have a pint or two before they go home. Martin McGrath doesn't work, so he relies on the generosity of those around him to supply him with drink. That only goes so far for so long.'

'Martin doesn't sound like he's well liked,' Lauren observed.

'It's like this—Keelnamara is like a family. You may despise your uncle, but you still invite him over because it's Christmas. He's one of us, whether we like it or not. Do you get my meaning?'

'I do,' Lauren replied, trying not to answer in an Irish accent like every guy in every bar in South Buffalo did on St Patrick's Day.

'If that's all you'll be needing, I'll be heading home now. I've got a long day at work tomorrow.' He stood and gave Lauren another wink.

'You never did tell us about your nickname,' she said before he had a chance to walk away.

'Aye. I did not.' The smile returned to his face. 'In these parts there are a lot of families with the same last names. So to differentiate between them folks stick a word, usually a physical characteristic in front of their Christian names, like the Red Sheas, or the Squinty Sheas with their bad eyes, or the Giant Sheas. They're really tall, that lot. But sometimes someone in your lineage does something infamous that gets passed down to your descendants. Most of the time it's whispered behind your back.' He lowered his voice dramatically. 'Legend has it that a distant relative of mine was a highway man, so we became the Robber Sheas.'

'I don't know if you're telling the truth or pulling my leg because I'm American,' Lauren teased. The man knew how to tell a story, that was for sure.

'You tell me, love.' That cheeky grin of his gave him a mischievous look. 'You know what they call Martin McGrath's family?'

Lauren shook her head. 'I don't even want to take a guess.'

Robber reached down and picked up Reese's empty pint glass. 'The Luckless McGraths,' he said, and turned to head back over to the bar. 'Have a grand night, folks.'

TWENTY

LAUREN WHITE-KNUCKLED the steering wheel the entire way back to Mrs Fitzgerald's. Reese had only had three beers, but that was two beers too many and they decided not to risk it. Lauren had learned to drive a stick in high school, but that had been decades ago, so Reese talked her through the gears and clutch while she slowly crept down the opposite side of the road to the one she was used to driving on. When they finally pulled into the driveway, Lauren had the overwhelming urge to get out and kiss the ground.

'No more beer for you,' she told him, climbing out of the driver's side. 'I don't ever want to do that again.'

'You did great. Why do you think you can't drive a stick? I barely helped you at all.'

She began to tick the reasons off on her fingers. 'One, it's pitch black out. Two, I've never driven on the other side of the road. Three, I haven't driven a stick since I was a teenager, and four, the two-lane road is only six feet wide.'

'Now you're just being a drama queen,' Reese said as he followed her down the stone path to the back cottage. 'I don't know what you're complaining about. I'm the one that had to watch you flirt shamelessly with that Irishman.'

'I was *not* flirting with anyone,' she said, juggling the car keys in one hand and trying to fish the house key out of her pants pocket with the other.

'I know flirting, and you were definitely flirting. He wasn't wearing a wedding ring, either.'

'Believe it or not, he thought we were married.' She shouldered the door open and flicked the light switch on.

'I believe that. Sometimes I forget that we're not. You personify the expression "the old ball and chain". I feel like we're bound to each other forever. Like herpes.'

She tossed both sets of keys on the kitchen table, glad her back was to Reese. 'I'm not going to dignify that with an answer. I'm going to bed.'

'Sweet dreams,' he called after her, 'of Robber Shea.'

Lauren shut her bedroom door. She was tempted to lock it, not because she thought Reese would try to come in, but to keep her from going back out. In the end, she left it open. She should have started typing her notes into her iPad but that last exchange with Reese had her mind twisted. Ever since Reese had almost died a year ago she'd been struggling with conflicting feelings for him. They were compounded by a hospital chapel conversation she'd had with his mother, who told Lauren her son had feelings for her. She'd never had the guts to get confirmation of that. She was too afraid of losing him, like she'd lost every other man in her life. But when he made comments like that, even jokingly, the feelings bubbled to the surface again. Lauren had hoped she'd put all of those emotions aside in Iceland a few months back, where she'd decided she was better off leaving things as they were—keeping him in her life, if only as a partner and friend. She could live without romance. It never lasted, at least, not for her. And what if Reese's mother had misread the situation? Not only would Lauren make a fool of herself, she'd lose her best friend and her partner forever. It was better this way.

Still, he'd actually sounded a little jealous just then.

After three pints of Guinness, she reminded herself. *What we have is good and I'm not going to mess that up like some pathetic lovelorn teenager. We're better together than most married couples I know. Isn't that worth something?*

Isn't that everything?

Getting undressed, she could hear Reese bombing around the front room, trying to figure out how to work the TV. After much swearing, it finally roared to life, the sounds of a cheering crowd at some sort of sports game filling the little cottage. She crawled into bed and pulled the covers up to her chin.

No, she thought and closed her eyes as the crowd went wild on the big screen, *it's better this way.*

TWENTY-ONE

'DON'T SCREAM.'

Lauren's eyes snapped open to a man's hand over her mouth and his weight pressed into her body. She struggled against him, trying to get her arms out from under the covers where they were trapped. 'Shhhh. It's me,' Reese whispered, his lips right next to her ear. 'There's someone creeping around outside.'

She relaxed her body but her mind went into high alert as Reese pulled his hand away. She blinked against the darkness, trying to get her eyes to adjust.

Reese was standing next to her bed in sweatpants and an old Buffalo Bills T-shirt. He was pulling back the blinds with the tips of his fingers just enough to look out the window. When she sat up, he motioned to her to come next to him.

'There,' he whispered. 'See that?' The beam of a flashlight traced its way around the back of the house.

'Come on,' she whispered, tugging his arm.

They made their way quickly and quietly through the little guesthouse to the back door in the kitchen. Both of them paused to get ready, Lauren taking a deep breath. Moonlight poured through the kitchen windows, casting long shadows. Outside, they heard the sound of something getting knocked over and a beam of light came in through the living room window off to their left. 'He's looking through the front window,' Reese whispered. 'On three.'

They silently counted out three and Reese turned the knob. Lauren's bare feet hit the cold, wet grass sending a chill through her body. She and Reese came around the corner only to see the light bouncing across the yard toward the hedges.

'Go! Go! Go!' Reese yelled, sprinting ahead. Setting off after the intruder in a dead run, he crashed through the bushes into the next field over. Lauren followed, while broken hedge branches clawed at her arms as she pushed her way through.

Lauren was nowhere near as fast as Reese, even when she had the air for it. She could see Reese in the moonlight gain on their Peeping Tom. They raced across the field toward a second row of bushes that separated the Fitzgerald's property from the road.

Reese pushed forward and leapt on the man, causing the two of them to tumble to the ground. She'd almost reached them when she saw something cylindrical come down and Reese cried out.

'Reese!' she yelled. Whoever he was chasing stumbled forward, smashed his way through the second set of hedges and was gone.

The sound of a car peeling off filled the night air. When she stopped short, Reese was rolling on the ground, clutching his right arm. 'That son of a bitch hit me with his flashlight. If I hadn't blocked it with my arm, he would have split my head wide open,' he panted.

Lauren knelt down next to him. 'Are you OK?'

'Yeah.' He sat up and tried stretching out his arm. He flexed his fingers and winced. 'Help me up.'

Lauren got her arm around his back and helped him to his feet. Once he was standing, he shook himself, like a dog shakes off water after it gets out of a pond, trying to expel the adrenaline rushing through his body.

'Your nose is bleeding,' she told him, picking the grass and twigs from the front of his shirt.

He dragged his sleeve across his face, then looked down at the line of blood left behind. 'The fucker elbowed me in the face,' he panted.

Lauren walked over to the gap in the bushes and stuck her head in. Whoever it was had crashed straight through to the other side and disappeared.

'He's gone,' she said, stepping back. 'He must have had a vehicle parked on the road waiting. Did you get a look at him?'

'No,' he said, with disgust in his voice. He brushed at the muddy skid mark on his sweatpants that went from his left knee to his hip bone but only succeeded in smearing it more. He gave up and they started walking back toward their guesthouse. 'He had something covering his face. Some kind of mask, like fishermen wear.'

'Someone wants to know what we found at Jimmy's place today,' Lauren said, looking back over her shoulder at the destroyed shrubbery.

'Someone is going to get my foot in their ass,' Reese said. 'I'm charging Sharon Whitney extra for this. These were my favorite pair of sweats.'

TWENTY-TWO

AS MUCH AS Lauren hated to do it, she called Mr and Mrs Fitzgerald, who then woke up Garda Scannell. After Lauren hung up with his wife, Mr Fitzgerald jumped in his truck and took off down the road in the direction she and Reese surmised the fleeing vehicle went. They never saw Mr Fitzgerald's face, just his silhouette as he raced outside, and the taillights of his truck as he peeled out onto the road and out of sight.

Mrs Fitzgerald wandered back from the main residence into the guesthouse kitchen when Garda Scannell arrived. She had a pink terrycloth robe pulled tightly over her nightdress, her hair curled around tight old-fashioned rollers held with bobby pins. She immediately began fussing over Reese's arm, making him hold ice wrapped in a towel on it.

Scannell stood in the kitchen of Mrs Fitzgerald's guest cottage rubbing the sleep out of his eyes, with his Garda coat thrown over a rumpled uniform he'd probably snatched off the floor. He wasn't happy at being woken up in the middle of the night. 'My twins were screaming when I left,' he complained. 'That woke up the older two. I left my poor wife trying to get them all back to sleep.'

Lauren relayed the latest events to him.

He wasn't convinced it had anything to do with the missing painting. 'Could have been some poor bastard looking for nightcrawlers. Always people around trying to hunt up bait in the middle of the night in Keelnamara. And the Fitzgeralds have a great yard for it.'

Mrs Fitzgerald nodded. 'My husband is always running people off, but he never can catch them. We must have extra fat earthworms here.'

Scannell covered a yawn with his hand. 'We're mostly fishermen by trade in Keelnamara, you know. Old Whitey Donnell probably shat himself and dropped his worms to boot.' He gave a harsh-sounding snort. 'That'll teach him to nose around on other people's property.'

'He didn't hit like a fisherman,' Reese said, yanking up the sleeve of his sweatshirt to show Scannell a big purple bruise blossoming on his arm.

'Then you've never been hit by one before,' Scannell said dryly. 'You have to be strong to pull in those nets.'

We'd never think of someone searching for bait, Lauren thought. *Are we being a bit paranoid?* From the look of fury on Reese's face, he wasn't buying the idea that their intruder was just someone looking for worms.

Scannell went on to tell Lauren, 'Sheila McGrath was none too happy I'd come asking Martin questions about the break-in at his uncle's place. I questioned him in the driveway for almost twenty minutes. Martin denied breaking into the cottage, saying he knew ten different ways to get inside without kicking in the door.'

'What did he say about the night of Jimmy Breen's death?' Lauren asked, watching Mrs Fitzgerald take the towel from Reese, dump the almost-melted ice in the sink, then wring it out.

His eyes cut over to Mrs Fitzgerald. Lauren could see him weighing his words carefully. 'Said he'd been drinking with him earlier in Robber's, then drove out to the abandoned resort to finish a bottle of whiskey alone in his car. Said being out of prison was tough on him. He likes to drink by himself where no one can know his business.'

'How'd he get to the walking path after they found Jimmy's body?' Reese asked.

'Said he got so drunk he decided to leave his car and walk home. Saw the lights on the walking path and stopped to check it out.'

'That's no alibi.' Reese accepted a fresh batch of ice cubes from their host with a grim smile and thank you nod.

'True. It isn't.' Scannell was rubbing the start of dark stubble on his chin. Lauren suspected he was the type that had five o'clock shadow at noon. When she first got on the job she'd had a partner who kept a razor in his locker and had to stop back at the station at least once a night to shave or else he'd resemble a budding werewolf by the time the shift was over. 'In the end, Sheila came out crying and Martin told me to piss off, so I did, having nothing to hold him on.'

Lauren glanced at the clock. It was three in the morning. From the tone of his voice, she knew Scannell was finished with them and their questions. 'You should go to bed, Mrs Fitzgerald. It's late and I'm sure your husband will be back soon.'

'I'll walk you up front, Theresa,' Scannell said. She now dabbed at Reese's nose with a wet paper towel, trying to get all the dried blood from under it. 'I'm just a phone call away if there's any other *odd* happenings.' The feeling they were getting on Scannell's last nerve intensified with his emphasis on the word 'odd'.

'I'll definitely call you when we're on the way back to Jimmy's cottage today,' Lauren said.

Scannell held his arm out to Mrs Fitzgerald. 'Very good. I'll see you in the morning then. Good night, folks.'

And that, Lauren mused to herself as Scannell escorted Mrs Fitzgerald to the main house, *is being blown off, Irish style*.

TWENTY-THREE

'I KNEW SHEILA wasn't going to come with us after what Scannell said about his talk with Martin,' Reese said, picking his way carefully through the clutter of Jimmy Breen's house. With the tips of two fingers, Lauren peeled what looked like a greasy T-shirt off the back of a kitchen chair sitting in the middle of the living room, and let it fall onto a stack of old auto magazines.

'I would have at least thought she'd open the door for us.' They'd knocked on Sheila McGrath's door for a full minute, then stood there on the stairs in silence for another five. This time the curtain in the window didn't even flutter.

Lauren had called Garda Scannell on the way over to the cottage. He sounded tired from being woken up in the middle of the night, but not unpleasant. He agreed to meet them at Jimmy's place. He told Lauren he'd spoken to Detective Quill, who'd driven to Keelnamara from Killorglin first thing that morning and was eager to speak with them. That surprised her, as she'd given Scannell her card and Quill hadn't called her back yesterday.

Scannell had secured the cottage door using crime scene tape to keep it from flopping open because the latch was broken, so Lauren and Reese knew no one had tampered with it. Lauren had used crime scene tape herself to hold doors closed in the past. It might deter someone from trying to enter that way, but anyone intent on getting in wouldn't have much of a problem with forcing a window open. It wasn't exactly Fort Knox, which Reese pointed out to Lauren. They'd unlocked the back door, come in through the kitchen, which was now buzzing with flies, and made their way to the living room. As long as they stayed away from the bathroom, the stench was almost bearable.

Almost.

'Not one person claims to have ever seen the painting,' Lauren said, scanning the wreckage of the living room again. 'Sheila or Martin would've grabbed it before selling the cottage if they knew where it was. I'm thinking there's a good chance it was never here at all, but Jimmy knew where it went.'

'Martin would have taken it for sure,' Reese agreed.

'I don't think Sheila McGrath has it.' Lauren rubbed at her nose to try to get the smell out. 'But we do need to talk to her again. She was holding something back.'

'Maybe we should grab that milk jug she asked for and drop it off. Sort of a peace offering,' Reese suggested.

'Good idea. You go look for it in the kitchen. I'll start checking the bedroom. I want to get through as much as we can before Garda Scannell gets here with Detective Quill.' She was still getting used to referring to police in Ireland as Garda instead of officer. It just didn't roll off her tongue as easily and she was sure she'd slip up at some point.

'Have fun with Jimmy's dirty drawers.' Reese stepped over the partially disassembled engine that had blocked Lauren's way yesterday.

'Will do,' she called back, maneuvering around the piles of garbage to the bedroom door. She snapped a picture of the room with her cell phone camera before she waded in.

Thankfully, most of the debris in the bedroom was made

up of clothes. It looked to Lauren like Jimmy Breen had never thrown out a piece of clothing in his life, no matter how ripped, stained or worn out. There was so much strewn about, you couldn't see the floor. The smell was more subdued in the bedroom: stale, like sweat, instead of the putrid odor wafting from the bathroom.

She wasn't sure if he didn't believe in actually using dressers or hampers, because he owned both, and both had been overturned in the ransacking. Overturned easily because they'd been empty. All the clothes Jimmy owned were already trampled down on the floor. Lauren could see shoe prints on some near the far corner, and they didn't look recent. He must have picked a shirt off the ground, worn it, and thrown it right back down. Kicking herself for not bringing latex gloves with her to Ireland, she made a mental note to ask Garda Scannell if he could spare a couple of pairs when he got to the cottage. As it was, she used her pen to lift and turn over T-shirts and work pants and yellow socks with the toes worn through.

The mattress was on its side next to the bed frame, its guts spilling out onto the floor. In one corner old records were stacked against the wall next to a black turntable from the seventies. They'd been rifled through. Lauren realized that the painting could conceivably fit into a jacket sleeve, so she started to look through each album, one by one. From the kitchen she could hear the sounds of Reese banging around in the cabinets.

She put a copy of a Beach Boys album in the checked pile she'd made and caught something out of the corner of her eye. Something red, white and blue.

A cardboard box that looked like it had been pulled from under the bed, parting the dirty clothes on either side, had been dumped out onto the floor. A Buffalo Bills bobble-head doll sat on a stained yellow towel next to it.

She made her way over to the box, squatted beside it and tipped it back up with her pen. Underneath was a hockey puck with the logo of the Buffalo Sabres on it, a playbill from the now closed Studio Arena Theatre, some American coins, a little stack of receipts and a small black cassette tape.

She picked up the papers and leafed through them. She did a quick calculation in her head. 'Hey Reese!' she called. 'I think I might have something here.'

There was more banging and crashing as he made his way to the bedroom. 'I got nothing so far in the kitchen. I can't even find the milk jug. What'd you find?'

'Come take a look at these,' she said, holding out the receipts.

Taking them from her, he flipped through the stack. 'Western Union. Two hundred pounds a month. But these are from'—he squinted to read the date—'almost twenty years ago.'

'It's more than two years' worth. Someone was wiring him cash.'

'It's says here the Western Union he used was located inside a shop called Murphy's in the town of Killarney.' Reese handed back the receipts.

'I wonder if these were payments from whoever had Jimmy steal the painting.'

'Why'd the payments stop then? A couple of grand isn't much compensation for stealing a multi-million-dollar painting.'

'Maybe they didn't stop. Maybe the pick-up place changed or maybe there's another box of receipts around here. One thing's for sure, we need to go to Killarney and show Jimmy's picture around that shop. Maybe they have records that go back that far.'

'Doubtful,' Reese said, using the toe of his shoe to move the rest of the items from the box around. 'But it's worth a shot.' He picked up the little black tape. 'What's this for?' He turned it over in his hand, checking for markings.

Lauren took it from him and slid her glasses down so she could get a closer look. She hadn't been able to bring herself to get bifocals just yet. 'It looks like a tape from an old-fashioned answering machine. I wonder what it's doing in a box full of his Buffalo mementos.'

From outside they heard the sound of a car crunching up the gravel drive.

'I hope that's Scannell and not Martin McGrath,' Lauren said, tucking the receipts and cassette tape into her inside jacket pocket.

The back door creaked open. 'Miss Riley, Mr Reese?' Garda Scannell's voice called from the kitchen. He must have seen the front door still sealed and gone around the back.

'In here,' Lauren called. 'But don't break your neck trying to come in, we'll come out to you.'

'We'll be on the lawn.' He let out a gagging cough, the smell getting to him as well.

Standing in the overgrown grass and weeds when they emerged was the solid Garda from the night before and a taller, thinner man in a smart-looking tan trench coat. He was in his early fifties with a receding hairline over a high forehead and long thin nose that made Lauren think of Ichabod Crane for some crazy reason. Clearing their throats as they walked, they joined the two Irish cops.

'How's the arm?' Scannell asked Reese.

'I won't be pitching in the police league any time soon,'

he said, stretching it out. 'Better my arm than my head, right?'

Having seen Reese's hatless head and matching scars in the guesthouse kitchen, Scannell now scrambled to change the subject. 'Sorry about not coming inside,' he said. 'I could barely breathe in there. Mr Reese, Miss Riley, this is Detective Simon Quill, Killorglin station.'

'Very nice to make both of your acquaintances,' he said. 'I'm sorry I didn't ring you yesterday. Garda Scannell didn't give me your cell number until this morning.' When Lauren and Reese's eyes both cut to Scannell, he added, 'In fact, he didn't mention this trip to Jimmy Breen's cottage with you today either. I found that out on the drive up here.' The pleasant façade slipped for a second and a note of annoyance with his colleague crept into his voice.

'No worries,' Reese told him, trying to smooth over the situation. 'We stopped at Robber O'Shea's pub for a pint. The Guinness is good there.'

'That it is,' he smiled, showing off slightly crooked teeth. 'It's not often I get to meet real private investigators from America, who also happen to be actual detectives from America.'

'We're not here on behalf of the Buffalo Police Department,' Lauren told him. 'We were hired by the woman who bought this cottage. We have no official powers or authority.'

'Oh, that I'm aware of,' the detective answered, but not unkindly. 'I actually have some things I'd like to talk to both of you about, if you'd follow us back to the station house.'

Lauren and Reese exchanged glances. Something was up. 'Of course. Lead the way,' Lauren said.

The Garda station house was actually in Glenbeigh,

about twenty minutes to the south over the Caragh Bridge, back off route N70. They followed Scannell's patrol vehicle while discussing the possibilities along the way.

'Do you think he wants to read us the riot act for getting involved in local affairs?' Reese asked, lolling his hand out the window to catch the bay's breeze.

'Possibly,' Lauren conceded. A tour bus rumbled past heading in the opposite direction, causing Reese to quickly pull his arm back into the car or risk losing it. 'Though he didn't seem all that territorial,' she said. 'He was pleasant enough, for what it's worth.'

'Maybe he has hero syndrome,' Reese said, now on the lookout for buses. 'You know, he wants to be the one who finds the long-lost painting? Maybe that was why Scannell didn't call him and give him your number or tell him we wanted to go through the cottage again. Maybe our new Garda friend wants to be the one to locate it.'

Lauren considered that. Finding a stolen Picasso would definitely be a feather in any cop's cap, no matter what country you were in. And European law enforcement was much more serious about art theft than their American counterparts, from what she'd managed to read in the short time she'd had to research. There was a lot to learn. It was a much more serious problem than she'd realized. Millions of dollars of artwork and artifacts were stolen every year. Many were never recovered. She wished Sharon Whitney had given her two or three days to prepare, at least.

'We'll just keep these receipts to ourselves for now. We'll go through them and head to the shop as soon as possible,' Lauren said. 'They're probably nothing, but they're all we've got to go on right now.'

'Agreed,' Reese replied, turning into another dreaded roundabout. 'I forgot to ask you before we left the States, does this job come with benefits? I'm thinking dental, eye exams—'

'Shut up and drive or you're fired.'

'Then you'd have to drive. I'd rethink that position.'

The Garda station was an old refurbished coast guard station that backed onto a cliff overlooking the bay. Two cars sat in the car park in front of the small, squat building. One had to be Detective Quill's unmarked vehicle, Lauren assumed, and the other Garda Scannell's personal car.

They hadn't waited for Reese and Riley. Lauren watched them walk into the building as Reese pulled their rental into an empty spot.

Throwing the car into park, Reese adjusted his hat in the rearview mirror before he got out. He'd ditched the base-ball hats for an Irish tweed cap Lauren hadn't even known he owned.

'What?' he asked Lauren when she gave him the side eye. 'When in Rome. Besides, my Buffalo Bills hat makes me stick out like a sore thumb more than I already do, ex-cuse my cliché.'

'You don't stick out.'

'Really? Because while I'm sure I'm not the only biracial man in County Kerry, I haven't seen too many black folks since we've been here, have you? Especially none with a road map etched on their bald noggins. Besides, this looks damn good on me.'

Lauren bit back the urge to apologize as they crossed the asphalt to the door. Reese would never admit it, but he was self-conscious of the scars that crisscrossed his head. He tried to mask it with humor, but Lauren knew better. What's worse was that they were scars she'd caused, even though he told her time and again he didn't blame her. They were the price that cops paid for working the job. She reached around and put her scarred palm over the spot in her side where she'd been stabbed. Other people had done these things to them. Still, she couldn't help blaming herself.

The office was what she'd expected from a non-manned station: a desk with an older model computer, some filing cabinets against the wall, a copy machine that had seen better days. There was a small room next to the bathroom with a framed glass door and window. Lauren surmised it was an interview room for witnesses, with a desk and chairs but no camera set up that she could see. Also the window looked out over the bay. Unless the rules of interrogation were different in Ireland, you'd want video recording and no distracting views.

Off to the right was an adjacent room with a round table and five chairs poised around it. Cabinets lined the walls, probably filled with office supplies. A coffee maker and electric kettle sat on a rolling cart in the corner, neither plugged in, sugar packets and powdered nondairy creamer in a basket on the shelf underneath.

Quill took a seat at the table in front of a laptop and black leather folio, almost exactly like the one Lauren carried in Homicide. 'Have a seat.' He gestured to the two chairs across from him, as Scannell took the spot next to him.

'I'd offer you a coffee or tea,' Scannell said, looking over at the cart, 'but I usually bring that in from home if I know I'm going to be working out of here for a few days straight. I usually only man it a couple of hours a day. Just long enough to take care of permits or complaints about neighbors. You'd find it hard to believe if I told you about the number of sheep that stray off in the middle of the night.'

'I'm fine,' Lauren replied. In truth she was actually dying for a cup of java. They hadn't had time to hit a local store to get supplies. Thankfully, Mrs Fitzgerald had brewed some for her that morning with breakfast. The tea sat untouched while she drank the entire pot, minus Reese's one cup.

'No worries, brother,' Reese told him, then got straight to the point. 'I know this isn't a meet and greet, fellas, so what's up?'

Detective Quill sat very straight, folding his hands in front of him on the table.

I know that pose, Lauren thought, recognizing the body language immediately.

'We got the results of James Breen's postmortem this morning from Tralee University Hospital.' His voice was even, measured. 'Mister Breen did not die from a fall or heart attack. It's been ruled a homicide.'

Reese sat back in his chair and beat Lauren to asking the first question that popped into her head. 'Any suspects?'

Quill was careful in his answer. They hadn't been brought to the station as cops, Lauren realized, they were there as witnesses. 'As you know, Garda Scannell spoke to the nephew about the break-in at the house. He also questioned him about his whereabouts at the time of James's death. All I can tell you about that conversation is that he has no solid alibi. However, we still have a lot of evidence to process from the scene, witnesses to talk to, and security camera footage to track down, although I can tell you there aren't many cameras in Keelnamara. This murder investigation is still in its infancy,' he said, looking from Lauren to Reese and back again. 'Apparently you're both homicide detectives back in the States?'

Lauren piped up, 'We're here as—'

Quill held up a hand, cutting her off. 'Excuse me, Miss Riley. I know why you're here. And being detectives yourselves I know you'll understand why we won't be able to let you back into James Breen's home until our investigation allows for it. That's why we called you out of the property and brought you here. I'm waiting for our Divisional Crime Scenes Unit out of Tralee to arrive. They'll dust for prints and look for any trace evidence. Although,' he wrinkled his nose, 'considering its current state, I don't know how much more we'll be able to recover, given they went over the place yesterday. Garda Scannell shouldn't have granted you permission to go back into that house until he'd spoken to me.'

Lauren looked to Reese, then said, 'We understand completely. And we'd like to offer our assistance in any way we can.'

'That won't be necessary,' Quill said. 'While I appreciate the offer, contrary to what you might think, law enforcement in County Kerry is quite capable of investigating its own crimes. We'll be setting up an incident room here in the station. A detective inspector is on his way to head up the investigation, along with a few of my fellow detectives. I'll be assisting, along with the Crime Scenes Unit and Garda Scannell, to investigate the murder.' He opened the laptop that had been sitting on the table next to him. 'Now I have some questions for the both of you.'

Lauren and Reese spent the next half-hour answering questions from Detective Quill, while Scannell took handwritten notes and interjected something every now and then. Most of Quill's questions centered on Mrs Whitney and why she believed the painting was in Ireland. Lauren had to dance around some of them, citing client confidentiality, but in truth, Sharon Whitney buying Jimmy Breen's house was a matter of public record. And the theft of the painting had been widely covered by news outlets.

Quill asked if Lauren had copies of the original police reports of the robbery and she agreed to make them for him. Those too were a matter of public record, and she told herself that if the shoe were on the other foot, she'd appreciate getting copies right away instead of going through the red tape of a formal request to a police department in another country.

Quill was calculated and professional the entire conversation, never once veering into the casual manner they'd shared with Garda Scannell the day before. There'd be no swapping stories with him over a pint when they were finished with all of this.

'Thank you for your time,' Quill said, shutting his laptop with a snap. 'I'd like to have those copies as soon as possible. Would you mind if I followed you back to your bed and breakfast?'

'Not at all,' Lauren told him, stopping her hand from creeping toward the receipts in her jacket pocket. Jimmy Breen being murdered changed everything. Quill was slowing her down; she wanted to get over to the shop in Killarney as soon as possible. They only had one lead and she wanted to jump on it.

TWENTY-FOUR

LAUREN AND REESE kept quiet on the walk to their car, with Scannell and Quill trailing behind them. It wasn't until they were safely ensconced in the vehicle that Reese let out one of his signature low whistles. 'Can you believe this?' he exhaled. 'Now we're involved in a homicide investigation.'

Lauren pulled her seatbelt across her chest and buckled in. 'Quill clearly doesn't want our input.'

Slipping the key into the ignition, Reese started the car. 'He wants our information, though,' he said as he slowly backed up, easing out of the parking lot, allowing Quill and Scannell to follow.

'So would we, if the roles were reversed,' Lauren said. She thought for a moment, staring out of the window at the blue-green water. 'Why, after being home for twenty years, would someone kill Jimmy now?'

'Maybe someone in Keelnamara is desperate for cash,' Reese offered.

'They'd have to have a buyer,' Lauren countered. Reese and Riley did their best work when they talked out scenarios, pulling apart information piece by piece. 'You can't take a Picasso to the local pawn shop to fence like it was a Rolex watch.'

'Maybe it took the murderer this long to *find* a buyer.'

'Maybe,' Lauren conceded. That was a good point. For

the kind of money that painting could fetch, someone smart would be willing to play the long game.

Straining against the seatbelt, she twisted around to look at the Gardai following them, then turned back and pulled the little stack of receipts out of her jacket pocket. Now that she had a few minutes, she began to examine them more closely.

'Hey Reese,' she said, pulling one that was printed on pale pink paper out of the stack, 'this one's different. It's from a pharmacy in Killorglin. It looks like it's for a prescription.'

Reese glanced over at the paper in her hand. 'What's it for?'

She squinted at the fading ink. 'I can't pronounce it. I'll spell it out for you.'

He shook his head when she was done. 'I never heard of it. Do they have HIPAA laws in Ireland?'

Lauren took out her phone and Googled chemists in Killorglin. 'It doesn't matter. Google Maps shows a brand-new daycare center where Beamish's Chemist used to be.'

'Did you Google what the drug was used for?'

Before she could punch it into her phone, Mrs Fitzgerald's house appeared as they crested the hill, with their little guesthouse behind and the bay spread out beyond both. Mrs Fitzgerald's car was gone. She'd said at breakfast she was going into Killorglin to work in her real estate office, and told them to call her if they needed anything. Mr Fitzgerald's blue truck, which had been parked in the long drive-way, was also gone. Mrs Fitzgerald had told them he'd been helping out some fellow fishermen and had been leaving for Killarney before sun-up every day. 'They're short a man on their boat. We all lend a hand to one another in these parts,' she'd explained. They had yet to meet him face to face.

'Could be Jimmy got the clap in America,' Reese said as he pulled into the driveway. He stopped in front of the garage and threw the car into park. Lauren stashed the receipts back in her jacket pocket before she had a chance to Google what the medicine was for. 'That's the gift that keeps on giving.'

Lauren gave him a look as she gathered up her things. 'Focus, please. No jokes. Detective Quill doesn't seem the type to appreciate our lowbrow sense of humor.'

He adjusted his hat again. 'Everyone appreciates my sense of humor except you.'

She grabbed the door handle. 'Remind me to fire you later.'

All four exited their vehicles at once, as if they'd rehearsed it. An awkwardness hung between them, now that they were aware of their different interests in the same case. That fact was bound to cause a clash in the very near future.

Scannell and Quill followed them down the stone path that cut around the main house to the guesthouse in silence. From Scannell's body language, Quill must have given him a dressing down. The huge hare was back on the lawn, jaw working, working, working. It didn't hop away as they approached but merely sat with ears pointing straight up, watching their progress.

Reese had both sets of keys since he'd been driving, so he stepped in front of the other three to unlock the door. As soon as he swung it open, there was a collective gasp of disbelief.

The guesthouse had been trashed.

Every pot and pan had been pulled out of the small kitchen's cupboards, every plate and cup smashed on the ground. The oven door hung open and the microwave had been yanked out of the wall and thrown in the corner.

'Don't touch anything,' Quill said, reaching into his

trench coat and pulling out his sidearm. He pushed in front of Reese to take the lead.

The intruder had used the same search methods in the living room: pillows and cushions slashed open, drawers dumped, couch tipped over.

The doors to both Lauren's and Reese's rooms were ajar. Definitely not how they'd left them that morning. Lauren used her hip to nudge hers the rest of the way open. She wasn't nervous about finding the perpetrator inside like she'd been at Jimmy's the day before. Having Quill behind her with a gun was a great equalizer.

Devastation similar to Jimmy's cottage had been visited upon her room, with one notable exception: her iPad and files were missing from her nightstand. 'Son of a bitch,' she whispered, stepping over a broken lamp to double-check they weren't scattered on the floor somewhere.

'It's all clear in here,' Reese called from across the hall.

'Same,' she called back. 'Did they take anything?'

'Not that I can tell. Just ransacked.'

She turned to Quill, her voice rising in anger. 'They took my iPad and case files.' Lauren walked past him, forcing Quill to follow her so they weren't standing around staring at her underwear strewn all over the floor.

When they met up with Reese and Scannell in the living room, Lauren noticed Reese's look of disgust that mirrored her own feelings. 'This is unbelievable,' he said, hands on his hips.

'Whoever broke into Jimmy's must have hoped you'd found the painting,' Scannell said.

'Well,' Lauren said, head still swiveling around to take in the damage, 'that's good news for you and my client.'

'Why's that?' Quill asked.

'Because that means whoever murdered Jimmy Breen

doesn't have the painting and is still hunting for it,' Lauren replied. 'And apparently he's not giving up until he finds it. He'll be looking where we're looking. He's bound to slip up.'

'The two of you have put me in a position,' Quill said. 'This person is a killer. I can't leave you in Keelnamara unprotected. Maybe I should call a hotel in Killarney for you to stay in.'

'We'll be fine right here,' Reese threw in before Lauren could snap something back at Quill. 'We still have our job to do. We'll assume the risk.'

'I've got to call Mrs Fitzgerald,' Scannell said, trying to diffuse the tension. 'And we should check the main house to see if the bastard got in there as well.'

'I agree,' Quill said. 'You two come with us and wait outside while we check. I'm going to have the Crime Scenes Unit in here to dust for prints and take pictures after they're done with James Breen's place.'

'You're the boss,' Reese replied, following them back out through the kitchen door, Lauren trailing slightly behind.

They leaned up against their car, shoulder to shoulder, watching the two Irish cops looking for any signs of a break-in up at the Fitzgeralds'. 'What are we gonna do about our files?' Reese asked. 'They got your iPad, our notes, the crime scene photos.'

'It's not 1957, Reese.' Lauren crossed her arms over her chest as Quill inspected a window. 'I scanned everything before we left and saved it to the Cloud.'

TWENTY-FIVE

MRS FITZGERALD RUSHED home from her office as soon as she got the call from Scannell. Apparently, Mr Fitzgerald was still out on his boat in the middle of Castlemaine Bay and wouldn't be able to survey the damage until they brought their catch in at the end of the day.

Standing in the middle of the driveway, wringing her hands together, Mrs Fitzgerald was beside herself. 'Are we in danger?' she asked Detective Quill. 'Will they come back here again?'

'I'm thinking whoever did this is a coward, waiting until everyone left before they broke in,' Quill replied. And they had broken in. During Quill and Scannell's check of the property they'd found the window in the guesthouse bathroom had been shattered. Smeared muddy footprints had been left on the side of the house where the burglar had climbed in and stood on top of the toilet seat.

'What if I'd have come home? Or my husband? What would have become of us?'

'I believe they would have fled.' Quill put a reassuring hand on the tiny woman's shoulder. He hadn't told her Jimmy Breen had been murdered yet. Quill said he wanted to withhold that information until he could speak to his next of kin, Sheila and Martin. 'Whoever it was, they weren't looking for a confrontation.'

'If you want us to find other accommodations,' Reese told her, despite the conversation he'd previously had with Quill, 'we understand.'

'Nonsense.' Her mouth set in a hard line as fear morphed into indignation. 'You're my guests and I'm not going to let some foolish treasure hunter run you off.'

Quill and Scannell stayed with Mrs Fitzgerald to take the report. Looking for fingerprints in a guesthouse may have seemed futile, but the Crime Scenes techs from the Garda had come over from Jimmy's place and were now dusting black powder all over and dutifully photographing footprints as Reese and Riley excused themselves.

Lauren had asked if there was an office supply store in town where she could download and make copies of her missing files. 'I don't want to use up all of your ink in the front house,' she told Mrs Fitzgerald. 'There's a lot to print.'

'You could use the printer at the substation,' Scannell offered.

'Thank you, but you still have work to do here and I need all the paperwork pertaining to my client's case, not just the files I'm sharing with you. It isn't anything you need but it's confidential.' Lauren could imagine what they'd think if they saw what Mrs Whitney was paying her. Or how she'd feel if she knew some random cops in Ireland were going over the terms of her divorce from Mr Whitney. Lauren would never get another PI job in Buffalo again. 'I'll make sure you get your copies, Detective Quill.'

Quill gave them the address of an office supply store in Killorglin. Lauren figured they could head over there, make copies, then go over to Killarney, hit Murphy's shop, ask about the money transfer receipts, and be back by supper time.

'I'll start cleaning up this mess as soon as they're finished,' Mrs Fitzgerald assured them, walking with Reese and Riley to their car. 'We've got rollaway beds in the shed for when larger parties book the house and Mister Fitzgerald will have that window boarded up in a snap.'

They thanked their host, who disappeared back into the main house as soon as they got in their car. Lauren could imagine her making a flurry of phone calls. The news would be all over Keenamara within the hour. She wondered how long it would take for word about Jimmy's murder to get out.

Lauren punched the address of the office supply store into their GPS. As Reese turned onto the road, she started brainstorming with him. 'Let's list off possible suspects. Who knew we were in Keelnamara?'

'Every person in Keelnamara,' Reese replied, following the pleasant British woman's directions.

'OK,' she conceded. 'Let's narrow that down. Who knew we were at Jimmy's place yesterday?'

'Mister and Mrs Fitzgerald, Sheila and Martin McGrath, Garda Scannell, Detective Quill and your boyfriend at the bar.'

Lauren ignored that last jab. 'Did you mention it to any of your newfound friends at Robber O'Shea's?'

'What do you think I am? Some kind of amateur?' he asked, giving her the side eye. 'I was gathering information from Jacky, who discovered poor Jimmy's body. He said Jimmy had no business being on the footpath so late at night, unless he was heading to work for someone. But none of the residents claimed to have hired him for anything.'

'So someone may have lured him out there.'

'That's what it looks like,' Reese agreed.

'Why didn't you tell me that last night?'

'Because you stormed off into your room after I teased you about your boyfriend and slammed the door.'

'I didn't slam the door.'

'Anyway,' Reese went on, 'Mrs Fitzgerald has a key to the guesthouse and I don't think Scannell or Quill broke in.'

'That leaves Sheila and Martin McGrath.'

'And your boyfriend.'

Lauren sighed. 'And my boyfriend.'

Reese's eyes cut to the rearview mirror and back. 'Or it could be whoever's in the white car that's following us. I saw the same make and model parked at Robber O'Shea's when we walked out last night.'

TWENTY-SIX

LAUREN ADJUSTED THE rearview so she could keep eyes on the car that was following them without turning around. 'Can you make out the driver?' Reese asked, slowing down just a fraction to force the driver to catch up.

She shook her head. 'This road leads right into Killorglin. When we're done making copies there, we can get on the N72 all the way into Killarney. All he has to do is hang back and wait for us to park. The streets are so narrow in this country, there's nowhere for him to hide.'

'For us either,' Reese replied. 'Just be ready.'

Lauren's hand snaked around her side to rest over her stab wound scar. 'I always am, now.'

With all the talk she'd heard of Killorglin since she'd gotten to Keelnamara, Lauren was expecting a thriving, edgy metropolis. What she found was a charming small town, with a narrow main street lined with shops. When the British lady on their GPS informed them they'd reached their destination, they parked on the street in front of the office supply store and exited, scanning for the white car and coming up empty. 'He must have turned down one of the side streets when I stopped to back into the spot,' Reese said.

'Or we're jumping at shadows,' Lauren replied.

'It was no shadow that hit me with a flashlight, or trashed our guesthouse, or killed Jimmy Breen, for that matter.'

'True,' Lauren said, walking into the shop with Reese bringing up the rear. 'Maybe Detective Quill has someone tailing us.'

'Could be,' Reese agreed. 'That's what I would do.'

While Lauren could have just gotten access to the files in the Cloud from her phone and saved herself the trouble, she preferred having hard copies to work with. She located a sales associate and was led to a desktop workstation at which to make prints. She had Reese grab some folders. 'Presentation is everything,' she told him when he grumbled.

The color photographs took longer to print, especially since she needed two copies of everything. When Reese came back with the folders, she could tell he was getting antsy. He had a lot of nervous energy he needed to burn off, especially when cases took an unexpected turn. 'I'm going to look for a coffee shop,' he announced as a picture of Sharon Whitney's foyer slowly emerged from the printer. 'And I've got to try to return these phone calls. Don't people understand I'm busy over here? I don't have time to play phone tag.'

'I'll handle this. You go.' Lauren plucked the picture out of the tray and added it to the stack as the next one began to print. She pictured Reese upon his return, sitting across from her ripping a napkin to shreds, then grabbing hers and doing the same thing. Jimmy had been murdered and they had been violated. When working a murder you had to separate yourself from it to remain objective. It wasn't personal. Until it was. And now whoever killed Jimmy was going to have the Garda and Reese and Riley after them.

Reese returned holding two cups of coffee. As Lauren predicted, he sat staring at the world's slowest color printer, absently tearing strip after strip off his napkin until there was only a pile of shredded paper on the desk in front of him. Lauren reached over and swept the whole mess into a trash can next to the desk.

When the last picture was printed, she gathered up their paperwork and package of folders, paid the cashier at the counter and they left to head over to Murphy's store in Killarney.

TWENTY-SEVEN

COMING INTO KILLARNEY, they had to squeeze past tour bus after tour bus as they tried to locate the shop named on the old receipts. They finally found the mom-and-pop grocery store squashed in between two shops that catered to the tourist trade. Trying to find a parking spot on the street proved to be a feat in itself. The tour buses were parked end to end all the way to the next intersection. Lauren had read that Killarney was the start and finish for the Ring of Kerry, but hadn't really known what that meant until then.

Reese managed to find someone pulling out of a spot and quickly parallel parked down and across the street from Murphy's. They could see tourists pooled around the front entrances to the establishments on either side of the little grocery store, arms loaded with shopping bags.

'I always wanted to see the Ring of Kerry,' Lauren remarked, standing on the curb as Reese hit the lock button on the key fob.

'And here you are, investigating a murder and the grand theft of a Picasso. It's a dream come true for you.' He looked both ways up and down the street. 'Any sign of our new friend?'

She swept the vehicles lining both sides of the narrow road with her eyes. 'I don't see the car. It's hard to tell with all the buses though.'

'Let's do this then. Stay sharp.'

Lauren inwardly winced at his choice of words as they crossed the street. It was the damn knife wound in her side that was threatening to end her police career. Try as she might to deny it, she really wasn't operating at one hundred percent and probably never would be, no matter how many physical therapy sessions she attended.

Bells jingled as Lauren opened the door to Murphy's, announcing their arrival.

Time had passed Murphy's general store by. It had all the essentials lined up neatly on worn wooden shelves. Boxed laundry soap, canned green beans and baking soda were on sale in prominent displays at the head of each of the three aisles. The daily newspaper sat stacked next to the cash register in front of a bored-looking twentysomething girl sporting blond hair streaked with pink. She didn't look up from scrolling on her phone when they came in, just shifted on her stool behind the counter. 'The ATM's outside.'

Reese cleared his throat and she glanced their way. 'Hello, Miss,' he said, tipping his Irish hat to her.

'We don't have a public bathroom,' she said, probably for the tenth time that day, but her phone had sunk down by her side. Clearly, he'd gotten her attention. Lauren hung back, deciding to let Reese take the lead on this.

'That's not what I came in for,' he said, moving in front of Lauren, unleashing his 1,000-watt smile on her. 'I was wondering if you could help me with something.'

Clearly mesmerized by Reese's smile, accent and grass-green eyes, she slid both her arms onto the counter and leaned in toward him. 'What can I help you with?' she asked, looking up at him through thick, black-mascaraed lashes.

'Have you worked here long?'

She nodded, totally oblivious to Lauren's presence. 'My granddad bought the place in the seventies and then my Da took it over from him. I've been working here since I was high enough to reach the register.'

'Well, the things that I came to ask about happened long before you were tall enough to reach the register. Is your father around, so maybe I could ask him?' He bent forward and mirrored her, so that he was leaning on the counter as well, their hands almost touching.

She didn't move away from him. 'No, but my grand-dad is in the back. My Da keeps retiring him, but he keeps coming into work.'

'Do you think you could get him for me?'

Tucking a strand of pink hair behind her ear, the girl slid off her stool. 'I'll be right back.' She adjusted her short shorts for Reese's sake before disappearing into a back room.

Reese turned his head and cocked an eyebrow at Lauren. 'Now *that* is how you flirt.'

'You're unbelievable,' was all she said and handed him the case file she had just printed out. He was getting the job done, no need to feed his ego about it.

From the back room they could hear the voice of a man who was seriously hard of hearing, yelling, 'Who's here ta see me? An American? What American?'

The girl ushered a man well into his eighties to the front counter. His pleated khaki pants were hitched up to his chest, almost under his armpits, and were held in place with gray suspenders. He eyed Reese and Riley up. 'Me grand-daughter, Maoliosa, says yer looking for me,' he practically screamed, his thick round glasses making his watery blue eyes look huge. 'I don't know you.'

'No, sir, you don't,' Reese said loudly so he could hear. 'My name's Shane Reese and I'm a private investigator from the States. I came across some old Western Union receipts from your store and I was wondering if you kept records of transactions.'

He gave his granddaughter a skeptical look. 'A private investigator, he says. Like on the telly.' He turned back to Reese. 'And from America, no less.'

'Yes, sir. I'm looking into an old case and I was hoping you could help me with these receipts.' He held them out to the man who brought them right up to his glasses, then as far out as he could, trying to focus on the faded writing.

'How old did you say these were?'

'You would have done the money transfers between eighteen and twenty years ago.'

The man's bushy eyebrows knit together. 'Now that's a tall order. We don't have records from that far back. Why don't you tell me who gave you the receipts? Or don't you know?'

Reese put the file on the counter and extracted a photo of Jimmy Breen from the time of the theft. 'Did this man ever come in here?'

Mr Murphy let the receipts drop to the counter and took the picture from Reese. 'This is Jimmy Breen,' he said, holding the picture so close to his face it practically touched his nose. 'He did some work for me a couple of years back when my roof was leaking. Poor bastard. May he rest in peace.'

'Did he ever do money transfers here? It looks like he was getting about two hundred pounds a month.'

'That wasn't Jimmy Breen,' the granddaughter piped up. 'We only ever had one person who got a regular monthly wire transfer, since I can remember. It switched over from pounds to euros in 2002 when we joined the EU. He didn't come this month, though, and come to think of it, the transfer didn't come in either.'

'Who was picking up the money?' Lauren asked.

Noticing Lauren was with Reese for the first time, her smile disappeared. She narrowed her eyes at Lauren and tossed her hair in Reese's direction. 'Why, Robber Shea, of course.'

TWENTY-EIGHT

'ROBBER SHEA WHO runs the pub in Keelnamara?' Lauren asked. 'Are you sure?'

'Maoliosa's known the man her entire life,' Mr Murphy said, with a note of indignation. 'Of course she's sure. He's been coming here for twenty years picking up that money. Said it was from a silent partner in the pub from the States. All you Yanks want to own a piece of Ireland.'

The tinkling of bells filled the background.

'Did Jimmy ever pick the money up for Robber?' Lauren asked.

'Never.' Mr Murphy was sure. 'Robber came in like clockwork, first of every month.'

Lauren wanted to ask another question, but Reese grabbed her arm and steered her toward the front of the shop. 'Reese—'

'Thank you, Mr Murphy, and you too, Maoliosa,' Reese called to them over his shoulder. He pushed Lauren through the door and out onto the crowded street before they could respond.

'What's up with you?' Lauren demanded, trying to pull her arm away, but Reese held tight, propelling her forward into the throng.

'A guy from the pub last night just came into the store. He went down the cleaning supply aisle. Don't look now.' Reese guided her through the knot of tourists. 'He followed us out.'

Lauren looked. The man in the pressed button-down shirt from the night before was indeed threading his way through the crowd in their direction.

'Cripes, Riley, you'd never make it as a spy,' Reese hissed, and shouldered open the first door he came to: O'Halloran's Pub.

Unlike Robber O'Shea's, the inside of this pub was bathed in the sunlight pouring in from the picture windows that made up the front of the tavern. Patrons stood four-deep at the bar with shopping bags and fanny packs, sipping Guinness and taking selfies on their phones, trying to get the bar mirror in the background. An oversized chalkboard announced that Stephen Scales and Friends, famous musician and his bandmates, would be playing the uilleann pipes that evening at seven. A white-haired local sat at a table in the corner, where he was regaling five young backpackers with some highly animated tale, his arm flailing about as he drank from one of the three pints of Guinness parked in front of him. It was exactly what Lauren had pictured a traditional Irish pub to look like, albeit overrun with tourists at the moment.

'I think we should invite our new friend to sit and have a drink with us,' Reese said, hanging just inside the door, camouflaged from the window by its heavy wooden frame.

Lauren nodded, taking up a position next to Reese.

They didn't have to wait long. The stranger from Robber O'Shea's came in, looking into the crowd, trying to catch a glimpse of them. Reese stepped forward and grabbed the man's arm, using the grip they'd been taught in the police academy, and began walking him toward an empty table in the back corner. 'Hello friend,' Reese said as he guided him through the mobbed bar using the pressure point technique.

'It seems like you're really interested in what me and my partner are doing today, so why don't we sit and have a chat?'

'Easy, mate,' the man replied, trying to pull his arm away. Reese just smiled and applied more pressure, sitting the stranger down in a chair before letting him go.

Lauren and Reese sat at the table across from the now red-faced man, who was rubbing his wrist. 'That was unnecessary,' he said, and straightened his olive-colored windbreaker.

'What's unnecessary is you following us around the Ring of Kerry,' Lauren replied. 'What can we do for you?'

The man raked his fingers through his brown hair that was graying at the temples, then signaled to the waitress. She made her way over, her tray loaded with dirty dishes. 'Get me and my friends here some drinks, would ya, love? I'll have Powers on the rocks. And you, my friends?' He waved his index finger between them.

'Two waters,' Lauren replied with a smile, but didn't take her eyes off their new acquaintance. He was a greasy-looking man, with a square jaw and a nose riddled with broken blood vessels. *Wino nose*, her father used to call it. Lauren's Uncle Dwayne had the equivalent of a lumpy potato above his mouth, every blood vessel burst from the nonstop boozing he did.

The server nodded sweetly and ambled away, in no hurry at all. The stranger turned his attention back to Reese and Riley, bringing his shoulders to his ears in a dismissive shrug. 'You caught me. I must be getting rusty in my old age.'

'Who are you?' Reese prompted, not falling for his friendly act.

'My name is Shamus Gorham. Pleased to make your acquaintance.' He stuck out his hand, which Reese and

Riley ignored. It hung there for a few seconds before he pulled it back.

'Why are you following us, Shamus Gorham?' Lauren asked.

He cocked a bushy eyebrow at her. 'You really don't believe your client is the only one who has an interest in that painting being found, do you?'

Reese exhaled and sat back in his chair. 'You work for Mr Whitney.'

'Aye. And I have for many years now. Keeping track of Jimmy Breen, making sure he didn't buy a mansion or jet off to Bora Bora.'

'You weren't tracking him when he died,' Reese pointed out, being careful not to say murdered.

Shamus shook his head. 'It wasn't a full-time job. I just had to check on him from time to time, make sure nothing wonky was going on. I used to live here in Killarney, originally from Dublin, so I had to ease my way slowly into Keelnamara's good graces. Got a nice little flat there with my lovely bride. The fine folks in the townland think I travel for an insurance company and they are on my route. I told them I fell in love with the place, although the truth's not far off.'

'You're a private detective?' Reese asked.

'More like a hired gun,' he said, as if that clarified everything. His cockiness was grating on Lauren's nerves. 'I was let go from the Garda when I lived in Dublin. Moved out here to the coast. That was a long time ago. I consider myself an unofficial private investigator. Although I don't have a license, per se, I still have connections to the Garda. It's been useful. The type of people that hire me don't want to leave paper trails behind.'

'What got you fired?' Reese asked, just as the waitress strolled back over and put the drinks down on the table. Before Shamus could reach into his pocket, Reese produced enough Euros to cover his whiskey. Giving Reese an appreciative smile, she tucked the bills in her apron and thanked him before moving on to the next table.

Shamus grinned. 'I took a fancy to a lady with a dodgy past. We did some things I'm not proud of. Things that were frowned upon.'

Lauren wasn't falling for his lame attempt at an explanation. 'And then what happened?'

He picked up the rocks glass full of whiskey. 'I barely avoided prison and married her. A real love story that is, right there.'

'So Howard Whitney hired you and you've been watching Jimmy Breen for twenty years?' Lauren tried to clarify.

Shamus shrugged, shoulders almost touching his ears. 'You know the warring parties in this matter split the insurance money, don't you? Three million American dollars. That's a million and a half Mr Whitney had to invest in a guy like me, because that painting is worth a hell of a lot more now, I can tell you that.' He took a long drink before wiping his mouth with the back of his sleeve and setting it down again. 'It seems to me that keeping it out of his ex-wife's hands was more his motivation, though. There's a lot of bad blood there.'

Reese reached over and pulled the whiskey glass away from him. 'How'd you find us?'

'Are you joking? I heard about the sale of the cottage and then about the arrival of two private investigators from the States. You two are the number one topic of conversation in Keelnamara. You'd be amazed at how much information you can get in the local pub. I figured if I followed you, maybe you'd lead me to the painting.'

'You didn't happen to visit our guest cottage this morning, maybe cut open a few pillows and mattresses in your quest for the Picasso?' Reese asked.

'I've been following you since you left your place this morning. I know you don't have the painting yet. You wouldn't have bothered meeting with the Garda because you'd have no more business here.' Lauren wanted to swat the smug smirk off Shamus Gorham's face. 'You would've taken it and left.'

Lauren wasn't convinced. He could have easily watched them leave, ransacked the cottage looking for the painting, and caught up with them again at the Garda station or waited at the house for them to return. 'What's Whitney promising you if you recover it for him?' she asked.

He clapped his hands together and rubbed them like some old-time villain in a silent movie. 'If I can actually find it and deliver it to him myself, three million dollars. If I can give him the exact location of the painting, say you two track it down to a storage shed in County Clare, one million. It's a win-win for me, no matter which of us finds it.'

'I'd rather have three million than one,' Reese pointed out.

'Three million, one million,' he parroted with that maddeningly wise-ass grin. 'I couldn't spend that amount of money in these parts in ten years. I just want to keep my flat's rent paid and my wife happy. If Jimmy's dead and the painting is lost forever, my income just got significantly cut. Do you see my problem?'

Lauren did see the problem, and he was sitting right in front of her. She didn't know how much he'd heard of their conversation back in Murphy's store, but she was willing to bet his next stop was going to be Robber O'Shea's. 'What are you suggesting?' she asked.

He slouched in his chair, taking the glass of whiskey back from Reese. Swirling his melting ice cubes around, he said, 'I haven't a clue what the Mrs is paying you, but I know it's not three million dollars. What do you say we team up and split the profit from my boss? One and a half for you and one and a half for me.'

'Your math skills are lacking, friend,' Reese told him.

'Aye. That may be, but what have you got to lose? What loyalty do you have to that woman?'

Lauren pushed back from the table and stood up. 'If the problem is loyalty, it's not with my client, it's with you. If you're willing to scam your boss of twenty years, what would you be willing to do to us?'

'Keep your friends close, love, and your enemies closer,' he admonished. 'It makes sense for us to work together.'

Reese stood as well. 'I think we're good,' he said. 'I'm as close to you as I ever want to be.'

'Suit yourself,' Shamus said, seemingly nonplussed that they were declining his offer and leaving. 'But when I find the painting and you go home empty-handed, I hope you practiced what my dear wife has always preached.'

'And what's that?' Lauren asked, pausing next to her chair, Reese beside her.

He threw back the last of his whiskey and slammed the glass down on the table so hard several tourists turned and looked at them. 'Always get the money up front.'

TWENTY-NINE

'I THINK I need a shower,' Reese said when they got back to their car.

'I guess America didn't corner the market in skeevy ex-cops,' Lauren replied. Getting the copies made and the stop at Murphy's store had taken longer than either of them expected. Added to that was the time they'd spent watching Shamus drink whiskey they'd paid for. They wouldn't be back in Keelnamara until after dinner time. Still, when Lauren saw a sign for a chemist, she tugged on Reese's sleeve and pointed. 'Pull over! Right there!'

'What? Why?' he asked, searching the street around them with his eyes after pulling off to the side of the road, head swiveling back and forth.

'The prescription.' In the aftermath of finding their cottage trashed, Lauren had forgotten to Google what the medicine was for. She didn't want to run the risk of downloading bad information off the Internet when a pharmacy was right in front of her. 'I'll run in and ask what it is. You wait here.'

'I might have to go around the block a few times. I'm pretty sure I'm parked illegally and on the wrong side of the road.' As if on cue, a horn blared from behind.

'Just go. I'll be right back.' Lauren dashed from the car, crossing the road while Reese pulled out and turned down a side street.

Unlike Murphy's, the drug store was a modern chain, like you'd find on any street corner in America. Lauren stepped up to the automatic glass doors and they slid open for her. She made a beeline for the pharmacy counter in the back of the store, where a man in his forties wearing a white coat was waiting on a young mom standing next to an umbrella stroller with a sleeping toddler.

Lauren waited patiently in line while the mom got her prescription for ear drops filled, picturing Reese swearing profusely as he drove in circles around the block. 'Next,' the pharmacist called after the woman took the paper bag from him and pushed her baby down the aisle.

'Hi. Hello,' Lauren said, stepping forward and smoothing out the crumpled receipt on the counter. 'This may seem like a strange question, but would you be able to tell me what this drug is used for?'

He picked it up and squinted at the fading ink. 'It's the name of a medication that used to be prescribed for a number of things. Most commonly it was for endometriosis, although now there are much more effective treatments with less side-effects available. Where did you get this?' He turned the paper over in his hand. 'It must be fifteen years old.'

Plucking it from his fingers, Lauren told him, 'At least. Thank you very much for the information.' She turned and left the pharmacist standing with a baffled expression on his face.

What in the world was a handyman like Jimmy Breen doing with a receipt for endometriosis medicine? Lauren thought as she waved her hand in front of the doors to make them slide open.

It was her lucky day because just as she stepped out, Reese came around the corner. She jumped in the car be-

fore another motorist could lay on the horn and filled him
in on what she'd found out.

'I know endometriosis is a lady problem but could you
elaborate on that for me?'

'Really, Reese?' Lauren cocked an eyebrow at him. 'You
don't know how girl parts work?'

'I'm a cop, not a doctor. When you have to get your pros-
tate checked, let me know how that goes for you.'

'It's a condition where tissue grows outside of the uterus.
It can cause cysts and these bands of tissue can form. My
Aunt Linda had it and she had to have an operation because
the medicine she was on just wasn't working. It's incred-
ibly painful and a lot of women suffer from it.'

Reese shook his head. 'None of this makes any sense.
Jimmy had receipts for money Robber Shea was picking up
and a prescription for a medicine only a woman would use.'

'We need to talk to Robber,' Lauren said. 'Right now.'

Lauren called Scannell on their way back to Keelnamara and explained they'd gotten tied up in Killarney. She
didn't want to get into their run-in with Shamus the unli-
censed investigator over the phone. She figured she'd question Scannell about Shamus Gorham when they dropped
the copies of the files off at the Garda station the next day.
She wanted to wait until Quill wasn't around. Scannell was
much more talkative without him.

They'd almost made it to the pub in Keelnamara when
they were forced to a standstill by a shepherd and his flock
clogging the road. The ruddy-faced man was guiding hundreds of sheep from one pasture on the left side of the road
to one a quarter mile down on the other side. Minutes ticked
into a half-hour, and soon there were four other cars behind them, all waiting patiently for the man to tend to his
charges.

'Looks like we're stuck in rush-hour traffic,' Reese joked. 'I'm having a hard time staying awake.'

'Stop counting, there's too many of them,' Lauren said with a sigh. It figured that when they needed to get somewhere fast, they'd be held up by livestock, of all things. It was hard to believe that the beautiful soft woolen goods they'd seen in the tourist shops in Killarney came from these beasts, whose grayish coats looked dirty and matted.

The sheep herder finally wrangled the last of his flock through the wooden gate and swung it shut, giving Lauren and Reese a wave to go ahead.

After what seemed like an eternity on the narrow two-lane road, they pulled into Robber O'Shea's lot. A lone car sat in front of the curtained window, but not a single light was on. The double-sided sign hanging on the front door was turned to CLOSED. 'I thought pubs were open until eleven thirty in Ireland,' Reese said as they surveyed the vacant parking lot.

'It is a weekday. And,' Lauren glanced at her phone, 'it's just after eight o'clock. Maybe it was a slow bar night.'

'OK then,' Reese put the car in reverse and pulled out of the lot. 'We'll stop by tomorrow after we drop that paperwork off to Detective Quill. Mrs Fitzgerald will know what time Robber O'Shea's usually opens. But right now, we're going to have to stop at that gas station down the road and grab every snack in there because I'm starving.'

Lauren's stomach rumbled in response. 'I guess I am too. I forget to eat sometimes.'

'Really, Olive Oyl? And here I was thinking you were dieting to maintain that grossly emaciated frame of yours.'

'Just drive.' She tried to sound stern. After the day they'd had she wasn't in the mood to trade jabs with Reese. Their cold case robbery had turned into a fresh homicide. They'd had their lodgings broken into and been followed by a creepy ex-Garda. This was supposed to be an easy trip, to look around a cottage and come home. It had literally morphed into something much, much darker over a matter of hours.

I should have known better, she thought as she gave the closed Robber O'Shea's one last glance in the rearview mirror as they drove off in the direction of the gas station. *Nothing is ever simple for me.*

THIRTY

BACK AT THE GUESTHOUSE, Reese was full of pent-up energy. They'd eaten snacks standing at the counter of the gas station, the young clerk staring at them with eyes as wide as Mrs Fitzgerald's china saucers as they shoveled flavored potato chips and pretzels into their mouths. Reese hadn't worked out in days and now he was feeling antsy and guilty, pacing around the living room, swinging his arms until finally he dropped to the hardwood floor and started doing push-ups. An errant piece of pillow stuffing skittered away from him and disappeared under the cushionless couch. 'Is that necessary?' Lauren asked him, even though she knew for him it was.

Mrs Fitzgerald had done an amazing job of cleaning up as best she could with what she had to hand. There was nothing to be done for the couch until she sewed the cushions and pillows back up, but she'd swept up all the broken glass and dishes in the kitchen, even replacing them with new ones. Broken knickknacks had been cleared away, cabinet doors rehung and all the debris littering the floor removed.

'Got. To. Stay. In. Shape,' he replied, puffing out a word every time his chest hit the ground.

She sat in the rocking chair by the window, watching him. That, at least, had remained in one piece. Reese had flung his Irish hat on the kitchen table as soon as he'd walked in. Now his shaved head glistened with sweat, despite the chill in the room, as he pushed himself, muscles straining.

She used to be able to do a few push-ups, back in the day, when she was a young cop. Now she wasn't sure if she'd be able to do even one. She felt a twinge of guilt for not doing the exercises her therapists had taught her while she was in Ireland. She'd never get back to full duty if she didn't build up her strength.

Sometimes Lauren forgot how much older she was than Reese. Watching him now, that age difference was abundantly clear. She knew this was one of the reasons she'd never acted on her feelings, and had pushed them aside. She was twice divorced, had two grown daughters and was over forty. Really, what did she have to offer him? He deserved a blushing young bride and a house full of babies, if that was what he wanted. Lauren felt like any relationship they might have beyond their partnership would be robbing him of those things. Things she'd already had.

It would be even worse if he didn't feel the same, which was entirely plausible. She would never be able to live down the humiliation of revealing her feelings, only to get a sympathetic pat on the head.

'...one hundred!' he huffed, rocking back onto his knees. He was out of breath, smiling, glad to have released some of his frustration. 'Eyes up here, Riley. I'm not a piece of meat.'

'More like a slab of beef,' she countered, 'with the same IQ.'

He pulled his shirt over his head and wiped his face with it. 'Stop hitting on me.'

He turned his green eyes to hers, waiting for her witty comeback.

She wanted to say, *I'm not hitting on you* or *Put your*

shirt on or *You wish*, but all of those phrases stuck in her throat. Instead, she got up without a word, walked to the hallway and into her bedroom. 'I was only kidding!' she heard him call after her.

She flattened herself against the door, heart pounding. *I'm not a sappy teenager pining over a boy*, she told herself. *I'm not an over-the-hill woman with an unrequited crush. I'm not that pathetic.* She felt ashamed. A man had been murdered. She needed to do what she did best: work the case. Whatever conflicted feelings she had for Reese needed to be tucked away for good. *I need to work this job, maybe find the killer and the painting, then go home with our relationship intact.*

In her head it sounded like a solid plan. She took a few more deep breaths and decided she needed to go back into the living room or he'd definitely think something was up. She looked at herself in the mirror over the dresser and ran a hand through her hair. *OK*, she told herself as she walked toward the door. *Go back out there and act normal.*

She found Reese fully dressed and drinking tea at the kitchen table while he surfed the net on his phone. Looking up, he asked, 'You all right?'

Shaking her head, she sat across from him at the table. 'I felt out of breath all of a sudden. I just needed a minute for it to pass.' That, at least, was the truth.

He set both elbows on the table, tea mug cradled in his hands. 'I'm telling you right now, when we get home, you're going to see that specialist. You're white as a ghost right now. Well, paler than usual.'

'Ha, ha. I know—' She was cut short by her phone buzzing in her pocket. She fished it out and looked at it, relieved by the distraction.

The number on the screen was local to Buffalo, that much

she could tell by the area code, but it was unfamiliar. She read it off to Reese and asked if he knew who it belonged to. Shaking his head and shrugging at the same time, he responded, 'I have no idea.'

Against her better judgment, she answered. That was the mom in her, always afraid of the late-night phone call from an unknown number about one of her daughters.

'Hello, Miss Riley.' The voice was aged, warm and smooth, like the Irish whiskey she favored on cold winter nights, but not one she recognized.

The connection was lousy, so Lauren switched the phone from her left ear to her right, supposedly the good side. 'Who is this?' she asked.

'Howard Whitney. I hope you're having a good time in Keelnamara. My associate, Shamus Gorham, informed me that you had a nice talk with him in a local pub today.'

Lauren didn't bother to ask how he'd got her cell number. With his money and connections, he probably knew her bra size and where she made her first communion. 'Why are you calling me, Mr Whitney?' she asked bluntly.

'Don't get your hackles up. You don't think I would let someone beat me almost to death and steal what's mine and get away with it, do you?'

'I don't know you very well, but I suppose not,' she conceded, then added, 'You didn't answer my question.'

'Straight to the point then. Good,' he said. 'I want you to know that my ex-wife will never get her hands on that painting. Never. I will do everything in my power to make sure of that.'

'Did you tell Shamus to thwart me?' *People are throwing threats around like confetti*, Lauren thought.

'I know Mr Gorham probably offered to split the three million with you. I know what kind of man he is, that's why

I hired him. I'm here to tell you I'll pay you the three million if you turn the painting over to me instead of Sharon. I'm sure that's more than she offered you.'

It was more, but not that much more. 'Everyone in this situation has ulterior motives. None of you have clean hands,' Lauren said. 'I'm finding it hard to put my trust in anyone involved. I never thought I'd use these words in real life, but I have a real fear of being double-crossed, so forgive me if I refuse your generous offer.'

He laughed out loud into the phone. 'You really are a sharp woman, Miss Riley. I wish I'd hired you first.'

'With all due respect, Mr Whitney, I'm starting to wish I'd never answered your ex-wife's phone call in the first place.' *Just like I wish I'd never answered this one.*

'Then why not jump ship and come work for me?'

'If you knew me at all you'd know that as soon as I found out Jimmy Breen was murdered my priority switched from finding the painting to his homicide investigation.'

'Murdered? That's something Shamus Gorham didn't mention.'

Lauren resisted the urge to facepalm herself. She didn't know if Mrs Fitzgerald was even aware yet that Jimmy had been murdered. She hoped the information she'd just accidentally leaked to Howard Whitney wouldn't come back and bite her in the ass somehow. 'The Garda just got the autopsy reports back today.'

'You're investigating his murder with the Irish police?'

'No,' she said. 'Not exactly.'

'If you find the murderer, you'll find the painting,' Mr Whitney pointed out.

'One might lead to the other,' she had to admit. 'Yes.'

'And you'll still turn it over to Sharon despite my offer?'

'You said it yourself, Mr Whitney,' Lauren reminded

him. 'She hired me first. You have a good night.' With that, she hung up.

Reese had been listening to the entire conversation intently. 'Darth Vader wants you to come over to the dark side?' he asked.

Lauren nodded. 'You know, he and Sharon really should've stayed married. They were made for each other.'

Reese set his mug down and stretched his legs out, putting his stocking feet on the table, only to have Lauren swat them off. 'Hey!' he protested, then went on, 'They've wasted the last twenty years of their lives trying to stick it to each other. Sounds like they're still married to me.'

'Oh, Reese,' Lauren said with a knowing smile. She slumped down in her chair and crossed her arms over her chest. 'You have no idea.'

THIRTY-ONE

THE NEXT MORNING there was an enormous breakfast waiting for them, thanks to a shaken Mrs Fitzgerald. She was shocked at the news of Jimmy Breen's murder. She'd found out from Sheila McGrath, who'd phoned her as soon as Detective Quill finished doing the notification. 'I went over to Sheila's house and sat with her until well after dark. She told me that Martin had jumped in his car as soon as Detective Quill left.' Mrs Fitzgerald shoveled food onto their plates as she talked. 'I stayed with Sheila as long as I could. He still hadn't returned when I finally had to come home.'

She apologized to Lauren and Reese, saying she'd been too emotionally exhausted to check in on her guests when they came back that evening. Mr Fitzgerald had wanted to stay home with her but Mrs Fitzgerald had insisted he go out on the boat that morning. 'We all have our jobs to do, despite the dreadful news,' she said, finally sitting down after the last pancake was in front of Reese. The kitchen smelled of frying eggs and cinnamon.

Her heart went out to Mrs Fitzgerald, who watched her two guests with sad eyes. Lauren and Reese inhaled piles of pancakes and eggs, while she sat there sipping her tea, waiting for one of them to finish so she could whip the plate away and replace it with something else she'd cooked up. Lauren had managed to buy a few staples to keep at the guesthouse while they were staying there so they wouldn't eat poor Mrs Fitzgerald out of house and home every morning. But having eaten only chips and pretzels at the little gas station down the road from the pub the night before, her breakfast was a godsend.

Lauren could tell their host was the type of woman who had to keep busy—clean, cook, rearrange the furniture—to ward off thoughts of the murderer who'd come to her house just one day before. She was fully dressed when they got to the front house, hair done, and a touch of makeup already applied. She must have gotten up with her husband before sunrise to get herself put together and start making their food.

Thinking Jimmy had died of a heart attack was something the locals could wrap their heads around. Murder was something else. Something unbelievable and frightening. Watching Mrs Fitzgerald clearing away dirty plates and setting new dishes in front of Reese, Lauren wondered if she was regretting sending her husband off to work.

'Do you know what time Robber O'Shea's opens?' Lauren asked her as she set a coffee cake down. 'We need to ask him a few more questions.'

'Michael opens the pub at ten thirty to cater to the folks who like to have a pint with their lunch,' she said, cutting into the cake and laying a square on a plate, which Reese gratefully accepted. Lauren wondered if Mr Fitzgerald was included in that group but didn't dare ask for fear of insulting their host.

'Jimmy's funeral is scheduled for tomorrow morning at the church. Poor Sheila McGrath has decided to forego tonight's wake with the news of the murder.' Mrs Fitzgerald reached up and touched the gold cross that hung at her throat with the tips of her fingers. 'She said she didn't want people gawking at her brother, one of them possibly the devil that killed him. She just wants to lay him to rest in peace.'

'Call us if you need anything and thank you for the wonderful breakfast,' Lauren told their host, who was rinsing dishes to load in the dishwasher. She gave them a wave and turned back to her plates, basically washing them by hand.

Lauren was itching to get on the road to the Glenbeigh Garda station. On the way, they discussed how much they wanted to share with Quill and Scannell. 'Really,' Lauren said, 'what do we have except a couple of odd receipts that were stuffed under his bed for the last twenty years? It's not like he threw anything away.'

'We definitely have to tell them about Shamus Gorham,' Reese said, with just a touch of disapproval in his voice. Lauren knew he was trying to keep her on the straight and narrow. She had a tendency to come dangerously close to crossing whatever lines had been put before her during investigations.

'Shamus has been getting paid to watch Jimmy. It would make no sense for him to kill his golden goose,' Lauren pointed out.

'Irregardless, I say we tell them everything and let them sort it out.' Reese pulled to the side momentarily to let a truck pass. 'We can't obstruct a murder investigation.'

'Agreed.' Lauren only semi-agreed. Doing what Mrs Whitney hired them for was not obstructing anything. Lauren would eventually share everything with the Garda. Like she had told Howard Whitney the night before, Jimmy's murder was the priority. And like Whitney had pointed out, you find the murderer, you find the painting, and vice versa. Whose fault was it that she and Reese were uncovering more information than the Garda were?

She hated when Reese had to be her moral compass. 'And *irregardless* is not a word.'

The parking lot in front of the substation was filled with cars. People walked back and forth in the windows that lined the front of the building, some in uniform, some not, making it look alive with activity. Reese found the only empty spot left and pulled in. Lauren slung her canvas messenger bag, now filled with hard copies of the files for Detective Quill, over her shoulder and followed Reese into the small station house now crammed with Gardai.

Scannell was sitting at the front desk, a frown creasing his face as he held a phone receiver to his ear with one hand and jotted down notes on a yellow legal pad with the other. He saw them come in and held up an index finger, signaling them to wait where they were.

He said goodbye to whoever he was talking to and stood up. 'Good morning,' he said, coming around the desk. 'I hope you have that paperwork with you. Detective Quill was going to send me by Mrs Fitzgerald's to get it. I tried ringing you last night, but your cell said you were out of service range.'

Lauren pulled her phone out of her pocket and thumbed the screen to check. 'You did?'

'Happens all the time,' he said, dismissing it with a wave. 'If you were in transit between here and Killorglin, sometimes the reception can be spotty.'

'Good to know,' Lauren said, tucking her phone away. 'I have your files right here.' She patted the messenger bag. Two Gardai walked by carrying the telltale tackle boxes of evidence collection technicians around the world. 'Is there somewhere we can go to talk in private?'

The little area they had used the day before was now occupied by an imposing-looking man, giving a morning briefing to Quill and what looked like another group of detectives. Scannell led them to the interview room with the glass door and unlocked it.

Inside were a scratched-up metal desk and four sorry-looking chairs. Some cardboard boxes sat stacked in the corner. A very conspicuous camera with a cobweb stretched across the lens pointed down at them. 'We don't use this room to interview witnesses anymore,' Scannell explained. 'We take them to Killorglin if we can help it.'

The three of them sat down and Lauren handed over the file folders while Reese filled him in on their findings from the day before. He started with the receipts that apparently belonged to Robber Shea but had somehow ended up in Jimmy Breen's possession.

'Robber inherited the pub from his father,' Scannell told them. 'If he had a silent business partner in the States, that's news to me.'

'We went by there last night around eight o'clock to talk to Robber, but the pub was closed,' Reese said.

Scannell's brow furrowed. 'That's odd. I stopped in around six for a pint on my way home. He told me he had to work a double shift. Declan, his night publican, called in sick again.'

'Maybe Shamus Gorham tipped him off that we might be stopping by,' Lauren said.

'How would Shamus be involved?' Scannell asked in a puzzled voice.

'As Mr Murphy was giving us the information about Robber Shea receiving the money, Shamus Gorham showed up in the shop.' Lauren went on to tell him about ducking into the random pub and having a sit-down with him, where he admitted to working for the husband. Scannell's eyebrows shot up when she said Gorham had been keeping tabs on Jimmy Breen for years. She then told him about the late-night phone call from Howard Whitney, and how he'd tried to hire her away from his ex-wife. 'I told him he'd have to stick with Gorham.'

Even with the explanation of Shamus Gorham's involvement, Scannell still looked confused. 'I'm originally from County Wexford. I've only been with the Garda ten years. Been stationed here in Keelnamara for the last three. It's my job to know everyone's business here. I knew that Shamus was ex-Garda. He tells everyone at Robber's he sells insurance or some shite like that now. But this is the first time I'm hearing about him doing investigative work on the side.' He stood from his chair. 'Let me go and get Detective Quill.'

Lauren looked over at Reese as the door swung shut behind Scannell. Reese raised an eyebrow. 'I think things are about to get interesting,' he said.

Quill pushed through the door ahead of the shorter Garda. 'Tell me what you told him about Shamus Gorham,' he said in his serious way, his thin mouth creased in a tight line.

Lauren relayed it all over again, with Quill sitting across from her, arms folded across his chest. 'It appears you know of Shamus Gorham,' Lauren said, reading his body language.

'I worked with Shamus in Dublin over twenty years ago.' His voice was tinged with disgust. 'He left the Garda as a disgrace. I haven't seen him since.'

'You haven't bumped into him at the pub over the years?' Reese asked. 'Keelnamara only has one tavern.'

'Here in Ireland we have a national police force. You can get assigned anywhere in the country. I've been stationed in Cork, Tralee, Dublin, and now as a detective, in Killorglin. Keelnamara doesn't have much crime to speak of.

This is the first time I've had to be called in for an investigation here since I got to County Kerry. And I live on the other side of Killarney, so no, myself and Shamus Gorham haven't been running into each other over pints.'

Lauren, realizing Reese had just insulted their best source of information, tried to steer the conversation back on track. 'He said he wanted to work with us to find the painting.'

'If Shamus Gorham said the sky was blue, I'd stick my head out the window to double-check,' Quill retorted. Whatever had happened when they worked together in Dublin must have been truly corrupt because Quill obviously hadn't forgotten or forgiven it.

'We told him we were happy in our present arrangement,' Lauren assured him.

'Do you know of any connection between Gorham and James Breen?' Quill pressed.

'Just what Gorham told us. Maybe Robber Shea or Sheila McGrath can tell you if they had any kind of relationship.'

Quill nodded and made some notes on a legal pad.

'What about these receipts?' Reese asked, holding the slips of paper out to Quill.

Quill took them, flipped through them once and handed them back. 'Make me copies and leave them with Garda Scannell,' he said as he stood up, obviously not interested in the receipts at all.

Lauren opened her mouth to protest that they warranted further follow-up, but Quill turned his attention to Scannell. 'We need to locate Shamus Gorham,' Quill told him. 'I want to know everything about the man since he got to County Kerry. If he got a parking ticket in the last ten years, I want to know where he was parked. And I want him found and in the interrogation room at Killorglin station. Today.'

He took the files out of Scannell's hand without even glancing at them. Reaching for the doorknob, he suddenly remembered his American guests, half turned and said, 'Thank you, Miss Riley, Mr Reese. I have to report all this back to the detective inspector. You can be on your way now,' before walking out. As he opened the door, they saw the man who'd been briefing Quill earlier throwing orders at the assembled Gardai in the next room, who started scrambling around the station.

'The detective inspector?' Lauren asked.

Scannell nodded. 'Detective Inspector Riordan,' he confirmed. 'I'll walk you to your car.' He seemed a little embarrassed at the way Quill had treated both him and them. The trio stood simultaneously, then filed out the door in an awkward silence.

'We can show ourselves out,' Lauren told Scannell as she cut her way through the front of the station with Reese on her heels.

Scannell followed them into the car park anyway. 'I'm sorry about Detective Quill back there. Obviously there's bad blood between the two men. But Shamus Gorham has never caused any problems since I've been here in Keelnamara. I had no reason to suspect him of anything.'

'I'm still not sure you do,' Lauren said. 'But we don't know what Quill knows about him either.'

'County Kerry is only so big. Gorham has been keeping his nose clean as long as I've been here. He's a crawling bastard, to be sure, but other than annoying me with his presence in the pub, I can't say he's been much of a bother.'

There's always more to the story, Lauren thought as she studied the disgusted frown on Scannell's face. A dirty cop was a dirty cop. And in a place this size, Gorham had to be more than just a thorn in the local Garda's side.

'I'll be in touch,' Scannell said as Reese hit the key fob and unlocked their doors. 'I'll keep you abreast of the situation.'

'Thank you, Garda Scannell,' Lauren told him, opening the passenger side door.

'You can call me John,' he said, giving them a wave. 'Everyone around these parts does.'

'Thanks, John,' she said, but doubted she'd say it again. The first-name basis didn't seem to flow as naturally as it should.

A female Garda with dark hair pulled back in a tight bun gave their car a disapproving look as she walked through the car park, heading for the station door. Lauren's case in Ireland was shaping up very differently from her case in Iceland. She would have thought it would've been the other way around. Maybe it was because she'd been in Reykjavik, which was a big city and offered some anonymity, which the tiny townland of Keelnamara did not. Even though the Icelandic detective she'd been paired with had proven to her that everyone in Iceland was connected somehow, here in Ireland the connections were much, much closer, which added a layer of suspicion. In Iceland she'd been considered little more than a tourist. Here she was an outsider sticking her nose where it didn't belong. People in County Kerry had been handling their own affairs for generations. Lauren wouldn't expect much help from the locals going forward.

'Is it ten thirty yet?' Reese asked as he turned the car in the direction of Robber O'Shea's.

She glanced at her phone. 'Just about.'

THIRTY-TWO

IT WAS 10:32 when they arrived at the lot of Robber O'Shea's. Despite the morning light fighting through the gathering clouds, sparkling off the water of the bay, and the flock of seagulls dipping and dive bombing on the beach behind the building, both Lauren and Reese knew something was off the moment they pulled into the car park.

The sign on the door was still turned to CLOSED and the same lone car from the night before occupied the same spot in front of the pub. Anyone in the building would already know they'd pulled up just from the sound of the vehicle, so there was no need to park anywhere but right next to it. Exiting their rental, Lauren and Reese checked out the vehicle. 'Keep an eye on the bar,' Reese told Lauren as he cupped his hands around his face to block the glare and peered in the driver's side window without touching the glass.

'The car looks OK,' he said, straightening up.

It was the quiet that was disconcerting. The only sound was the screeching of the gulls behind them. The pub should have been open. A thick wooden doorstop sat unused to the left of the frame on the step.

They made sure to keep their eyes on the curtain for any movement as they made their way to the door.

'Maybe Robber just forgot to turn the sign around,' Lauren said in a low voice. She looked over at Reese who'd immediately bladed himself off to the side. They'd worked together so long, she knew he'd check the left while she took the right as they made their entry.

'Doubtful,' Reese replied, matching her tone. He gave Lauren a nod to indicate he was ready.

She tried the knob. It was unlocked. The door swung open.

The pub looked almost exactly as it had two nights before, but even darker now that it was empty. The May sunshine didn't penetrate the heavy curtains, which should have been opened, at least a crack. Lauren and Reese stepped into the interior of the pub, which seemed bigger now, devoid of its patrons.

The tables sat empty, silverware laid out on napkins, waiting for the lunch crowd. Some steel-tipped darts jutted from the bullseye in the dartboard hanging in the corner. No one manned the bar and from somewhere in the back, a phone began to ring, startling them both.

'Hello?' Lauren called, while her hand went subconsciously to her side, where her gun would have been back in the States. She realized what she was doing and immediately pulled it back. The phone continued to ring.

'This is creepier than a cemetery,' Reese said under his breath. His aversion to cemeteries approached phobia-like status.

He and Lauren made their way over to the bar rail, lifting it up and ducking under to the bartender's side. The decorative knobs stood lined up, advertising lagers, stouts and hard cider. The one at the farthest end had a single drop dangling from the tap, ready to fall into the sink below it. The cash register was on and seemed like it hadn't been tampered with, its digital read-out displaying 0.00 in red, ready for the next order to be rung up.

A single empty rocks glass sat on the polished wood on top of a cardboard coaster. Next to it was a threadbare white dish towel. As abruptly as it'd started, the ringing stopped.

'Let's check the office,' Lauren said, eyeing the door with an 'EMPLOYEES ONLY' sign on it. The ringing had been coming from back there.

From outside the bar, they heard the sound of approaching sirens.

Lauren and Reese exchanged glances. 'That's not good,' she said. It was more than just one emergency vehicle. From the amount of noise, every cop car at the Garda station must be heading their way.

Reese grabbed the door handle to the office, pushing it open.

Robber Shea was sitting in an office chair propped up against the wall. His hands had been duct-taped to the arms, his face beaten to a bloody pulp. Lauren could see scuff marks on the wall from where the chair had scraped against it during the horrific beating. Robber's head was tilted back at an unnatural angle, dried blood crusted under his nose and around his gaping mouth. An oval patch of black spread out across his white shirt, two ragged holes punched through the fabric. His cloudy eyes stared blankly toward the ceiling.

All the drawers in the office desk had been pulled open and dumped. Robber's computer screen was on lockout from someone trying to access it without the password. Whoever had been trying to get into it had left a smear of blood on the space bar. A duffel bag with men's gym clothes was open next to the chair, a gray sock hanging half in and half out.

Robber's wallet, contents sifted through and discarded, sat face up on the floor next to his foot, along with two teeth, lying in a pool of dried blood.

A fisherman's knife was stuck into the cheap particle board of the desk, blood crusted on the blade, black handle clean as a whistle. Whoever had killed Robber had been cocky enough to leave the murder weapon, but no prints, behind.

'Son of a bitch,' Reese whispered as they heard the rumble of cars come tearing into the lot, their sirens blaring.

THIRTY-THREE

OUTSIDE THE BAR, Detective Quill had put Garda Scannell in charge of keeping an eye on Reese and Riley, while he and the two other detectives he'd brought with him secured the homicide scene. The surly-looking detective inspector stood just outside the crime scene tape, head bowed, back to them, talking into his cell phone. The Crime Scenes technicians waited in their vehicles until they got the OK to go in and process the pub. Parked in the last space at the far end of the lot was a young Garda who had a sobbing gray-haired woman in his backseat.

'That's Robber's cook,' Scannell told Reese and Riley as they leaned up against the side of their rental car. 'She showed up for work, saw his body and drove down to the petrol station, hysterical. We got the call a few minutes after you left the station. I didn't think you'd be heading over here.'

We told you about the money transfers, Lauren thought. *But Quill wasn't interested.* 'Did she work yesterday?' she asked.

'Aye. Until six. I was here when Robber let her go. There was no one to cook for. It was a slow evening and Robber told me if he didn't get any more business soon, he'd close the place up for the night. I was here until seven when my wife rang and told me to get home,' Scannell admitted. 'And I was the only customer at the bar when I left.'

He was the last person to see Robber alive then, Lauren thought. *He was also the one who supposedly sealed up Jimmy's place.* Lauren had met enough bad cops in her day to know a uniform didn't make you exempt as a criminal. Garda Scannell had just made it onto her list of possible suspects, and if Quill was any kind of detective, he'd've made his list too.

'We stopped in the lot around eight,' Reese said. 'That car was the only one parked out here.'

'That's Robber's.' He shook his head in disbelief. 'There's parking around the back as well. Whoever did this could have still been here when you stopped by.'

And we could have interrupted his murder if we'd bothered to get out of our car and check. You could have been the one parked back there, Lauren thought. *If we hadn't been so worried about getting something to eat and just done our jobs, like Mrs Whitney is paying us to do—*

She stopped herself mid self-admonishment. A question had formed while she was thinking of Sharon Whitney. 'Garda Scannell, when Jimmy Breen died, did anyone from your department call either of his former employers in the States?'

'No,' he said, looking confused. 'Why in the world would we?'

The same lightbulb that had gone off in Lauren's head popped on in Reese's as soon as she asked the question. 'Did you call the FBI?' he asked. 'Tell them the suspect in an old art theft had died?'

'Bloody hell, we thought he died of a heart attack. It was the coroner that insisted on the postmortem. No one would be calling the American Federal Bureau of Investigation about it.'

'Do you mind if I step over there and make a phone call,

John?' she asked, hoping the familiarity would make him more amenable.

He nodded. 'Just stay where I can see you. I don't want to bring the wrath of Detective Quill or the detective inspector down on us all.'

Leaving Reese with Scannell, she walked across the lot toward the road. She tried to work out the time difference in New York. If her math was correct, it was around six in the morning back home.

'Hello?' Picking up after the seventh ring, Mrs Whitney's voice was cloudy with sleep.

'Hello, Mrs Whitney. It's Lauren Riley. Sorry about the early morning phone call but I have to ask you an important question.'

'Did you find it? My Picasso?' Her voice rose in hope and excitement. Now she sounded wide awake.

'No, not yet. I need to know who called and told you Jimmy Breen had died,' she said, dashing Mrs Whitney's hopes. 'It's very important.'

There was a moment of baffled silence, then, 'He said he was with Interpol. He said he'd worked with the FBI in the past on my case over in Ireland.'

'Did he say anything else? Ask you anything?'

'Just the same basic questions I've answered a thousand times. What the size of the painting was. What the frame looked like. I told him that frame was worth thousands of dollars in and of itself. Handcrafted and one of a kind. He should have known that. There's a close-up shot of it in the insurance paperwork. You have a copy of that, too.'

Lauren had seen the frame. It was a huge, gaudy, ornate gold thing that reminded her of something you'd see around a print of a vase of calla lilies hanging in a funeral parlor.

'You didn't get the agent's name, did you?'

Now she sounded flustered. 'He must have given it to me, but I was so focused on securing the painting, I hung up and called my lawyer right away. I was fixated on buying Jimmy Breen's property before my husband could get his hands on it. It must have slipped my mind to write it down. Is something wrong?'

'Yes, but nothing you need to worry about right now. Did the agent call your home phone or your cell number?'

'My landline. Sometimes I think I'm the only person left who has one.'

'Did he say how he got your number?'

'He said it was the number they had on file for my case. I've had the same number since I moved out of the house where the robbery took place. I mean, how often do you change a landline number?'

Lauren's parents still used the same number she'd learned in kindergarten. 'Did he say anything else to you?'

'Just that with the passing of the only suspect, the case was officially closed. That's why I didn't bother calling our local FBI branch. I know the agent who was assigned to the case here retired years ago. I thought private detectives were my only option if I ever wanted to get my painting back.'

The woman in the back of the Garda's car let out a wail. 'What was that?' Mrs Whitney asked in alarm. 'What's going on over there?'

'Sorry again about the time,' Lauren said quickly, before the distraught cook could keen again. 'I'll keep you updated with our progress.' She clicked off the line, preventing Mrs Whitney from asking another question.

'Well?' Reese asked when she came back to the car.

Lauren wanted to see how Scannell would react to the information. 'Someone called our client posing as an Inter-

194

THE PARTING GLASS

pol agent. Asked her a bunch of questions about the painting and told her the investigation was officially over.' She
dug her notebook and pen out of her pocket and began to
jot down notes while they were still fresh in her head.

'Shamus Gorham would know Interpol could be involved
in something like this. He'd know how to ask the right questions without raising suspicion,' Scannell said.

And so would you. Lauren continued to jot notes.

'We know when Gorham came into the shop yesterday
where Robber picked up his money transfers, we were talking to the owner about it. He could have come here and
waited for everyone to leave and then made a move,' Reese
told Scannell.

'If Shamus killed Jimmy and ransacked his house, he
might have found Sharon Whitney's phone number,' Lauren
said, tucking the notebook away. Now she watched Scannell's face carefully. 'Maybe he thought by talking to her,
he'd get a clue about where Jimmy might have hidden the
painting.'

'That makes no sense,' Scannell threw in. 'If she had
any inkling where he'd stashed the painting, she'd have
paid someone to retrieve it by now. Instead she sent you.'

'Nothing about this case makes sense,' Lauren tossed
back, jerking a thumb toward the pub. 'The one person who
may have had some answers about Jimmy's murder is duct-
taped to a chair in there.'

'I think our focus has rightfully shifted to Shamus Gorham as a suspect,' Scannell said. 'Let's sit tight until Detective Quill and the team are done. We'll have to get witness
statements from you, as well as DNA swabs and fingerprint
exemplars. It's going to be a long day.'

'Do you have a pick up order out on Gorham?' Reese
asked. From the look on his face Lauren could tell he wasn't

crazy about giving up his DNA, even if it was just to rule him out.

'Our equivalent of it, yes,' Scannell answered. 'County Kerry is only so big. We'll find him.'

Lauren glanced at the pub's closed curtains and thought, *Unless someone else finds him first*, before her eyes slid back to Garda Scannell.

THIRTY-FOUR

THEY DIDN'T GET out of the substation until almost five o'clock. Thankfully, Scannell had gone into Glenbeigh to fetch some lunch as they recounted their reasons for heading over to the pub.

Lauren was glad Scannell had left, as she explained the discovery of the money transfers again, this time to a much more receptive audience. When she was done, Quill took the original receipts from her and gave Lauren a receipt for the receipts.

During the course of the day, even more detectives showed up to help with what was now a double homicide investigation. The little substation was crammed with Gardai, detectives and support people. Finally, Quill got the OK from the detective inspector—who wanted nothing to do with the American interlopers—for Reese and Riley to leave, cautioning them on their next moves. 'I respect why you're here and I'm glad of the assistance you've provided, but I can't stress enough that we can't have you interfering with our investigation,' he said, hands stuffed in the front pockets of his gray flannel pants.

'We understand,' Reese said, but didn't sound very understanding. They'd provided the only leads in Jimmy Breen's homicide and discovered Robber Shea's body. Lauren knew Reese was expecting a little professional courtesy. She had been expecting a little herself. Their job was to locate the painting, but she couldn't see how they'd be able to investigate that without crossing over into the homicides.

Quill went on about how they'd send extra patrols around Mrs Fitzgerald's place and double-checked that he had both of their phone numbers in his cell. They were being dismissed and they knew it.

'One last thing,' he said as they were about to leave. 'Two homicides that look to be connected are very rare in these parts. The press has already got wind of the situation. I fear that within an hour or two reporters from across Ireland will be descending on Keelnamara.'

Lauren held up a hand to cut him off, not caring if she was being rude. 'We know. No talking to the media.'

'And no spouting off—'

'On social media either. I promise, I won't post a thing on Facebook.'

Quill didn't look convinced, probably because of all the old news stories that popped up as soon as you Googled her name. Lauren didn't shun the media like a lot of cops. They could be a great tool in an investigation, and she had good relationships with a number of the local reporters in Buffalo. But she also didn't run to them to get her name in the paper or her face on television. And while she might have enjoyed the attention a little when she solved her first couple of cold cases, that wore thin pretty quickly. She hated how the sheer number of news stories she'd generated gave the impression that she was some kind of glory hound. Lately that hampered more investigations than it helped.

Back in the passenger seat of their car at the Garda station, Lauren laid out her suspicions about Scannell to Reese. The more she thought about Scannell, the less she trusted him. 'Unfortunately, it makes sense,' Reese said. 'He heard the stories in the pub just like anyone else. I can't imagine a Garda makes a huge salary.' He adjusted the rearview mirror to watch Scannell talking to another Garda by the station's front door.

'Do you think he's the guy who was poking around our yard?'

'Hard to say. I think he's a little heftier than the guy I rolled around with.' He studied Scannell for another second, then pushed the mirror back in place. 'I don't really think he's our guy, but we can't just dismiss him either. He could be working with someone else. We'll just have to be careful what we share with him from now on.'

'Agreed,' Lauren said, then asked, 'what do we really know about Garda John Scannell?'

'Not much,' Reese admitted. 'He lives close to the Fitzgeralds with his wife and kids. That's about it.'

'He did get to our place pretty fast. He could have driven home, changed into his uniform then come back.' Lauren didn't like the information gap. She was sure she could get something out of Mrs Fitzgerald, but the last thing they needed was for Scannell to find out they were asking about him. They'd have to tread very carefully.

'Where to now?' Reese asked, clenching and unclenching the wheel, as he did when he was anxious. He needed to stop talking and *do* something.

We've been driving around in this car for the vast majority of our time here, Lauren thought. Distance was a trick in this rural landscape. Back home in the city, every space was filled with something: a building, a house, a bodega, a church. Here, it was land and sea and sheep. It seemed like it was miles between landmarks, because it was. And time was playing tricks on her as well. Everything seemed to have slowed down. Everything was a little off-kilter, just

enough to throw her off balance. She'd worked a lot of homicides, but never one like this. They were racing against
a murderer to find a painting that had stayed quietly stolen for twenty years, only to now become the center of a
bloody scavenger hunt the local detective didn't want them
to be a part of.

Lauren pulled her notebook out of her jacket pocket.
She looked it over for a minute, tucked it away again and
announced, 'Endometriosis.'

'What?'

'Who's the only woman involved in this entire scenario
here in Ireland?'

Reese put the car in gear. 'Sheila McGrath.'

'Let's hope Martin is out for the day,' Lauren said as she
sat back in her seat. 'And Sheila is ready to answer some
questions.'

'Finally, I get to see what happens when you're off private investigating without me.' He eased onto the road,
making sure to look both ways. 'You go behind everyone's
back and do what you want to do.'

'Pretty much,' Lauren agreed. 'Though admittedly I
have had mixed results with my choice of methods.'

Reese ran his left hand up under his hat and over his
scars. 'Don't I know it.'

THIRTY-FIVE

'WHAT DO YA WANT?' Sheila McGrath yelled from behind her door. Lauren and Reese were stationed in front of it, each bladed off to one side, not only out of habit but necessity. The last thing they wanted was for Martin McGrath to come barreling out, knocking them over like bowling pins.

'We need to talk to you about your brother,' Lauren called, hoping she was loud enough to get through the heavy wooden door.

'He's dead. That's all you need to know from me. You'll get your house when the Garda are done with it.'

'I think maybe we can help each other, Sheila,' she called. 'I think there's more to the story and you know it. I think you're glad we're here and not the Garda. I think you know why Robber's dead. And I think you're scared.'

The door cracked open a hair. One muddy brown eye rimmed in red peered out at them. 'Is it true then? Is Robber dead?'

'What did you hear?' Reese asked.

The door swung inward a few inches, revealing the haggard-looking Sheila McGrath. 'I got four phone calls within five minutes about Bridie Stack showing up at the petrol station. She said someone murdered Robber in his own pub. Is it true?'

'Can we come in?' Lauren asked.

'Is it true?' she demanded, holding the door.

'It's true,' Reese told her. 'Can we please come in?'

She turned and walked into her living room, sinking down onto her couch and burying her face in her hands. Lauren and Reese cautiously followed, not knowing if her son was home. Reese stood, but Lauren knelt down, so she was eye level with Sheila. 'Where's Martin?' Lauren asked.

Hands still covering her face, she shook her head. 'I don't know. He never came home last night.'

'Sheila,' Lauren said gently, 'why was Robber getting money from the States?'

Her shoulders shook as she wept. 'He was picking up money for Jimmy. So there wouldn't be nothing to tie him to it, you see? He had it wired to Michael Shea, in case the authorities were watching him.'

'Jimmy was getting a monthly payout from someone in the States?'

She nodded a yes. 'Robber picked it up. And they split it. Only Jimmy didn't use the money on himself, it was for me.'

'For your endometriosis?' Lauren asked.

Sheila's face burned red. She was not the type of woman to discuss such things in polite conversation, much less in front of a man. 'It's a curse for a woman. It's not curable. Only treatable, and it gets worse over time. My husband and I wanted children, so I wouldn't get the hysterectomy they were trying to push on me. We have public healthcare in Ireland, but my case got so severe that to get the best and newest treatments I needed private insurance. I went on an expensive new medicine our health insurance didn't cover. I stayed on it after Martin was born. It made the pain bearable. And then my husband died.' She took a deep, shuddering breath. 'Jimmy was using that money to pay for *my* insurance. And that money got him and Robber killed.'

'How are you going to pay for the insurance now? With the money from the sale of Jimmy's cottage?'

She shook her head. 'I don't need it anymore. I got a hysterectomy two months ago. I had a thought that maybe I'd marry again, maybe have a brother or sister for Martin, but then I turned fifty. I hadn't gone through the menopause yet, but I knew my days of having children were done. I think I was holding out some hope that I wouldn't be alone forever, you know?' she asked Lauren, who nodded her head in understanding. 'I had the operation, cancelled the private insurance and enrolled in public.'

Lauren thought of her own brief marriage to Mark Hathaway. He'd wanted to have a baby right away and she hadn't. She'd wanted to wait. She had two young daughters and a career that was just starting to take off. In the end, that had been a deal-breaker for them and they'd divorced after a year. She'd been devastated at the time. Mark had seemed like her Prince Charming. Now that she was older she knew there were no such things as fairy tale romances. And people didn't always get the happy endings they wanted.

'Who was sending Jimmy the money?' Reese asked, snapping Lauren's attention back to the matter at hand.

'I don't know. I'd be better off not knowing is what Jimmy told me.'

'Where is the painting now?' Lauren pressed.

'I don't know that either. He wouldn't say. I never saw it.' Her voice was tinged with desperation. 'I'm telling you now, like I told you before, I don't know that he ever actually had it, he just wanted people to *think* he had it.'

'Did Martin believe he had it?' Lauren's eyes flashed

over to the picture of the young, happy Martin over the mantel, so different from the angry, jagged-toothed man who'd confronted them outside.

She nodded. 'Aye, he tried to convince Jimmy to sell it, if he had it. Said he knew people from when he was in jail that would pay a pretty price for it. Bad people. I think my Martin is mixed up in this business somehow.' Now she looked up from her hands at Lauren who was still kneeling down in front of her. 'Whoever killed Jimmy and Robber could be after Martin right now. If they think Martin knows where the painting is, he'll be next. They'll kill him. You have to find him. I promise you, I'll help any way I can.'

Lauren reached over to a small side table next to the couch and plucked a tissue from its box. She handed it to Sheila who immediately wiped her eyes with it, then asked her, 'Where would Martin go?'

Sheila gave a helpless shrug, still clutching the tissue in her hand. 'Yesterday I would have said Robber O'Shea's. Today, I have no idea.'

'Listen, Sheila,' Lauren said, standing up. 'You need to dial 999 and get the Garda over here and report him missing. We'll call Detective Quill directly and tell him what you told us.'

'Please,' Sheila McGrath begged. 'Please find him. Martin is all I have left.'

THIRTY-SIX

THEY HADN'T BEEN in their car five minutes when Garda Scannell called. They pulled off to the side of the road next to the sheep farm. Lauren put Scannell on speakerphone, and he told them that Quill was sending him over to take a missing person's report from Sheila McGrath. Scannell wanted to meet up with them at the old resort once he was finished.

Lauren and Reese agreed to meet him in the parking lot of the half-finished wreck of a building they'd been passing on the way to and from Jimmy's cottage. A faded sign out front proclaimed it the future Keelnamara Resort and Suites. They waited in their car for Scannell to pull up, but not before stopping and checking on Jimmy's place to make sure the crime scene tape crisscrossing the front door was still unbroken. It didn't mean someone hadn't gotten in another way, but the back door and all the windows did appear intact.

'Is this smart? Meeting a possible suspect at an abandoned building?' Reese commented, once they were parked at the resort, looking out over the empty shell.

'He's a pipeline for information even if we can't rule him out as a suspect yet,' Lauren replied. 'Along with every other person in Keelnamara, I suppose. We just have to be careful.'

When Scannell arrived, they huddled together on the as-

phalt against a wicked wind that had kicked up from across
the bay. The developers had cleared the land to build, so
no trees stood between them and the bitter gusts. Lauren's
coat flapped in the gale until she grabbed both sides and
zipped it up to the neck. She wished she'd brought one of
her heavier jackets with her. The weather in Ireland seemed
to fluctuate as wildly as Western New York's in the spring.
It was wetter in Ireland as well; the moisture seemed to
hang in the air. With the sky darkening over the water and
the wind picking up, the threat of a storm was imminent.
Scannell was nonplussed. Just like snow falling in May in
Buffalo was normal for Lauren, he was used to the Irish
weather flip-flopping without warning.

'So Jimmy did have the painting after all,' Scannell said
in wonder. 'All this time I thought he was talking out of his
arse after too many pints at the pub. Poor Robber Shea for
getting involved. Bless his soul.'

Lauren could hear a sincerity in his voice that made her
want to kick herself for suspecting Scannell, but ignoring the possibility was dangerous. She should have known
Quill would send him over to talk to Sheila McGrath. He
seemed to be delegating the grunt work around the area to
Scannell, keeping him at arm's length from the actual homicide investigations. Or maybe it was just Lauren's suspi-
cious mind imagining that. 'At some point he had it, or at
least Jimmy convinced someone in the States that he did,'
Lauren said, flipping up the collar of her coat. 'And now
Martin McGrath is missing.'

'Martin could have lit out to go back to Dublin,' Scannell said. 'He was always bragging about his big city crime
connections.'

'Speaking of connections, have you located Gorham
yet?' Reese asked.

'Not yet. It's only a matter of time though,' Scannell replied. 'Quill's so hot for Shamus Gorham you can practically see the steam come off him every time his name comes up.'

'He's looking like a pretty good bet at this point,' Lauren admitted as her eyes swept over the complex. They were standing in front of a chain link fence with a heavy padlock securing the gate that cut the parking lot of the unfinished resort in half. The doors and windows had either never been installed or had been taken out, and the open black holes gave the whole complex a creepy, organic look, as if it were a giant sleeping insect with hundreds of dead, black eyes. If Reese had a phobia of cemeteries, it was nothing compared to Lauren's aversion to this particular abandoned building. It reminded her too much of the warehouse where she and the young sociopath David Spencer had had their final showdown a little over a year ago. Just looking at the cavernous entrance made Lauren's stomach knot up. She quickly glanced back to Scannell, and hoped the red that she felt creeping across her cheeks would be chalked up to the bite of the ocean wind.

'There's a small flaw in that theory though,' Scannell said.

'What's that?' Reese asked.

'We ran the prints we collected from Jimmy's cottage and the ones we recovered from your guesthouse through our national data bank. The hits came back right away. Robber's prints were all over Jimmy's house and Martin's prints were all over your place.'

Lauren let that soak in for a moment. 'Could Robber's have been old? They were friends. I'm sure he must have gone to his house at least once or twice.'

Scannell shook his head. 'Not such good friends that Robber's prints would be on the underside of his dresser drawer. Or on the kitchen knife still sticking out of one of his cushions.'

'I doubt Martin McGrath ever rented the guesthouse from Mrs Fitzgerald either,' Reese said, holding the edge of his cap so it wouldn't blow off.

'She said never,' Scannell confirmed.

'It's too bad there's only one pub in Keelnamara,' Lauren said, putting a hand to her forehead to stave off the migraine that was brewing. If Scannell was the real killer, he'd have to be an actual super villain to be able to plant those fingerprints ahead of time and act so concerned about finding the 'real' killer. But it *was* possible and he would have had access to both Martin's and Robber's fingerprints. Then again, so would Shamus Gorham, if his 'connections' actually existed. 'I think I need a drink.'

'There's a restaurant in Glenbeigh my wife and I fancy. If you'd be wanting something to eat and drink, we can wait there for Detective Quill. He and I spoke when I was on the way over here and he told me he'd like to talk with you both again.'

'Sounds good,' Reese told him. He was never one to turn down an opportunity for food. 'We'll follow you.'

Garda Scannell got a chuckle out of that. 'Only one road to Glenbeigh from here, mate. Just drive south. Hard to get lost in these parts.' Which was ironic, since Lauren and Reese had already managed to do just that.

'We'll still follow you.'

THIRTY-SEVEN

As soon as the door to Scannell's patrol vehicle closed, Reese practically exploded, 'What the hell is going on in this place?'

'Just drive,' Lauren told him. Scannell was already pulling onto the road. 'We have to talk this out before we get to the restaurant.'

Reese threw the car into gear. 'It's easy,' he said, craning to look over his shoulder as he backed out of the driveway. 'The money stops coming, Robber kills Jimmy and Gorham kills Robber.'

'So why are Martin's prints in our guesthouse? And Robber never came to pick up the money this month,' Lauren pointed out.

'Because he knew it was going to stop once news of Jimmy's death got out.'

She shook her head. 'Mr Murphy said he always came on the first of the month. His granddaughter said the money never came in this month. Robber knew it wasn't coming, even before Jimmy died.'

'Then it was Shamus Gorham,' Reese said. 'He wanted that painting. Maybe Mr Whitney decided to stop paying him. Gorham tries to get Jimmy to tell him where the painting is. When Jimmy dies without giving it up, he calls Mrs Whitney fishing for information.'

'How does that explain Robber breaking into Jimmy's

house or Martin breaking into ours? Could Scannell have planted both of those sets of prints to throw off any investigation?'

'Wait,' Reese said, holding a hand up to Lauren's face to stop her from talking. 'Back up. I'm confused.'

Lauren sighed and turned her head to look out of the window. 'Me too.'

The Old Glenbeigh Fish Market was neither old nor a fish market. It was a brand-new higher-end restaurant that overlooked the bay and specialized in local freshly caught seafood. 'My friend built this place two years ago on the grounds of the old fish market, hence the name,' Scannell explained, picking the menu up off the table. The hostess had seated them away from the only other two couples having dinner, at Scannell's request. Even with the obvious play for privacy, each couple in turn made their way over to their table to ask Scannell about the murders.

'I can't really talk about the details,' he told a white-haired lady wearing lime-green polyester pants, and her husband, just like he'd told the middle-aged couple before them who had finished their meals and were now sitting at the bar drinking whiskey.

'Shouldn't you be out there looking for the maniac, John?' the husband asked. He had the same thick accent that Sheila and Martin McGrath had.

In the States, that would have come off as an accusation of laziness, but Lauren realized that in such a small, tight-knit community, two murders must be absolutely terrifying to the locals. Scannell's voice took on a reassuring tone. 'There's a whole slew of detectives down from Killorglin, some on the way from Killarney, and Detective Inspector Riordan is in charge. Just wait a few minutes and you'll see Detective Quill come in.'

That promise made the pair hurry back to their table, eager to see the detective make an appearance. 'Quill told me he can't stay. He just wants to ask you a few more questions.' He flipped a page of the menu. 'He does want me to keep an eye on the two of you, though.'

'Any word on Gorham or Martin McGrath?' Lauren asked, not addressing the part about Scannell having to watch them.

'He did not say.' Scannell barely looked up from the daily specials.

Why do I get the feeling Quill is going to have Scannell keep tabs on us until either they solve the murders or we leave, whichever comes first? Lauren thought as the waitress filled her water glass. They were being kept occupied. Scannell probably wanted to be at home with his family, as it seemed Quill had pretty much cut him out of the homicide investigations. She wondered if Quill suspected him too, and this was his way of keeping an eye on all three of them? That would be putting her and Reese in terrible danger. Was Quill that kind of detective?

Not that Scannell seemed to mind. Lauren equated him with the guys that worked in the slower districts back home. He was content to take reports and talk to the people he served. He wasn't looking to go to the big city or to make detective. She prayed he was exactly what he seemed to be, a good guy who just wanted to keep his friends and neighbors safe, then go home to his family at the end of the day. If she'd developed that attitude early on in her career, it would have saved her a ton of heartache. Reese was always calling her a drama queen, but right now she felt more like the court jester.

Their order was already on the table, about to be eaten, when Detective Quill showed up. Despite his still sharp-looking attire, he was starting to look fatigued, with purple bags forming under his eyes. Lauren wondered if he'd sat up all night going over Jimmy's murder in his head, like she tended to do, only to get slapped with a second gruesome homicide case today.

He sat down as Reese took his first bite of salmon and got straight to business. 'Shamus Gorham and Martin Mc-Grath are both still outstanding, if that was to be your first question.'

Lauren was impressed by Quill's even composure. Nothing seemed to shake him. But then again, he didn't live in Keelnamara and wasn't from County Kerry. Unlike Scannell who lived among the residents, the two horrific murders weren't personal for him.

Lauren set her water glass down next to her plate of salad. 'Do you think they're working together?'

Quill shook his head, shrugging off his overcoat and folding it neatly over the back of his chair. 'Highly unlikely. They were at most passing acquaintances at the pub, from what the local residents say.'

Scannell held up his fork. 'I can attest to that.'

'Does anyone put Gorham and Jimmy together?'

'They drank together on occasion. I can connect just about every person in Keelnamara through Robber O'Shea's tavern in one way or another. The two centers of any Irish townland are the church and the pub. Thankfully, Father Gallagher has an airtight alibi.'

So Quill does have a sense of humor after all, Lauren thought. *Dry, but it's there*. 'Did you find any indication when you searched Robber's that he had the painting?'

'For what it's worth to you, I did not. I did, however, find a great many bills that were overdue. Michael Robber Shea had a bit of a gambling problem, it seems.'

Gambling added a whole other level to the puzzle. 'Could the killer have been someone Robber owed? Like a bookie?' Lauren asked.

'It seems like it was online betting with some side wagers going on in the pub, but we're looking into that angle.' *That's the same thing he'd say to a member of the press,* Lauren thought, *noncommittal and nonspecific. He really wants us to butt out.*

'Jimmy Breen was using the money Robber was picking up to pay for his sister's private health insurance,' Lauren offered, hoping that giving up some information would cause Quill to drop them a few more crumbs. 'Maybe Robber got greedy and didn't want to split the money anymore. Maybe him killing Jimmy had nothing to do with the painting and everything to do with keeping the entire monthly payout. Especially if there was gambling involved.'

'That could be,' Quill agreed. 'I think the key may be who was sending the money in the first place. We're trying to pin down where the money transfers were coming from right now. It looks like it was being sent from various sites in your hometown.'

Someone in the States has been covering their tracks, Lauren thought. There were money wiring services in most of the city's corner stores and bodegas. The amount the person was sending to Ireland was far from astronomical and wouldn't raise any eyebrows.

'In the meantime,' Quill went on, 'I've been told to assign Garda Scannell to assist you.'

'You mean make sure we stay out of your homicide investigation,' Reese said pointedly. He wasn't afraid to voice what Lauren was thinking.

Quill's even gaze met Reese's. 'That as well. We can't have you two running a parallel investigation alongside a double homicide. And frankly, I'm at a loss. I talked it over with Detective Inspector Riordan and we'd both prefer to send you back to the States and notify you if we recover the painting. However, you've managed to become witnesses to one crime and victims of another.' He gave them an ironic smile. 'And we'll be needing to keep you close for the time being.'

'Are you ordering us not to look for the painting?' Lauren asked pointedly.

'I can't do that. I can threaten you with arrest if you interfere with our investigation. I know that wouldn't be your intent, just the outcome, if you're still keen on pursuing the painting.' He leaned forward, palms flat on the table so neither one of them would make any mistake about the intent of what he was about to say. Lauren saw the tips of his fingers turn white as he pressed them into the wood. 'What I'm asking you, nicely, as fellow detectives, is to go back to Mrs Fitzgerald's. Get a good night's sleep. Let Garda Scannell show you the sights around town tomorrow, and maybe the day after we'll have another sit down and see where we're at in my homicide investigations. Can we agree on that?'

Quill was politely telling them to back off or else, just as Lauren would do to him if the roles were reversed. Two dead bodies took precedence over a painting any day, no matter what the price tag.

'I hear you loud and clear, Detective Quill,' Lauren told him.

'Good.' Quill pushed himself up from the table and grabbed the jacket off the back of the chair. 'I'm glad we understand each other. Enjoy your meal. I have a long night ahead of me.'

'Goodnight,' Reese and Riley said at the same time.

From their tones, Quill could easily interpret them as saying another two words to him, not quite as polite.

Pointing at Scannell as he backed up, Quill said, 'Ring me when you've seen them to their cottage.'

'Will do,' he replied. After Quill was out of earshot Scannell turned back to Reese and Lauren. 'I don't agree with him keeping you totally out of the investigation, but he's the detective. I'm just a local Garda.'

'He answers to someone too,' Lauren said. 'That Detective Inspector looks like a real hard ass.'

'That he does,' Scannell agreed. 'I don't know what it's like for you in the States, but here things are pretty political once you start making rank.'

'Things are the same all over,' Reese assured him, digging back into his food. He may have just been sidelined, but he was not about to miss a meal over it. Lauren, on the other hand, had lost her appetite.

While they had been talking, patrons had trickled in and now all the tables around them were occupied. Feeling the eyes of the locals on her, she pushed her plate away. Reese and Scannell exchanged cop stories while Lauren ruminated silently over the case. It wasn't in her nature to let things go; to let other people finish what she'd started. What had begun as a simple trip to try to find a stolen painting had morphed into something much more sinister. She'd never been involved in a homicide case with so many moving parts before: multiple suspects, multiple motives, and a grand prize someone was willing to kill for. On top of all that, she couldn't help thinking that if she and Reese hadn't visited him, Robber Shea would still be alive.

Not to mention there was still the possibility, however remote, that they were sitting with the killer right now.

Reese turned down the server's offer of an after-dinner

drink, opting for another water. Whether it was out of politeness or because he was on duty, Scannell declined as well.

Lauren checked the time on her phone. 'You must want to get home to your family. It's not fair that you have to babysit us all night.'

'It's not babysitting.' Picking up his cloth napkin from his lap, he folded it neatly and placed it on the table. 'Jimmy and Robber were my friends. Their murders happened on my watch. When I drop you at your place, I'm going back to the station. Detective Quill might be in from the Killarney District House, but he'll move on to the next case when he's finished in Keelnamara. I'll still be living here. I'm supposed to be working with him on these homicides, and he's trying to cut me out as well. I may not show it, and that's the Irish in me, but I'm mourning my friends, and the best way for me to do that right now is to stay in the game. Jimmy and Robber were good men.'

Lauren's eyes widened. Either he was the world's best actor or Scannell was going rogue. *Things change when it's personal*, she reflected. 'We'll help you any way we can,' she told him. She didn't know the politics of the Garda, but she knew some things were universal. He was willing to put his career in jeopardy. Lauren had more than enough experience of that course of action; it'd been her default mode for the last three years.

If he is the killer, Lauren thought, *taking Shamus Gorham's advice is the best bet: Keep your friends close and your enemies closer.*

Scannell nodded. 'I thought so. Let's get you back to Mrs Fitzgerald's place. We'll meet up in the morning before Jimmy's funeral. I'll try to find out as much as I can.'

THIRTY-EIGHT

LAUREN AND REESE stopped at the front house to speak with a distraught Mrs Fitzgerald before going back to their cottage.

'I've known Michael Shea his whole life, his parents and grandparents as well. He'd been best friends with my eldest son, Aiden. I rang him up and he expects to drive in from Dublin the day after tomorrow. He said the murders are all over the news.' She sat at her kitchen table, hair disheveled, eyes puffy and red. 'I can't believe it.'

Lauren sat down in the chair next to her and slipped an arm around the woman's thin shoulders. 'I'm so sorry,' she said.

'First Jimmy Breen and now Michael Shea. Where will it end?'

Lauren knew she didn't want to hear the real answer. It ended with the painting and however many bodies it took for the killer to get his hands on it.

'Is your husband home?' Reese asked, voice tinged with concern for the tiny lady.

Mrs Fitzgerald shook her head into Lauren's shoulder. 'He went to be with Michael's father over at his place, with some of the other men. Robber has three sisters but they're scattered across Ireland with their own families. They left after university and never came back, except to visit. I think Caitriona Higgins down the road managed to get ahold of one of them. She told me they're on their way home to Keel-namara now.' She dabbed at her eyes with a white hand-kerchief clutched in her hand. 'Robber's mother passed two years ago. And that's a blessing, because her children were her heart.'

'Do you want us to stay here with you until your hus-band gets back?' Reese offered.

She reached out and patted the back of his hand. 'That's lovely of you to ask, but no thank you. I won't let anyone scare me out of my house. Besides,' she gestured to a .22 rifle propped against the wall, 'I'm not afraid to defend myself.'

Lauren made a mental note not to come to the front house for any reason during the night without calling first. She didn't know how the Irish felt about guns and using them, in general, but she knew scared people made mis-takes and hoped Mr Fitzgerald announced himself prop-erly when he got home. Mrs Fitzgerald saw Lauren look at the gun and went on, 'I suppose I was in denial about Jimmy. That it was some kind of mistake. That he wasn't really murdered.' She sniffed back more tears. 'But now Robber is gone.'

'If you need us for any reason, we'll be right out back. And don't be afraid to call 999 or Detective Quill either,' Lauren said. Mrs Fitzgerald straightened up and tugged at her floral tunic, trying to get herself together. Lauren knew that every household in Keelnamara had to be on edge and terrified. The killer was bold, breaking into houses in broad daylight and murdering two men in cold blood. She pictured the local residents locking their doors for the first time in years, if ever. She'd forgotten to ask Scannell when the last murder in Keelnamara had occurred. She was willing to bet it was long before he came to work there. This crime spree was unprecedented in these parts.

Mrs Fitzgerald clutched Lauren's hand in hers for a moment. 'Thank you. I feel better just knowing you're both in the guesthouse.'

They said their goodnights and went out the back door. Lauren and Reese promised her they'd double-check both houses and the grounds before heading inside for the night. The weather had steadily deteriorated during the day, leaving the night with a frigid, biting wind and no moon. As they checked all the doors and windows, Lauren could hear the waves on the beach not a quarter mile down the hedge-lined lane. The salty sea wind stung her face and chilled her to the bone. Shivering in her too-thin coat, she breathed a sigh of relief when Reese came around the back of the guesthouse and, giving a thumbs-up, they went inside together.

Lauren marveled again at how fast and efficiently Mrs Fitzgerald had cleaned the mess inside. What she had started the day before after the initial break-in, she'd come back and finished during the day while they were out, despite her grief over Robber's murder. Or maybe she'd needed to do something to channel all that grief, like she had with the big breakfast. Maybe she cleaned to take her mind off the terrible things going on in the place she'd been born and raised.

Reese went over to the kitchen cabinet, opened it up and took out two teacups. 'Let's have a drink together now that I don't have to drive.' Setting one cup in front of him, he positioned the other directly across the table and sat down.

'I hope you don't mind if I keep my coat on,' Lauren said, taking a seat as Reese produced a flask from an inside pocket of his jacket. He unscrewed the top and poured brown liquid into each of the cups. She was perpetually cold, which was ironic for someone who chose to live in

Buffalo, which had six-month winters. 'When did you have time to buy a flask?'

'I brought it with me, but I had Robber fill it when I was at the bar drinking with my new friend, Jacky.' He lifted his teacup. 'To Robber Shea.'

Lauren lifted hers and clinked it to Reese's. 'To Robber.'

She threw the entire cupful down her throat and then held it out for more. Reese laughed and poured them both another shot, as warmth spread through her throat and chest. 'Jameson?' she asked, savoring the flavor.

'I know you love it,' he said. She kept a bottle in her kitchen cabinet for emergencies. Many a night the two of them had thrown back some whiskey and brainstormed over a case, or to shut the door on a bad day.

She slumped down in her chair, suddenly tired. 'Two dead bodies,' she said, toying with the teacup's thin china handle.

'I wouldn't expect anything less, traveling with you, Miss Murder She Wrote.'

'That's not funny.'

'It's not,' he agreed, sipping from his cup with his pinky arched. 'But it's unfortunately true.'

Forget the Guinness, the whiskey was good. Sitting across from Reese drinking Jameson in an Irish cottage loosened Lauren's tongue. 'Nothing can ever be simple. I would give anything for a straightforward case of two brothers fighting over a Thanksgiving turkey leg where one gets forked to death.'

'With fifteen family members sitting around the table as witnesses,' Reese added.

'And caught on video,' she sighed.

Reese held up the metal flask and shook it. Some liquid sloshed around, but not much. 'I should have bought the whole bottle.'

'My grandmother swore that whiskey was the cure for whatever ailed you.' She looked down into the last few drops left in her cup and murmured, '…what ails you.'

'You OK, Riley?' Reese asked, noticing the strange look that crossed her face.

'Why would Sharon Whitney think Jimmy Breen died of an illness?' She stabbed the tabletop with her index finger. 'Unless he told her he was using the money transferred to him because he needed medicine. Which means she was in contact with him after he got back to Ireland. After the theft.'

'Son of a bitch,' Reese whispered, sinking back in his chair in disbelief. 'How did we miss that?'

'Where is it?' Lauren started to frantically pat her jacket pockets down. 'Where is it?'

'What are you looking for?' Reese asked, watching her frisk herself.

Lauren held up the little black cassette tape she'd tucked away at Jimmy Breen's house. 'This. We need to find an old-fashioned answering machine right now.'

THIRTY-NINE

LAUREN CALLED MRS FITZGERALD's cell phone before they
went up front, just to make sure they didn't startle the woman
and end up riddled with bullets. Lauren could see the empty
space in front of the garage as they walked to the main
house. Her husband was still out comforting Robber's father.

Mrs Fitzgerald was in her nightgown with a blue terrycloth robe pulled over it when she answered the back door,
her hair pinned up for the night. The rifle had been moved
next to the back door, just in case, Lauren guessed, the bad
guys tried to get into her house by pretending to be Lauren.

She let them both inside and Reese explained what they
were looking for. Lauren handed her the tape, to illustrate
the point.

'I used to have an answering machine that played those
little tapes,' she said, looking down at it. 'That was years
ago. I still keep the landlines for the bed and breakfast
business, but I have all my messages forwarded to my mobile now.'

'Can you think of anyone who might have a machine to
play this for us?' Lauren asked.

Mrs Fitzgerald seemed to think on that for a moment.
'You know, up in the attic crawl space we have some old
junk. Not an answering machine, I'm fairly certain, but I
know there's at least one handheld tape recorder I used to

use back before you could record from your mobile. It's amazing how you can do everything with your phone now.'

'It is,' Lauren agreed, rushing their host. 'Can you point us to the attic crawl space?'

She led them up an intricately carved wooden staircase in the front foyer to the second floor. At the end of a hallway decorated in bold yellow floral wallpaper, Lauren could see the square cut in the ceiling with a little pull cord hanging down.

'I'm sorry, the step ladder is in the shed outside,' she apologized, wringing her hands.

'No worries, Mrs Fitz,' Reese told her as he stood underneath the hatch. He grabbed the cord and pulled. 'I can boost Ms Riley up there. It'll be like lifting a bag of feathers.'

Lauren gave him the side eye, but he was already bending over.

'You should see a cardboard box as soon as you poke your head inside,' Mrs Fitzgerald said as Reese made a basket with his hands to help Lauren. The wooden trap door swung on its creaky hinges as she put her foot on his woven fingers and propelled upward into the darkness of the crawl space.

Using the flashlight feature of her phone, Lauren looked around the cramped area. The beams of the roof were barely four feet above her head, truly making it a crawl space. In the far corner an overflowing box of Christmas decorations sat next to a longer box that Lauren assumed held the family's fake tree. She twisted in a semi-circle from the waist, balancing on Reese's hands. Off to her left she spotted a cardboard box labeled *Odds and Ends* in black marker.

'Got it.' Lauren reached in and hooked it, dragging the box over to the lip of the opening. She tucked her phone in her pants pocket before grabbing it with both hands.

Gripping the cardboard, she nodded down to Reese, who slowly lowered her to the ground. It was heavy, with black wires jutting out of the top, even though someone had unsuccessfully tried to fold it shut.

'People leave everything at bed and breakfasts,' Mrs Fitzgerald explained as they trooped back down the stairs. 'Most of the time they just buy a new gadget when they get to the next town. I end up with piles of useless junk. What I can't donate to the church winds up in that box.'

Reese tried to take the box from Lauren, but she walked ahead of him into the kitchen. It was no time for chivalry. Mrs Fitzgerald removed the lace doily from the center of the table and Lauren set the box down. When she unfolded the flaps, more wires and cords popped out. Reese came to stand alongside her, and they started going through the contents together.

Inside were old-fashioned cameras that still used rolls of film, chargers for obsolete phones, phones that were obsolete, travel alarm clocks, wristwatches that needed new batteries, and handheld video game systems that were all the rage six Christmases ago.

'Does anyone ever want their stuff back?' Reese asked, pulling a clip-on step-tracker out of the box.

'I've had to overnight wedding rings, credit cards and passports more times than I can count.'

While Lauren's hand was sifting through the goods, her eyes shifted to the kitchen clock. It was just after ten. The sound of the grandfather clock ticking in the living room seemed to rival the thunder that was creeping closer. She plucked out a CD player missing its headphones and set it down on the table.

Her fingers brushed against a solid plastic rectangle with telltale buttons on the side. She pulled the little black tape recorder from the bottom of the box. 'Bingo,' she said, pushing the button that popped open the door where the cassette would go.

'That's the one that actually belongs to me,' Mrs Fitzgerald said. 'I used to audiotape walkthroughs with it when people were moving into or out of flats. Now I just video them on my mobile.'

Lauren hit the ON button and nothing happened. 'The batteries are dead.' She slid the back compartment open, revealing two corroded Duracells.

Reese started digging through the box again. 'One of these chargers must fit.'

One after another, he tried plugging various power cords into the side, only to find the connection was too big or too small. After the sixth or seventh cord, one felt like it might fit. He took the recorder and power cord over to the wall outlet and plugged it in. Hitting the play button, the mechanical sound of the wheels turning was just audible. 'Got it,' he said, holding up the working player to Lauren, who immediately grabbed it and popped the tape in.

'—*This wasn't part of our deal.*' The unmistakable voice of Sharon Whitney filled the kitchen.

'*The deal has changed. I was only supposed to grab the picture. Your husband wasn't supposed to be home.*' A male voice now, agitated.

'That's Jimmy Breen,' Mrs Fitzgerald whispered, leaning in to hear better.

'*You were supposed to kill him if he was,*' Sharon Whitney countered.

'*You lied to me so I would kill off your husband and now you're going to pay me to keep your precious piece of shite safe,*' he told her.

'*I was desperate. Howard said he'd sell the painting*

out from under me out of spite. I was trapped living with him, so he couldn't do it.' She was begging now. *'You don't know what he's put me through.'*

'I only struck the man so I wouldn't go to jail. I thought I just hit him hard enough to knock him out. Poor fragile Americans, ya got heads like eggshells.'

'It's not too late. You could come back and finish the job.' She was reaching now. *'Give me the Picasso and take care of Howard—'*

'No.' He cut her off. *'I want my money every month or I swear to heaven I'll pitch it in my fireplace and burn it. You know I'll do it.'*

'I know you will,' she repeated in a small voice. *'Please. I'll send the money. Just don't destroy the painting.'*

'Well now, that'll be up to you,' he said, sounding a little more confident now that he knew he had the upper hand with her. *'You keep my money coming, make sure no one's tracing it, and I'll keep it nice and pretty for you.'*

'When will I get it back?' she asked cautiously, as if she didn't want to provoke him into doing something rash.

'When I don't need to pay for fecking medicine anymore,' he snapped. *'Don't contact me again. I have your number. Don't change it. And when I'm no longer in need of your charitable services, I'll be more than happy to make arrangements to get it back to you.'*

'James—'

Jimmy clicked off the line, ending their conversation. The only sound now was the screechy *beep beep beep* noise that rotary phones used to make when the phone was disconnected. Lauren hadn't heard it in years. Jimmy must have hit the stop button on the answering machine too, because even that cut off suddenly.

'Jimmy was blackmailing Sharon Whitney,' Lauren said, still holding the recorder.

'What changed though?' Reese asked. 'We know she didn't have the painting so why stop the payments?'

'Unless he was making arrangements to give the painting back,' Lauren said. 'Sheila doesn't need money for insurance anymore. Maybe he was going to give it back and that's why Sharon didn't send this month's payment.'

'And Robber knew it,' Reese said, picking up Lauren's train of thought. 'He was going to be out of that steady monthly income he'd been using to pay his gambling debts. He killed Jimmy, trying to get the location of the painting out of him, maybe to keep the gravy train flowing. Only Jimmy wouldn't give up the location.'

'He broke into Jimmy's cottage but he couldn't find it,' Lauren added.

Reese was pacing the room now, excited by the pieces of the puzzle coming together in his head. 'Gorham calls Sharon Whitney after Jimmy gets killed by Robber, fishing for information. Then we show up and he tracks us. He watched Martin McGrath break into our place, just to make sure we didn't have the painting. Gorham must have overheard us at Murphy's store, then paid Robber a visit and killed him.'

Lauren shook her head. 'That's not how it happened. Something is missing.'

'No,' Reese said, skidding to a stop in front of the stove. 'It all fits. Robber killed Jimmy, then Gorham killed Robber and took off.'

'Without the painting?' Lauren asked, more to herself than Reese.

He didn't answer. Mrs Fitzgerald looked from Lauren to Reese and back again. Both were quiet, going over the facts in their heads.

It started to rain. The ticking of the clock was now muffled by the sound of raindrops lightly hitting the roof. An ominous peal of thunder reminded them that this was the calm before the storm.

'Martin had my notes,' Lauren finally said. 'That's the only thing he stole from the guest cottage. That's what he took. Gorham watched him leave with my iPad. He must have thought Martin was onto something. So Gorham headed him off, got my notes and then went to Robber's pub. And now Robber's dead and Martin is missing.'

'How much do you want to bet Martin is dead somewhere too?' Reese asked. At that, Mrs Fitzgerald's hand flew to her chest.

'Gorham is taking out everyone who may have had knowledge of where the painting is.'

'Stay here,' Reese told them. 'I'll go get the files. Just don't shoot me when I knock.'

Lauren glanced at the clock. 'Hurry.'

FORTY

DAMP FROM THE RAIN, Reese was back in Mrs Fitzgerald's kitchen in record time with the hard copies of the files they'd printed up. Moving the box to the floor, they used the kitchen table the same way they used the mess table in the Cold Case office: as a visual brainstorming board.

Lauren spread all the photos from the original crime scene in the upper left-hand corner, while pictures of Jimmy's apartment taken during the search warrant filled the right-hand corner. Insurance pictures of the painting in its frame were fanned out in the middle, as well as pictures of Jimmy in the interview room at the old police headquarters, Mr Whitney in the hospital with bandages wrapped around his head, and Mrs Whitney, looking distraught, holding out both hands, palms up, then another with palms down.

Reese sifted through the paperwork, trying to make connections, looking for something from twenty years ago that could tie this whole thing together. He'd always been more hands-on, needing to physically touch things. Lauren took a step back, hands on her hips, trying to visually make sense of everything within the context of what she knew now.

These are the facts, Lauren thought as her eyes bounced from one picture to the next: *Jimmy Breen thought Sharon Whitney hired him to steal the disputed painting. She told him Howard Whitney wasn't going to be home. She set her*

husband up to be murdered and Jimmy up to be the killer.
She never expected Jimmy to take the painting and run. He
was extorting money from her, knowing he'd never be able
to sell it.

Lauren reached over, picking up a picture of the Picasso displayed over an ornate white fireplace that was obviously decorative and had never been used. The entire room seemed to have been designed around the painting as the focal point. Lauren picked up a police crime scene photo of the wall after the Picasso was stolen. A faint outline was visible on the paint, not from sunlight fading it, because there wasn't a single window in the room, but maybe from the frame itself touching the wall. She held the before and after pictures next to each other, studying them.

'That is one ugly ass frame,' Reese remarked, looking at a close-up shot of it.

Lauren dropped both photos and started leafing through the ones taken during the execution of the search warrant at Jimmy's apartment. Located on the grounds of their mansion, it was situated over the Whitney's expansive garage and looked twice the size of his cottage in Ireland.

Jimmy hadn't become quite the packrat he was when he died, but he was well on his way. The apartment was littered with half-finished projects, tools and beer bottles. Some sort of small engine was spread across a towel on his eighties-style glass and metal coffee table, with two sets of screwdrivers lined up next to it. There were no decorations to speak of, no knickknacks or mementos from home, just the obligatory photo of JFK hanging on the wall.

Lauren sucked in a breath.

She put the photo down on the table and took a picture of it with her iPhone.

'You see something?' Reese asked, watching her pinch the screen with her thumb and forefinger.

'Maybe,' she said, putting the phone on the table. She turned to Mrs Fitzgerald, who had taken a seat and was watching them work in silent, rapt attention. 'Did you take a video of the walkthrough of Jimmy's cottage before the sale to Sharon Whitney?'

Surprised at being included in the conversation, her eyebrows shot up. 'Of course, dear,' she said, and reached around behind her to grab the pocketbook hanging from her chair. Digging around in it for a moment, she pulled her own cell phone out and started scrolling through her saved videos.

'Here it is,' she said triumphantly, handing the phone to Lauren. 'Just hit the arrow on the screen to play.'

With Reese standing over her shoulder, she watched the camera bounce slowly around the interior of Jimmy Breen's cottage while Mrs Fitzgerald narrated. Before the break-in the house was still horribly cluttered but livable. Jimmy seemed to have had some sort of personal system or order to his junk while he was alive. In the video it was evident he had distinct piles for certain types of items and definite paths between the rooms cleared out.

Lauren stabbed the screen, stopping the video. 'There,' she said, and placed Mrs Fitzgerald's phone next to hers on the table. 'Right there.'

'It's the same picture of John F. Kennedy.' Reese's eyes shifted back and forth between the two phones.

'It is, but what's different about it?' Lauren prompted him.

'The frame,' he practically whispered as it clicked in his brain. 'Jimmy changed the frame.'

'That doesn't sound like Jimmy,' Mrs Fitzgerald threw in. 'He wasn't one for home décor, as you both saw. Why would he reframe a dime store picture?'

'He'd do it to put something else behind it,' Lauren said, now pinching Mrs Fitzgerald's screen, zooming in on the JFK that had hung on Jimmy's wall next to the door of his bathroom.

The close-ups of both frames and the angle of the shots made it abundantly clear that the frame in his cottage in Keelnamara was substantially thicker than the one in his apartment in Buffalo.

Lauren took a screenshot of the image on Mrs Fitzgerald's phone before handing it back to her. She looked down at the frozen video of Jimmy's artwork. 'I'd wager he made that frame himself,' she said of the plain wood that surrounded the picture.

'That's what I'm counting on.'

'We have to get to Jimmy's cottage right now.' Reese spoke just as a bolt of lightning lit up the entire room. A second later a loud peal of thunder followed and the rain drummed even harder against the roof.

'Will you be OK here by yourself?' Lauren asked, stuffing her phone in her pants pocket. Reese was already standing by the back door with his hand on the knob.

A ringtone sounded.

'Mr Fitzgerald just texted me himself,' she said, looking down at her screen. 'He's on his way home.' She looked up at the two of them, that steely determination she'd shown when Detective Quill suggested they leave the guesthouse shining in her eyes. 'Go. Get that cursed painting before someone else dies for it. Burn it like Jimmy wanted to.'

Lauren was just about to reply that they couldn't do that when she spied the rifle, still propped next to the door. She opened her mouth to ask if she could take it with them when Reese followed her gaze and grabbed her arm.

'We don't need it,' he said. 'Let's just go.'

FORTY-ONE

THE NIGHT HAD turned from a light foreshadowing drizzle into a full-blown thunderstorm. Lauren and Reese plunged through the pounding rain from Mrs Fitzgerald's back door to their car. In the seconds it took, Lauren's clothes were soaked through to the skin. She sat in the passenger side, water dripping from her hair, running down her fogged-up glasses. She was shivering when Reese started the car. 'I can't see shit,' he complained, slowly easing onto the road and making a left.

It doesn't help that the residents of Keelnamara don't seem to believe in streetlights either, Lauren thought as the wiper blades swished almost uselessly in front of her.

'I'm practically driving blind,' Reese said.

Lauren peered into the darkness, their headlights only illuminating a few feet in front of them. 'Our saving grace is the fact that you can make a left or make a right, like Scannell told us. If you know which way to turn and keep the bay in sight, you'll never get lost in Keelnamara.'

'Thank you for the pep talk, but we already got lost once and I'm trying to drive over here.'

'I'm just trying to help.'

'Why don't you call Scannell while you're thinking of him. See if he can meet us over at Jimmy's.'

Lauren could've kicked herself for forgetting to do that,

she was so focused on getting to the painting. Now was not the time to get sloppy.

He answered on the first ring. 'Are you still at the Garda station?' she asked without saying hello.

'I just pulled into my driveway at home. Every reporter in Ireland is camped out at the station right now. I kept having to stand behind Quill and Detective Inspector Riordan as he appealed for information on the murders. What's the matter?'

'You need to meet us over at Jimmy Breen's. I think I know where the painting is. And maybe where Shamus Gorham is heading.'

'I'm coming now. I'll call the station and get Quill and the rest.' His voice picked up a notch. 'Wait for us there.'

'We're en route.'

'Don't do anything foolish. And be careful.'

Lauren hung up before he could admonish her further. 'They're on the way,' she told Reese.

'It feels good that it's not the dirty cop, for once,' Reese said, squinting into the darkness of the storm.

'Not the active duty cop, just the ex-cop,' Lauren agreed. She had to admit, she was glad Scannell was off the suspect list. She'd almost died at the hands of the fellow officer who'd stuck a knife in her side to cover up the murder his brother had committed. That same injury was still threatening her career. The thought of stout, barrel-chested Scannell killing two men over a painting had made her side ache. Now the thought of bringing down a greedy, disgraced ex-Garda was enough to make her power through any pain. It'd be a pleasure to see Quill put the cuffs on Gorham. Unless they were wrong.

'If Scannell shows up alone, we're screwed,' she said.

'He won't. At least I'm pretty sure he won't.' A note

of uncertainty crept into his voice. 'Unless he's working with Gorham.'

'Gorham is the key,' Lauren said.

'Do you think Martin McGrath ever figured out where the picture was hidden from your case photos?' Reese asked.

'I'm betting no,' Lauren said. 'I don't think he had time to. I think Shamus got to him first. But Gorham knows Robber didn't have the painting and we don't have it, so it must still be in Jimmy's place somewhere. I'm willing to bet if Martin didn't go back and tear the place into confetti already, Gorham's doing it right now.'

The wind they'd heard earlier was amplified in the storm, blowing hard rain against the windshield with an unearthly howl.

'No wonder the Irish have so many myths and legends about Banshees.' Reese leaned forward over the steering wheel, trying to see past the headlights.

'Banshees are the harbingers of death,' Lauren told him. 'If that's a Banshee wailing out there, that's not good news for us.'

'Maybe you're a Banshee,' he said. 'Every time you show up someone bites it. It makes sense. You are hag-like and I have heard you sing.'

'Time and place,' Lauren reminded him. 'This is neither the time nor place.'

'Sorry,' he said, obviously not sorry.

Reese had turned on the navigation system when they got in the car. Now the robotic English-accented woman's voice announced, 'In one half kilometer, turn right.'

'I can't see a thing,' Reese said, 'I need you to navigate for me.'

The blue line on the display screen in the dashboard told her they were heading the right way. Their arrow was inching toward the turn off but when she looked up at the road ahead, all she could see was rain splashing off the windshield and darkness. 'Slow down,' she warned, not wanting him to pass the driveway. There was nowhere to turn around if they missed it and they'd never be able to back up without chancing getting rammed from behind.

'Parts of the road are flooding. I don't want the car to stall out.'

'Here. Here. Turn here!' Lauren reached across Reese, pointing to the gap in the road that was barely visible.

Reese jerked the wheel hard and hit the gas, propelling them up the hill. Lauren could just make out the outline of Jimmy's cottage at the top.

The incline was so steep and wet that Reese had to stop halfway up, put the car in park and set the emergency brake. 'I don't want to get stuck in the mud at the top or slide down. I can't get any traction as it is. Let's get in, get the painting, and get out of here quick before this driveway becomes a waterslide.'

Pulling her jacket up over her head, Lauren ran from the car to the front door. Lightning flashed overhead and she could see the blue and white crime scene tape still in place, crisscrossing the door. A lone latex glove, probably dropped by one of the Crime Scenes techs, lay next to her foot. Reese came up alongside her. 'Kick it in?' he yelled over the wind.

'It's our client's house,' Lauren called back, sputtering to keep the rain out of her mouth. 'Technically.'

'Or technically, it's not,' Reese replied, then booted the flimsy wooden door in with one kick, almost taking it off the hinges.

Lauren ducked inside, feeling around the wall for the light switch. She clicked it on and she and Reese shuffled in out of the rain. Knowing what to do without having to debate it, they immediately grabbed a gutted 1980s green Barcalounger and tipped it in front of the door to keep it shut.

'That won't keep anyone out,' Lauren said, wiping the rain from her face, 'but it might buy us a minute or two.'

'More like a second or two.' Reese looked around the living room. 'By turning on that light we just announced to the whole town we're up here. This place might as well be a damned lighthouse.' They stood dripping in the living room, soaked and cold, trying to catch their breath from the sprint up the hill in the storm.

'There it is,' Lauren said, motioning to the portrait of John F. Kennedy she'd rehung on their first visit to the cottage.

She hadn't really looked at it then, hadn't noticed the heavy wooden frame around the cheap picture. Her own grandmother had had almost the exact same picture hanging in her basement for years. She'd gotten it when JFK visited Ireland during his presidency, and with her being *right off the boat*, as she'd liked to say, she'd had to go out and buy the picture to commemorate the trip. It'd been a huge deal to the Irish community in Buffalo when Kennedy was elected president. Obviously, that feeling had been reciprocated in Ireland.

Lauren walked over and stood in front of it. It portrayed John Fitzgerald Kennedy looking off to the side with a slight smile. He looked tan and healthy against the white collar of his shirt, peeking out from his suit jacket. It was a picture of a man in his prime, ready to change the world.

She ran a hand through her hair to slick it back, then picked up a sliced pillow and dried her hands on it as best she could. Grabbing onto the frame, she lifted it up and off the hook.

'It's heavy,' she said, squatting down and sitting on her heels. Holding it out and away from her so as not to drip on it, she turned it over to look at the back.

'That's because he made the frame so thick,' Reese said, coming to stand next to her. 'Isn't this the oldest trick in the book? To hide a picture behind a picture in a frame? Wouldn't that be the first place someone would look?'

Lauren traced the back of the frame lightly with her index finger. 'Unless you were handy,' she said, wedging her fingernail behind the wooden backing and prying. 'And you could make a false backing to fool people.'

The back popped off, revealing the JFK picture snuggly fitted against the glass. She licked the tip of her finger and tugged on the thick paper until she could grasp the edge and take it out of the frame. She handed it to Reese.

'Congratulations, Detective. It's a picture of John Kennedy,' Reese said, looking down at it in his hands. 'We're back to square one.' Crumpling it up, he threw it on the floor with the rest of the garbage. 'Sorry, Mr President.'

'You never listen to me,' Lauren told him, shoving the empty top of the frame with the glass still in it into his gut.

He grabbed it with an *'ooff'*, and looked at the thin piece of wood Lauren was holding up. The fourteen-by-ten-inch backing was barely thicker than normal. It was the part of a frame that barely mattered. All anyone opening the back of the picture looking for the painting would find was a picture of JFK. Lauren took off her glasses and brought the edge of the wood right to her face. Then she held it up to the bare bulb that passed for a ceiling light. 'It's a box,' she said. 'A very thin wooden box.'

'Son of a bitch,' Reese said by way of agreement, eyeing the backing.

She pointed to a pile of tools sitting on an end table. 'See if there's a pair of pliers over there.'

Reese rummaged around the table. 'No pliers, just this wrench.' He held up a small silver adjustable wrench.

'That'll do.' She held out a hand and he slapped the tool into her palm, making her wince. Scars crisscrossed it, the same as his head. *We're walking road maps of physical trauma*, she thought as she balanced the wood on her knee. *Let's see if those hard lessons taught us anything.*

Reese stood over her now, being careful not to drip onto the wood. Slipping the mouth of the wrench over the bottom left-hand corner, Lauren turned the wheel, slowly clamping down. 'Can you hold it steady for me?' she asked Reese. 'I only want to crack the wood.'

He knelt down beside her and grabbed the top corners of the frame, steadying it. 'I got you,' he said.

Twisting harder, Lauren heard the thin wood crack and saw the corner splinter up. She immediately turned the wheel the other way and took the wrench off the casing. A little piece of the corner came off with it, creating a small hole.

'Is there anything inside?' Reese asked, not daring to bend over any further.

Lauren pulled her phone out of her jacket pocket and turned on the flashlight app. She brought the splintered corner up to her eye and angled the light into the hole as best she could. 'I can't see much and I'm not tearing this box apart to take it out, but it sure looks like a piece of canvas with pink paint on it is in there.'

'Would he have damaged it, taking it out of that gaudy gold frame and sticking it in that little box?'

'Not if he left it on its stretchers.' She'd read a little about the anatomy of paintings on Google during the plane ride over. 'I'm no expert, but it should be OK.'

'If that's true, Riley, you're holding twenty million dollars in your hands.'

For some reason, Lauren's stomach roiled. She didn't know if it was the excitement of locating the painting after it'd been missing for twenty years, the fact that someone was killing people to get their hands on it, or that their client had hired the wrong people if she thought they were just going to turn it over to her after finding out she'd set up the theft in the first place. Maybe it was a combination of all three.

'Let's find some plastic to wrap that thing and get the hell out of here before Shamus Gorham shows up,' Reese said, snapping her out of her thoughts. He let go of the frame and started tossing garbage aside. 'A gazillion plastic bags in the world and I can't find a single one when I actually need it,' he complained.

'I can't believe it,' Lauren said, staring down at the wooden backing. 'I can't believe it was here the whole time.'

'Believe it.' Reese had moved into the other room and was now rummaging through the contents of one of the kitchen cabinets. 'I bet you're not the first person to check that picture when Jimmy's back was turned. Did you see how easily it popped off? He knew people would look there and all they'd find was the back of the JFK photo. Pretty ingenious.'

'You'd never know it wasn't a normal frame,' Lauren agreed, 'unless you saw the original on his wall in Buffalo. He hid it in plain sight.'

'All of the best secrets are.'

He moved out of Lauren's line of sight toward the stove. She heard what sounded like pots and pans being thrown around, then Reese announced, 'I found his stash!' He came walking into the living room with two armfuls of plastic bags. 'It was like visiting my mom's big kitchen cabinet,' he said, and began handing them to Lauren one by one. 'She's been hoarding plastic Wegmans grocery bags since 1998.'

Lauren started by slipping the whole thing inside a Tesco's bag and tying the handle in a knot. She then slipped that into another bag and did the same thing. She pulled layer after layer of plastic over the box to keep it dry from the rain. 'He used wood glue to bond the perfectly cut pieces together. He kept it protected from light and dust for all these years.'

'Maybe he liked the painting too,' Reese said. 'Maybe it was enough for him to know it was there and not hanging on Sharon Whitney's walls. What are we going to do about that, by the way?'

'I haven't thought that far ahead yet,' Lauren admitted. Lightning flashed again and she looked toward the window. She clutched the plastic-wrapped package to her chest. 'Where the hell is Scannell? I feel like a sitting duck here.'

'I agree. Let's get out of here. Call Scannell from the car and tell him to have Quill and the team meet us at Mrs Fitzgerald's. If Gorham isn't in custody, he's going to head here, especially if he just saw the light pop on in the middle of the night.'

After checking one last time that the painting had been as waterproofed as they could make it with old grocery bags, Lauren tucked the package up under her coat for the dash to the car.

When she nodded she was ready, Reese tipped the recliner out of the way and they both dashed down the driveway, not bothering to close Jimmy's door. *I doubt Sharon Whitney is going to be worried about water damage to the cottage*, Lauren thought as she jumped into the passenger seat.

'This is going to be a real bitch, backing down the drive-way.' Reese wrapped his arm around the back of Lauren's seat and craned his neck over his shoulder to see out the rear windshield. They inched down the hill. The car started to slide on the wet gravel a couple of times, causing him to ride the brake.

Lauren laid the wrapped painting on the passenger side floor, wedging the corner beneath the floor mat so it wouldn't slide around. The white plastic bags practically glowed in the dark. Once she'd secured it as best she could, she turned back around and called Scannell. 'It's going straight to voicemail after the first ring,' she said after the third try. 'He must be talking to someone on the other line. Detective Quill maybe.'

Reese managed to get them to the bottom of the hill and stopped. If anyone was coming from either direction, Reese and Riley would get T-boned as soon as they pulled out onto the road. The rain was still coming down in thick sheets, pummeling the car. 'Text him,' Reese said, biting his lower lip as he prepared to pull out, hoping for the best.

He gave the car some gas and gunned it out onto the road, quickly putting the car into drive and straightening out the wheel as they moved forward. 'Ha!' He laughed, hitting the steering wheel with the palm of his hand in triumph. 'That wasn't so bad, was—'

The entire car jolted forward as it was hit from behind. The only thing that saved Lauren from flying through the windshield was her seatbelt, which locked into place against her chest. A pair of headlights blazed through the back window, blinding her.

FORTY-TWO

'Go, GO, GO!' Lauren yelled as the car tried to maneuver itself alongside them.

'I think our back tire is flat,' Reese said through gritted teeth, fighting to maintain control of the vehicle.

They accelerated and the other vehicle fell back behind them, butting up to their bumper. Lauren could feel their car being pushed from behind again as Reese struggled with the wheel, trying to keep in the lane. 'I can't—' he began, but his words were cut off mid-sentence as their car careened off the road and down an incline. They bounced over an embankment and crashed through the construction fence encircling the unfinished resort complex.

Both front airbags deployed, crushing them into their seats and leaving them dazed for a second. Coming to her senses, Lauren beat at the bag until she could finally see. A wave of déjà vu passed over her as the car chase across the Skyway flashed before her eyes. She shook her head to clear it and caught a glimpse of the car that had run them off the road. When they had pitched down, the other car had shot forward with the momentum. It was now backing up, trying to angle itself with the access road.

'Come on!' she urged Reese, snatching the painting up from the floor of the car.

'Give me that.' He grabbed it from her. 'And get on the phone with 999 or Scannell or whoever. Right now.'

Headlights pulling onto the access road and heading toward them pushed them into motion. 'Head for that opening.' Lauren pointed before jumping from the car. Her mind
was still spinning after getting smashed with the airbag.
The thought of Reese's past head trauma flashed through
her brain as she ran into the storm. *I'll be the death of him
yet*, she thought as they ducked inside the darkness of where
a set of double doors should have been.

The complex was framed and had a ceiling, but other
than that was completely empty. The builders hadn't even
left construction material behind, or maybe they had but
it had gotten stolen over the years. The building itself was
open and cavernous, the air inside foul, smelling of mold
and rot. Rain blew in from the glassless windows, and on
the left side they could see the waves roiling angrily in the
bay, almost coming up to the walls.

Their footsteps slapped and reverberated on the wet
floor. There was no place to go but forward.

Reese clung to the package with one hand and pulled
out his phone with the other, hitting the flashlight app. It
barely made a dent in the darkness as they made their way
down a long corridor. Empty, doorless rooms lined each
side. They could have ducked into one, but without an exit,
they'd be trapped. They needed to find another way out of
the complex.

From behind, even with the storm raging outside, they
heard the echo of footsteps.

'Get on your phone,' Reese urged her again in a hushed
whisper. 'See if you can get the 999 dispatch.'

As Lauren struggled to breathe, punch in the numbers,
and jog just short of a full-out run, Reese tripped on some
unseen object. He pitched forward, the light from his app
bouncing off the bare walls. Lauren reached out, dropping

her phone and grabbing his arm as he stumbled. For an instant they almost tumbled to the ground together, then he shot his palm out, slamming it into the wall to stop their forward momentum and they came skidding to a halt.

'I'm good,' he said as she steadied him with both hands.

Lauren's phone was glowing in a shallow puddle on the floor. The screen was broken; a spiderweb of cracks branched out over her screensaver of Lindsey and Erin. Snatching it up, she shook it off as they continued down the corridor, praying it would still work. The footsteps were louder now, closer.

Lauren was panting and trying to dial 999 on the shattered cell when she heard Reese swear under his breath. Looking up just as it started to ring, she saw what Reese was cursing about. The corridor they'd rushed down ended abruptly in a gray cinderblock wall. Lauren ran forward a few steps and hit the wall with her fist.

'No, damn it!' She felt along the wall with her hands, trying to find a way out. Water from a hole in the ceiling ran in a steady trickle, splashing on the floor next to her. The only way out was to go back.

The sound of a shotgun racking filled the hallway, followed by the sound of an ejected shell bouncing on the ground.

'Give me the painting and I'll let you live,' a figureless voice in the inky darkness called to them, causing them both to spin around. Reese's phone light only penetrated about a foot into the blackness, keeping the speaker invisible to them.

'Get behind me,' Reese growled, grabbing Riley by the arm and shoving her back. He angled the package in front of him like a shield.

'If you blast us with a shotgun, you'll destroy your precious painting,' he called, and clicked off his flashlight app. Even though whoever had followed them into the complex must have known about the dead end, Lauren hoped he was just as blind as they were in the corridor.

'You'll have to hand it over then,' the voice called. 'Because I can still take out your legs.'

'You won't though, Gorham,' Lauren challenged, trying to keep him talking. 'If you have pellets loaded in that gun, you won't risk damaging the canvas. How much would Mr Whitney pay you then?'

'You're not a very clever bird, are you?' A flash of lightning lit up the abandoned resort, illuminating Martin Mc-Grath standing six feet in front of them, pointing a sawed-off shotgun at Reese's head. 'So much for American detective skills. And I can aim low enough to take out your ankles.' Lightning flashed again. He had stepped closer and lowered the gun so that it now pointed at their shins.

'Not if there are ricochets.' Lauren was reaching now. 'They might even bounce back and hit you. Leave a nice trail of your DNA behind.'

Reese held his phone out. Martin was close enough now to be in the circle of light it put out. 'You really think someone is going to buy that painting with four bodies attached to it?' he asked.

'I won't get anything near what it's worth, but I have some associates who are interested in it. And a fraction of what it's worth is still a hell of a lot of euros.'

'You killed your uncle and then you killed Robber,' Lauren said, still trying to buy time, to keep the dialogue going. 'Jimmy was like a father to you.'

'A father.' Spit flew from his lips. 'What kind of a father leaves his son high and dry? My uncle was going to take a payout from that Whitney woman. My mum didn't need the insurance money anymore, so he was going to give her the painting back. Just a few thousand euros for twenty years' worth of trouble. I tried to convince him to give it to me to sell, but he wouldn't. Said the painting was bad luck, the superstitious fuck. Even when I was trying to beat it out of him, all he'd say was that it was for my own good.'

'You pick up a little drug habit in jail?' Reese guessed.

Martin laughed so hard that the muzzle of the gun bobbed up and down. 'You must be the brains of the out-fit then.'

'I'm the looks, she's the brains.' Reese nodded his head toward Lauren but kept the light steady on Martin.

'When you were at my mum's house talking about how Jimmy's place got broken into, I knew it was Robber. I went up there to double-check it, then hit your place while you were out, tried to make it look like the same person done it. I figured I'd slow ya down by taking your papers and computer. Then I went over to Robber's and waited. Once that horse's arse Scannell left, I paid Robber a visit. He said he didn't know where the painting was either.' A sickening smile played across his mouth. Light glinted off his cracked front tooth, making him look like a demented jack-o'-lantern. 'I guess he was telling the truth, eh?'

'Robber was your friend,' Lauren said in a disgusted voice. If Martin was going to shoot her, there was no need to pretend he was anything other than what he was, a low-life, murdering scumbag.

'And Jimmy was my uncle,' he snapped back. 'And both of them were too prideful to give up the picture. It seems neither will you. I gave ya a chance. Let's—'

From out of nowhere a heavy metal flashlight connected with the side of Martin's head. Blood exploded from his temple, spattering the wall. He stumbled to the side, dropping the shotgun as another blow rained down on him, crumpling him to the ground. The shotgun skittered across the wet floor and Lauren dove on it. Breathing hard and lying in the muck, she got up on her elbows and pointed the gun at the now unconscious Martin McGrath.

FORTY-THREE

ANOTHER BOLT OF lightning flashed, revealing Shamus Gorham standing along the wall, slapping his bloodied flashlight against his palm. 'I think I broke my torch on Marty's skull.' Suddenly, it clicked on. 'There we go.' He pointed it up at his own face. 'This is my good one. I thought I busted it on you, friend, back in the yard the other night.'

'That was you?' Lauren panted, having a hard time catching her breath.

'It was,' he said, with that maddening fake-cheerful voice of his. 'I haven't used it twice in one week since I was on the Garda. I love this old girl. I'd have hated to buy another.' He looked down at Martin's blood on his hand from the flashlight, grimaced, and rubbed it on his black pants.

'I never thought I'd say this, but it's good to see you, Mr Gorham,' Reese said, dropping his phone's light down to Lauren, who was still pointing the shotgun at Martin's prone body. 'Is he alive?'

'He's breathing,' Lauren replied, sitting up, keeping the gun aimed at him. Martin gave a long, low moan but didn't move. 'Yeah, thank you. I think you showed up at exactly the right time.'

'I was sitting in my flat with my beautiful bride watching the storm when I saw the light go on up at Jimmy's place. I drove as fast as I could to get my arse over there.' He was still furiously rubbing his fingers on the fabric of his pants. Lauren knew the sticky sensation he was feeling. Blood always got into every crease in your hand and seemed impossible to get off, no matter how hard you scrubbed. 'I was inching my way to his front door just in time to see the world's shortest car chase come to an end at the bottom of the hill. I would've been here sooner, but it's a real bitch to back down Jimmy's driveway in this rain. It took me a minute to get here.'

Reese gave Lauren an I-told-you-so look. He told Gorham, 'I don't think we had another minute left. Martin was done with talking.'

Gorham gave Reese that skeevy smile of his. 'Don't go patting me on the back too hard, my friends.' The sound of police sirens cut through the howling wind. 'I didn't knock Martin senseless out of brotherly love. Locating that painting is still worth a million American dollars to me. I wasn't about to let this arsehole blow a hundred holes in it.'

'Truly, your humanity is heartwarming,' Lauren told him dryly.

'Humanity don't pay my wife's credit card bills,' he said as more flashlight beams pierced the darkness of the corridor. At least three different voices commanded Lauren to drop the gun and for all of them to put their hands up.

Lauren tossed the gun behind her, away from Martin and Shamus, and slowly stood up, lacing her fingers behind her head.

'Just for the record,' Shamus said out of the side of his mouth to Reese, hands high in the air, 'I would have taken the painting from you if I'd have gotten ahold of Martin's gun before Wonder Woman here jumped on it.'

Holding the wrapped picture over his head as Scannell and Quill appeared out of the darkness with a knot of Gardai trailing behind them, Reese assured Gorham, 'Of that, I have absolutely no doubt.'

FORTY-FOUR

DETECTIVE QUILL AND Garda Scannell took Martin, Shamus and the painting into custody.

Once Quill said it was OK, Lauren dropped her hands and wrapped her arm around her bad side.

Scannell called for an ambulance for Martin McGrath, who was still out cold. A huge knot was starting to emerge on the side of his head and a small cut was bleeding profusely onto the wet floor. 'Do you want medical attention as well?' he asked her, noticing how hard she was breathing. She'd have been lying if she said the old wound in her side didn't hurt, or that she wasn't winded. He didn't ask that though.

'No,' she said, and looked over at Reese, whose eyebrows were drawn together in a V of concern.

While Scannell waited for Martin to be taken away in cuffs on a stretcher, another Garda led them out of the derelict building. Unlike in the movies where the heroes would emerge just as the storm was passing, symbolizing their triumph of good over evil, they exited the resort back into the thunder and lightning. Lauren's glasses were simultaneously fogged and covered in raindrops, and she still wasn't able to catch her breath. Reese looped his arm through hers now that he was free of the painting, and helped her through the cluster of police vehicles.

As they sat shivering and soaked in the rear seat of Scannell's patrol car, Reese rubbed Lauren's back while she hung her head between her knees, gasping for breath. Thankfully, the episode passed before Scannell returned. 'Better?' Reese asked when she sat back up. She wiped her glasses with the bottom of her shirt as best she could and perched them back on her nose.

'I could use a coffee. Or whiskey. Or whiskey coffee.'

Rain pelted against the car windows. All she wanted to do was get out of the storm and into some dry clothes. Between the Garda, the EMTs and the passersby who pulled over to watch the scene unfold, she knew phones were probably ringing all over Keelnamara already, spreading the news of Martin's arrest. Sheila McGrath's heart was about to be broken all over again.

Through the window they could just make out the fluorescent yellow of Scannell's Garda raincoat as he approached the car. Reese exhaled a long breath. 'I gotta say, this whole caper did not turn out the way I thought it would.'

'It never does,' Lauren said as Scannell reached for the driver's side door handle.

At the Glenbeigh substation they were separated for questioning and statements, which was standard procedure, even in the States. Lauren was grateful she didn't have to type up this particular incident report. It was going to take some creative writing on Detective Quill's part to make sense of what had happened over the last two weeks in Keelnamara.

Thankfully, Lauren was interviewed by Garda Scannell, while Reese got stuck with Detective Quill. She went through what they'd found out, point by point. Sharon Whitney had set up the robbery in the hopes Jimmy would kill her husband. When that didn't happen, Jimmy fled to Ireland with the painting and blackmailed her to pay for his sister's medical bills, using Robber Shea as a go-between. When his nephew found out that Jimmy was arranging to give the painting back to Sharon Whitney, he tried to get its location out of his uncle, killing him in the process. Shamus Gorham, who'd been under contract with Howard Whitney to find the painting, tried to force Sharon Whitney's hand by calling and telling her Jimmy had died.

'So then enter you and your partner,' Scannell said as he paused from typing into his computer tablet. He had Lauren in the back room, Reese was in the interview room with Quill, and Gorham had been transported by some of the other detectives to Killorglin. It was still unclear to Lauren if Detective Quill was placing Gorham under arrest or not, and for what.

'Robber had already ransacked Jimmy's cottage and come up with nothing. Martin went back after he found out someone had broken in and put two and two together. He wrecked our place to make sure we hadn't found the artwork and then went to confront Robber. Robber had no idea where the painting was hidden, so Martin killed him too.'

'That's some good police work you and your partner did, finding that painting.' He'd taken off his rain jacket with *Garda* emblazed across the back. It was hanging from a hook on the wall, dripping onto the floor. His round face was flushed, either from the wind or the excitement of the arrest or both.

Lauren took a sip from the bottle of water Scannell had gotten her when they'd first arrived. She was still soaked and chilled to the bone. They didn't have any emergency blankets at the substation, so she sat shivering in her wet clothes. An empty tea mug sat off to the side. She'd drained that within the first five minutes of sitting down. Now she was waiting for the young dark-haired Garda who'd offered to get her some coffee to come back with it.

'I suspected you for a minute,' she admitted.

'I suspected that you did,' Scannell said. 'You and your partner struck me right away as the "Trust no one" types. You were more buttoned-up after you found Robber's body and knew I'd been in the pub with him. I'm a poor civil servant with four kids to feed. I'd have thought the same of you.'

'What's going to happen to the painting?' Lauren asked, not bothering to comment on Scannell's assessment of her and Reese's personalities. She'd just told him she'd thought he might have murdered his friends, after all.

'Detective Quill cracked open the casing just enough to confirm that the painting is in there, and then Detective Inspector Riordan called our headquarters in Dublin. They're sending someone out right now to take it into custody and put it into evidence. Of course, we have no way of knowing if it's the real thing or a forgery. That's for an art expert to figure out. Above my pay grade anyway,' Scannell said, tilting his tablet forward so it rested against his chest. 'Martin McGrath is going to be facing two homicide charges and that painting is the motive. It'll be up to the courts as to whether it has to stay here in Ireland until the trial, or if it can be returned to its rightful owner.'

Lauren wondered how swiftly the wheels of justice turned in Ireland. Technically, the painting belonged to the insurance company until the Whitneys paid back the three-million-dollar settlement they'd received. Then a judge had to decide which of them was the actual owner. Now that Lauren had evidence Sharon had conspired to kill her husband and steal the painting, it was looking good for Howard Whitney. Sharon Whitney wasn't the type to let things go without a fight, though. She'd hire a team of lawyers. There was a good chance that neither one of the two awful people fighting for possession of the Picasso would live to see it finally awarded to one or the other.

Lauren wasn't the superstitious type, but there did seem to be something to the idea that the painting was cursed. She was glad she'd never actually laid eyes on it and that it was out of her hands.

'What will you and your partner do now?' Scannell asked.

She pondered that for a moment. 'My former client paid for our lodging at the guesthouse for another week. I think we might hang around, do some sightseeing.'

'Former client?'

'Sharon Whitney staged the robbery of that painting, almost got her husband killed and committed insurance fraud.' She frowned at the thought of Mrs Whitney's fake righteous indignation over the loss of her precious paint-ing. 'I don't work for criminals. Occasionally I get hired by them, but once I find out the truth, I'm done. My integ-rity isn't for sale.'

Scannell nodded in approval. 'What will happen to that woman now that you've found out she set up the robbery in the first place?'

Lauren shrugged. 'The statute of limitations ran out on the robbery and assault years ago. She didn't possess the stolen property. She's guilty of conspiracy, but even the feds' statute of limitations has run out on that. So I really don't know what's going to happen to her. I do know that I won't be getting paid the rest of my fee. And that Shamus Gorham was right about one thing.'

'What's that?' Scannell asked as the young Garda nudged the door open with his hip, carrying two coffee cups in a to-go tray.

She plucked the coffee from the holder and took a big sip, immediately feeling warmed. She gave Scannell a satisfied smile, wrapped both hands around the cup and said, 'Always get the money up front.'

FORTY-FIVE

IT WAS WELL past dawn when the Detective Inspector declared he was satisfied with Riley and Reese and they could head back to their guesthouse. He was happy to hear that they'd be staying another week in case Quill had more questions for them, and in Lauren's experience, there were always more questions. Their car had had to be towed from the abandoned resort parking lot, so the same young Garda who'd brought them coffee was tasked with driving Lauren and Reese back to Mrs Fitzgerald's.

News vans were already parked along the road to the Garda station. Reporters who had been clustered in knots in the parking lot saw them exit the building and came charging at them with their cameramen in tow. Two more Gardai held them at bay as they shouted questions at Reese and Riley, who both tried to yank their jacket collars up to cover their faces as best they could until the patrol car that was driving them pulled up.

Catching sight of her face in the rearview mirror from her spot in the backseat, Lauren saw a nasty brush burn had formed across her left cheek where the airbag had hit her. Thankfully, their rental car had been newer and didn't use the old white powder that airbags used to release, otherwise she and Reese would still be coated in it.

Reese, for once, had emerged unscathed. Somewhere

along the way he'd lost his Irish hat, but that seemed to be the worst of it.

The young Garda talked and talked and talked from the front seat, not realizing his two passengers were half asleep in the gloomy morning light, not listening to him at all.

Lauren's eyes were heavy and it was all she could do to keep them open. The roads were still wet from the previous night's storm, but that didn't stop the sheep herders from holding the patrol car up while moving their flocks from one pasture to the next. *Even the sheep got dirty in the storm*, Lauren thought as they waited for the mud-spattered animals to pass. Her own legs were crusted in it from the knee down, and a greenish smear from the floor of the resort covered the front of her jacket.

She was so exhausted that when Reese finally put the key in the lock she didn't bother making any small talk or cracking jokes or talking about the crazy case they'd just solved. She went straight to her room and lay down on her bed fully clothed. Normally she would have felt bad because of the mud on her legs getting on Mrs Fitzgerald's sheets, but she didn't have the energy to care. Across the hall she heard Reese's door open and shut, then the squeak of the mattress as he lay down.

We made it through some crazy shit again, she thought as sleep closed in on her. *Me and Reese, we're still a great team.*

FORTY-SIX

MRS FITZGERALD CALLED on them later that afternoon to let them know that Sheila McGrath had postponed Jimmy's funeral service, given the fact that her only son had just been arrested for his murder. 'However,' she said, hands on her hips as she stood in the guesthouse kitchen, 'Mr Fitzgerald and I, along with most of the town, are going to Robber O'Shea's tonight to celebrate both men's lives, and you've been invited to come.' The Garda had released the scene and the women of Keelnamara had spent the morning tidying up, so Michael senior decided to open the pub that evening for an Irish wake. 'As distraught as he is,' Mrs Fitzgerald said, 'he knows his son would have wanted his friends to lift a pint or two in his memory.'

'That seems so personal,' Lauren told her. She'd managed to buy coffee and tea at the petrol station the night they had their chips and pretzels dinner there, and put on the electric kettle for their diminutive landlady. The three of them sat down together at the kitchen table, Mrs Fitzgerald with her tea and Reese and Riley with their coffee. She'd waited until late afternoon to knock on their door, kind enough to allow them a few hours of sleep after the craziness of the night before, which her neighbors had been ringing her phone about all morning. Keelnamara was abuzz with the news of Martin's arrest. 'I'd feel like we were intruding.'

'Nonsense.' She reached over and patted Lauren's hand. Her skin was cool and dry, but rough. Lauren wondered what Theresa Fitzgerald's life had been like growing up in this small fishing village. 'You exposed Martin McGrath for what he was. And that cursed painting is finally out of Keelnamara forever. We can sleep at night without having to lock our doors again. The entire town has a lot to thank you for.'

'As vain as this sounds,' Lauren said, 'I don't think I have any clothes with me suitable for an Irish wake.'

'Come as you are, dear,' Mrs Fitzgerald said kindly. 'We aren't people who put on airs.'

'That's good.' Reese rubbed his bald head. 'Because I lost my favorite Irish hat in the storm last night. And I wouldn't feel right wearing one of my ball caps.'

'I'm sure I'll be able to bring you one of Mr Fitzgerald's,' she told him. 'He quite likes his hats and has a vast assortment cluttering up my closet. The one I have in mind will look grand on you.'

A look of relief passed over his face. He'd never admit it, but Lauren knew Reese was self-conscious about the scars on his head. He'd tried to grow his hair out earlier in the year, with disastrous results. It had come in patchy and uneven, making the scars even more prominent. He'd shaved his head bald again and stuck with wearing hats.

Reese raised his mug in Mr Fitzgerald's honor. 'Cheers, then. I'll drink to that.'

His phone buzzed at his elbow. He reached down, flipped it over, glanced at the screen, then turned it facedown again.

'Who was on the phone?' Lauren asked. Reese usually didn't worry about answering the phone and having an hour-long conversation about baseball with someone while you were sitting right in front of him.

'Nobody I need to talk to right now,' he replied, then deflected onto Lauren. 'When are you going to call Sharon Whitney and let her know she's probably never going to see her beloved painting again?'

Lauren looked at the digital clock on the microwave. 'Hmmm. Good question. What time is it in Buffalo right now? I'd really love to wake her up in the middle of the night. But I think I should call Matt Lawton over at the FBI first.'

'I thought you said they can't do anything.'

'I don't think they can, but at the very least they'll be able to finally close the case out for good.' She scooped up her phone and headed for the back door, double-checking the time as she went. 'As much as I want to wake Sharon up with this news, I'd hate to do it to Matt.'

'It's not too late,' Reese said. 'Call him. You wouldn't care what time it was if someone had news that one of our cold cases just got solved, would you?'

Lauren thought back to the phone call she'd got in the middle of the night from Reese when she was in Iceland, waking her out of a dead sleep. He'd called to tell her they'd gotten a DNA hit in the Billy Munzert case. The same case Steve Harrott had just been sentenced for. She remembered her heart hammering in her chest as Reese told her Harrott was sitting in a jail cell. Reese told her he'd wait for her and when she got back the two of them would put the case against him together.

And they did.

Yes, she needed to call Matt first and right away. It was only a painting, but two men had ended up dying for it. She didn't owe Sharon Whitney a thing anymore. 'I'll be right back,' she told them and slipped out the back door.

Making her way to the driveway, Lauren could see Mrs Fitzgerald and Reese chatting in the warm glow of the kitchen lights through the window. Even though the storm had passed, a gloom hung over the sky, as if it could pour down again any minute. She pulled her cracked phone out, careful of the glass on the screen that was just barely holding together. She scrolled through her contacts list and hit MATT LAWTON. He answered on the first ring, telling Lauren that he was already aware of why she was calling.

She started pacing back and forth in front of Mrs Fitzgerald's car, careful not to put the phone against her cheek like she usually did, as Matt relayed to her that his boss had gotten a call from the special agent in charge of the FBI's art theft squad that morning, saying that the Picasso was recovered and had been taken into evidence in Ireland. 'I can't believe you did it,' he said breathlessly. 'I mean, I can, but I can't. The original suspect had it this whole time?'

'The whole time,' Lauren affirmed. She realized she could hardly believe it herself.

The hare was out on the lawn again, jaw working back and forth, back and forth as he chewed on a piece of grass.

'Amazing. It took less than a week to figure out what we couldn't in over twenty years.'

'It took two people getting murdered,' Lauren amended. 'And if the FBI hadn't helped Buffalo process that scene at Jimmy Breen's apartment and documented it so well all those years ago, that painting might have been lost forever.'

Lauren always tried to give credit where it was due. Whenever people asked her about solving a particular crime, she always tried to point out that it took an army of people, from evidence techs to photographers to the lab workers and everyone in between. No one person ever closed a case on their own.

'I have to ask you, because they emailed us pictures, do you think he made the fake frame here or in Ireland?'

She shrugged, even though Matt was an ocean away and couldn't see her. 'I don't think we'll ever know for sure. Personally, I think he had a hiding spot all picked out before the night of the robbery. Mrs Whitney probably gave him plenty of time to prepare for it. He clubbed Mr Whitney, took and stashed the painting and then waited for the inevitable search warrant. I'm thinking he built the frame with the fake backing before he flew home to Ireland. Before 2001, airport security wasn't what it is now. He could have wrapped the picture up inside his checked luggage.'

'Do you still have the tape recording?'

Lauren patted her jacket pocket. The tape recorder with the cassette was not leaving her person until she was back in Buffalo. Thankfully, Quill had been satisfied with making a copy on his iPad back at the Garda station. She'd recorded it onto her phone at the same time. 'I do. I can email a copy. Maybe I'll call Sharon Whitney and play it for her after I talk to you.'

'Email it to me, but don't call her. Just send her a bill and if she doesn't pay you, sue her ass.'

'I like the way you think,' Lauren laughed. 'I'm not going to send her any bill. I'd rather she keep the rest of my fee. It's literally blood money now.'

'My supervisor ordered me to go and talk to both Mr and Mrs Whitney tomorrow, let them know it's been recovered, if it hasn't already made the news. I'll brief them on what happened over there and what's going to happen to the painting.'

'Neither one is going to be very happy,' Lauren said.

'Sharon Whitney is lucky the statute of limitations is up, both locally and federally. As it is, she's going to have to pay back her half of the three million the insurance company paid out to her and the ex.'

The hare heard something, sat straight up for a moment, then bounded into the hedges at the edge of the property.

'You know what? Sharon Whitney and her ex-husband have been sticking it to each other for over twenty years, and she tried to suck me into that toxic vortex.' Lauren could feel the anger bubbling up in her chest.

At the grim turn in her voice, his got kinder. 'There's still the reward money the FBI was offering for the painting. You're there as a private citizen. You'll be eligible for it.'

'Who donated that money in the first place? Mr Whitney?'

'I believe so, yes.'

Now she was shaking her head. 'That's a hard pass.'

'Enjoy a few days over there on her dime then. I'll handle things in Buffalo with her. We'll meet up and grab lunch when you get back home, OK?'

'OK.' She hoped the relief she felt hadn't seeped into her voice. If she called Sharon Whitney now she knew she'd lose her temper, say ugly things she'd regret, even if they were the truth. Matt volunteering to handle things was a huge weight lifted off her shoulders.

'And Riley,' he added, 'no media interviews, please.'

Again with the admonishments on media interviews. 'Really? Do you even know me at all?'

Now it was his turn to laugh. 'Sorry. What I was thinking? Have a good night and try to relax. You earned it.'

Lauren said goodbye and clicked off the line. She looked at the kitchen window again. She could see Reese regaling Mrs Fitzgerald with some tall tale, his arms flailing wildly around his head, her laughing with her hand on her chest. Lauren was just about to walk back inside when her phone vibrated in her hand.

Stopping dead, she looked at the caller ID: SHARON WHITNEY. Lauren swiped *Ignore* and tucked it into her back pocket. Stepping back into the warmth of Mrs Fitzgerald's kitchen, she asked Reese, 'What crazy story are you spinning now?'

FORTY-SEVEN

LAUREN RIFLED THROUGH the clothes she'd brought from home for almost twenty minutes before she finally settled on a pair of black pants topped with a long-sleeved, dark green blouse. She added the double butterfly necklace her daughters had bought her for Mother's Day the year before. She didn't know why she'd brought it. Lauren hardly wore any jewelry when she was working besides the same pair of gold stud earrings she'd had for at least ten years. She'd stuffed the little black velvet box in her makeup bag at the last second. Somehow, it made her feel close to her girls just then, and she vowed when she got home she was going to visit them at both of their respective campuses before school let out for the year.

By trying to keep herself busy, Lauren almost forgot how terribly she missed her girls. Almost. She'd raised them alone. Her first husband had never even seen Erin, her youngest. He'd taken off while she was pregnant, leaving her with Lindsey, who was an infant at the time, and no money. Somehow she'd kept the three of them alive. Although looking back now, she still couldn't figure out how she'd managed it. Taking care of Reese and Watson ate up a lot of her free time now, but it wasn't the same. She fingered the silver-and-crystal-encrusted necklace at her throat. No, it wasn't the same by a longshot.

Along with jewelry, Lauren also rarely wore makeup. Looking in the mirror above the dresser, she was afraid she'd apply too much and look like a clown, but she wanted to cover up the nasty burn on her cheek. After nearly poking her eye out with the mascara wand, she let it dry completely before putting her glasses back on. The last time she'd worn it, she put them on too quickly and ended up with black hash marks on her lenses that she couldn't get off, no matter how hard she scrubbed.

This is as good as it's going to get, she thought, combing her fingers through her hair.

After all the time she'd put into getting ready, Reese merely gave her a quick onceover when she came out of her room, then asked, 'How do I look in this hat? Old-world charming, right?' as he tipped it this way and that at his reflection in the picture window.

It was brown tweed and matched perfectly with a camel-colored sweater he'd put on over a white button-down shirt. A pair of khaki-colored pants completed the outfit, and even though she'd never tell him, he did look classically handsome. He already knew.

'I wonder how long it takes to get an Uber around here,' she replied, before something stupid popped out of her mouth. 'I feel like having some more of that whiskey you brought here the other night.'

'I'll refrain from drinking if you'd like to indulge yourself,' he offered.

'Let's just play it by ear,' she said, and glanced at herself in the same window Reese was preening into. She suppressed a smile. She thought she looked pretty good for the first time in a long time. Maybe too long. There was not caring how you looked to other people, and there was letting yourself go. Reese might have argued otherwise, but she felt like lately she was dangerously close to letting herself go. Not tonight. 'Ready?' she asked.

'Ready.'

FORTY-EIGHT

MRS FITZGERALD WAS meeting her husband at the pub. He'd gone early to help Robber senior set everything up after the local women cleaned, so Reese and Riley hopped in her car. Patches of the road were still wet from the night before. Lauren had seen on the local news there'd been some flooding in the low-lying areas of the county. Mrs Fitz had to drive through huge puddles every time there was a dip in the road.

The parking lot of Robber O'Shea's was full again. Only this time it was with modest economy cars and beat-up older model trucks instead of patrol vehicles and unmarked detective cars. Parking on the side of the road, they had to walk along a line of cars that had been forced to do the same thing.

People were clustered around the front door, off to either side, smoking or vaping, depending on how old they were. The howling gale from over the bay had been replaced by a stiff, cold wind, causing the smokers to cup their hands around their cigarettes as they tried to light them. One man, who looked to be about ninety, with deep lines etched in his face, was puffing on a pipe while a kid barely out of his teens held his lighter to the bowl, trying to light it.

The smokers and vapers parted and greeted Mrs Fitzgerald and her guests as they walked up. Reese even got a clap on the back as they crossed into the pub. The bar was three deep with mourners and every table was full. It looked to

Lauren like every resident in Keelnamara was there, from white-haired ladies in wheelchairs to rambunctious toddlers running between people's legs with their tired-looking mums following behind, trying to keep up. There was even a hound in the corner chewing on a piece of rawhide, while his owner, a pretty twentysomething, sat at the table next to him with a baby cradled in her arms, her husband rooting around for something in a pink diaper bag.

Almost every head in the bar swiveled to watch as they walked in, then turned back to their drinks and conversations just as quickly. Reese and Riley were the heroes of the day, but it was a day of mourning and the business of mourning in Keelnamara was remembering. And that's what the residents were doing, remembering Robber and Jimmy, not in the way they passed, but in the stories and tales of their lives.

Mrs Fitzgerald marched right over to a man bellied up to the bar, holding court with some younger folks. For some reason, Lauren had gotten it in her head that Mr Fitzgerald was a mammoth of a man. The reality was that he was even smaller than his wife. If she was an owl, he was a dormouse, with white bushy hair that surrounded a wispy bald head and bright little eyes. She waved the two of them over.

Declan, the young bartender who had relieved Robber the night they came in, was behind the bar. He wore a smile, but it didn't reach his eyes. He set two full pint glasses down for Reese and Riley before they even got to the bar, then moved on to pour shots of whiskey for a knot of men in the corner. One of them stood slump-shouldered, head down, gray curls tight to his head. It was Robber's father, there was no mistaking it. He stood surrounded by his lifelong friends, looking down into a half-empty pint glass, heartbroken. The elder Robber was the only person who hadn't looked up when they came in. Lauren's heart ached for his loss. She knew there were no words to comfort a mourning parent. The pain was too great. A chasm as big as the Grand Canyon had just been ripped into his life. It was a hole that would never be filled.

'I know you were thinking that I made him up out of thin air, but this is Mister Fitzgerald, himself!' Mrs Fitzgerald beamed, snapping Lauren out of her thoughts of Robber's father. Dropping her arm around the back of him, she propelled him forward to finally meet his house guests.

'Sean Fitzgerald.' He stuck out his hand. 'Pleased to finally make your acquaintance.'

Reese and Riley both shook his hand and said their hellos, then Lauren let Reese be pulled away by his new friends from the other night. Jacky had made a beeline for him with a couple of his mates, proclaiming Reese to be the American Sherlock Holmes. They clapped him on the back and called to Declan for shots of whiskey.

Lauren sipped her beer. It was dark and creamy and delicious and exactly what she needed right at that moment. She'd save her taste for whiskey for later. It was better for her to work her way up to it.

Not having made friends like Reese, and not having a line of ladies waiting to speak with her like Mrs Fitzgerald, Lauren hugged her free arm around her middle and drifted toward the far wall where someone had set up a poster board of photographs on a top table. Two pairs of women sat on either side of the display, so engrossed in their own conversations they didn't even look up when Lauren came and studied the pictures. Whoever had made the display at such short notice had done a wonderful job of capturing Robber's life—from the time he was a baby playing on the stony shore, to the one that looked like it was printed off a

Facebook page only a week or two before. There was no denying Robber had led a happy, cheerful life in Keelnamara.

In Lauren's American-big-city mind, Robber's rural, remote life in Ireland should have been *less* somehow. Less exciting, less memorable, less fulfilling. From the pictures that were posted, and if the love and admiration that filled the room was any indication, Robber's life had been more than most, not less. She reached out and touched a picture of him riding a horse on a beach, his curls blown back by the wind. Her fingertips traced the line of the shore.

'It's truly a sin, it is,' a voice from behind her said. 'Robber was a good man, just helping out a friend.'

Lauren turned to see Shamus Gorham standing behind her in a cheap blue suit, a rocks glass full of whiskey in his hand. 'They didn't hold you,' Lauren said, surprised. He always seemed to magically appear when you least expected it.

'On what charges? I was hired to nose around, same as you. Didn't break any laws.'

'I'm not well versed in Irish jurisprudence,' Lauren admitted, 'but it sure seemed like Detective Quill would have found a way to arrest you for something.'

'Ahh,' he said, then held his index finger out while he took a long drink of his whiskey. 'He'd have happily charged me with simple trespassing, if he could've proved it. We're not like you Yankee police. We stick to the letter of the law around these parts.'

'Is that what got you fired?'

Now he wagged that same finger at her with a crooked smile. 'You're a quick one, you are. I chose my bride over the job. I'd do it again too.'

There was something earnest in the way he said that. Like loving his wife was his number one priority. For the first time Lauren noticed the gleaming gold band on his left hand. Maybe it touched her because her own two ex-husbands had never felt that way about her. As hard as she had worked to be the perfect wife and mom, she'd been expendable to both of them. Whatever his wife had been into and had gotten him involved with, he gave up the Garda for her and had no regrets.

'She must be quite a woman,' Lauren said.

'That she is. It's too bad she had a headache this evening. I'd have loved for you to meet her.' He held out his rocks glass and Lauren clinked hers to it. 'Cheers.'

'Cheers.' She tipped her head back and drank to the crooked cop's crooked wife. She wiped her mouth with the back of her hand, not very lady-like, but it was better than wearing a Guinness mustache. 'You've been watching Jimmy Breen for Howard Whitney for over twenty years,' she said. 'Why didn't you ever search his house?'

'Who says I didn't? I know very well how to pick a lock. And I know enough not to leave fingerprints or any trace behind. I must have taken the back off that stupid picture ten times over the years. It never occurred to me that the canvas was in the backing.'

'It would've been better for Jimmy if you had found it.' Wrapping her arm around her midsection, she leaned against the wall next to the photo display, hoping Gorham didn't notice her wincing.

'For Robber and Jimmy both,' he agreed.

'What will you do now that the painting has been located? Collect your million from Mr Whitney?'

He snorted. 'Do you really think Howard Whitney is going to give me a million dollars? I was happy enough sending him pictures of me searching Jimmy's place every once in a while, emailing him an embellished surveillance report that had him meeting with shady characters. I got my check every month, that was enough for me. I believe he'll send me just enough to keep my trap shut and not a penny more.'

'That's always the problem when a case is over,' Lauren agreed. 'Your client has no incentive to pay you anymore.'

'Victims become villains and villains become victims,' Gorham said. 'One day you're helping them, the next you're chasing after them. It's human nature, love.'

'It's hard to think of Howard Whitney as the victim in all this,' Lauren admitted.

'I knew what kind of man Mr Whitney was when he hired me. I also knew things were going to go bad once Martin McGrath came home.' He tapped his nose with his finger. 'A criminal knows a criminal. I didn't think he'd kill his own uncle, though. Mr Whitney was not happy when I rang him up to report Jimmy's demise.'

'Hey, Riley! Come over here and tell my friends that story about us chasing that guy through the Buffalo Irish Festival on St Patrick's Day four years ago,' Reese called to her from the bar where he was surrounded by men and women alike hanging on his every word.

'In a minute,' she called back. She had one more question for Shamus Gorham. 'What happened between you and Detective Quill? Why was he so hot that you were the killer?'

'Well now,' his shoulders lifted up to his ears and he gave her a fake sheepish grin, 'he could've made a big drug bust when we worked together in Dublin, got loads and loads of cocaine. He could've made a big arrest with it too. Only the drugs disappeared from the evidence lock-up and the suspect walked. That bust could've made his career. He could've gone right to a cushy desk job at our headquarters.'

'That's a lot of could'ves,' Lauren pointed out.

'It is. If only the evidence hadn't vanished,' he lamented.

'That was a long time ago,' Lauren said. 'Before they had cameras on evidence rooms?'

'Right!' He laughed, snapping his fingers, then said dramatically, 'The evidence room was practically screaming to be robbed.'

'And you know how to pick locks.'

'Why pick a lock when you already have all the keys, love?'

She had to smile with him. 'Do I have to ask who was arrested with the drugs?'

'My lovely bride was railroaded, as you Yanks like to say. She hails from a rather infamous Dublin family. Sins of the father, and all that. Quill fancied her, followed her all over creation for ages, got caught peeking in her windows. Surveillance, my arse! Even after he arrested her, he couldn't stay away from her.'

'She sounds like she really had a pull over him.'

'She's gorgeous, she is. Quill never got over her and he certainly never got over her carrying on with me.' He sighed at the memory of it. 'Time and age have mended her wild ways, but we Irish know how to hold a grudge.' He put his empty rocks glass down on the table. 'Did you know that my grandparents were married for fifty-two years, but didn't speak a word to each other the last twenty-five years of their lives? Not one word. I think I've given Quill even more reason to come after me, now that I saved you and your partner's lives and helped recover that fecking painting. I think he wanted to be the hero of this story.'

Lauren held up her mostly empty glass in a toast to him. 'At least you and your wife get to ride off into the sunset together, even if Mr Whitney doesn't come through with your fortune.'

'Riley! Come on! I'm at the part where you had to cuff the guy dressed like a leprechaun,' Reese called out in jolly exasperation, waving her over. 'You tell it better than me.'

'Don't you know, love?' Gorham motioned around at the room full of Keelnamara residents talking, drinking and laughing. 'This is the sunset, right here. Keelnamara is the pot of gold at the end of the rainbow.' He gave her a wink and wandered off into the crowd humming the tune to 'The Parting Glass' as he went.

FORTY-NINE

'WHAT'S A TRIP to Ireland without a visit to a castle?' Reese asked, hands on his hips, looking over the ruins of Wynne's Folly outside of Glenbeigh. They'd just gotten back from walking the beach at Rossbeigh Strand. The temperature hovered in the low sixties and the sun kept peeking out from behind the clouds, making it one of the nicest days they'd had since they'd gotten to Ireland.

Scannell had promised them the night before, just as they'd finished shots of Powers whiskey in the pub, that he would take them to see the sights the next morning. Lauren and Reese had agreed. The alcohol had continued to flow freely until Robber's father decided to close for the night. It was a good thing they didn't have a car because neither Reese nor Lauren were in any shape to drive back to the Fitzgeralds', who'd left hours earlier. Luckily, one of Reese's newfound friends was on antibiotics for a nasty puncture wound he'd got cutting fishing lines, and drove them home squashed into the front seat of his ancient pickup truck.

Scannell had been good to his word, showing up at the guesthouse bright and early, waking them, then waiting for the hungover pair to get ready. Quill had given Scannell the day off to take them around, while he and his team of detectives tied up loose ends. 'I don't mind it,' Scannell had told Lauren as he sipped some tea in their kitchen, waiting for Reese to get out of the shower. 'Between me and you, Quill is a bit of a tosser.'

Lauren bit back the urge to agree, only nodding her head in acknowledgment of the comment. She wondered what the patrol officers said about her back home in the States. She was pretty sure it was a lot less kind than 'tosser'.

Once Reese was finished with his marathon shower, they filed into Scannell's car for the dime tour of County Kerry. Lauren was grateful Scannell had followed through on his promise, even though her head was throbbing and her stomach heaved every time they hit a bump in the road. From the way Reese kept pulling his borrowed cap down over his eyes, he was feeling the after-effects of the whiskey as well.

'It does have an interesting history,' Scannell told them. 'A Brit named Lord Headley had it built in 1867. During World War One it was rented out to the British Military for a training center. It was burned by the Irish Republican Army during the Irish Civil War in 1921, and here it stands to this day.'

Lauren gazed up at the gray brick shell of a structure as she stood outside of Scannell's personal vehicle across the road, thinking on how it mirrored the modern abandoned resort just a few miles away. *People build magnificent things and then walk away from them when they're no longer of use or not worth the money to fix*, she thought. *Yet Jimmy Breen brought a small piece of canvas to Keelnamara, hid it away, and people were willing to kill for it.*

'Can we walk around inside?' Reese asked.

Scannell shook his head. He was leaning his pear-shaped frame against the car, arms crossed. 'Sorry, we can't. They've been doing maintenance on it to keep the walls from collapsing, trying to preserve it. This is as close as we get.'

'No worries.' Lauren was good with that. She had had enough of being inside abandoned buildings for a lifetime.

'Do you want to go over to the cemetery in Cromane? I can show you the old church ruins. Legend has it, Cromwell's men ripped the roof off of it.'

'Hell no,' popped out of Reese's mouth before he could stop himself. Reese had a serious phobia of cemeteries. He'd once told Lauren he wanted to be cremated and have his ashes scattered in Iceland, even though he'd never been there. As luck, or in Lauren's case, unluck, would have it, she fell into the investigation that took her to Iceland and told him he might want to rethink that position. He hadn't come up with an alternative yet, except to say that if he died and she buried him, he'd come back and haunt her for all time. Her response was that he already haunted her.

'Have you talked to your bosses back home yet?' Scannell asked.

'Let's go to that shop you were telling us about,' Lauren deflected. She didn't want to talk or even think about the police department just then. Or about the fact that given all the breathing problems she'd had since she'd been in Ireland, maybe they were right to want to retire her. 'The one where they make the sweaters from the sheep right there on the farm.'

'It's a little ways to the south, about half an hour. Mary Margaret Brennan runs the shop. She should be in today. The farm has been in her family for a hundred years. She handles the business end and her husband and sons work the farm and take care of the livestock.'

Sheep farming, mussel dredging, and running bed and breakfasts, Lauren thought as she climbed into the backseat, letting Reese sit up front. *It's not a bad life here on the coast of Ireland. No one's in a hurry, no one's trying to keep up with the Joneses. I could get used to this.*

Reese twisted around in his seat to ask her, 'Did you change the plane tickets?'

'While you were in the shower. Our flight leaves from Dublin day after tomorrow at six a.m.'

'Bollocks. I hate early morning flights.'

'Bollocks? Is Scannell here rubbing off on you?' she teased.

Scannell grinned at her in the rearview mirror. 'Reese and I had an in-depth conversation last night about the many different ways to weave the word *bollocks* into a conversation. It's as versatile as the way you Yankees use the word fu—'

Lauren held up a hand, cutting him off and laughing at the same time. 'I get it. And from what I heard in the pub last night, we don't have a monopoly on the f-bomb.'

'You'll both be well versed in the Irish and their slang when you leave here,' he assured her, putting the car into gear.

'That'll be grand,' she replied, using one of Mrs Fitzgerald's favorite expressions.

'T'will,' he agreed, exaggerating his accent as he pulled onto an even narrower road than the one that ran through Keelnamara.

They didn't get back to the Fitzgeralds' house until after five o'clock. Their host had a meal of mussels and potatoes set out for them when they arrived. The previous few days had been such a blur that it was a comfort and relief to have a home-cooked dinner. When they lowered themselves into the chairs at the kitchen table, they ate, drank tea, and let themselves relax. Everything had happened in such a whirlwind that neither Reese nor Riley had had any time to process it all.

Now, in Mrs Fitzgerald's warm, cozy kitchen, the weight of the events seemed to come down on them all at once. Lauren felt so bone-tired she could barely keep her eyes open.

The buzzing of Reese's cell made her eyes snap open. It was a reflex now. They both kept their phones on vibrate and when she heard one of them go off, she snapped to attention, thinking work was calling. 'I better get this,' Reese said, finally swiping the *Accept* bar on his screen and walking out into the backyard, like Lauren had done when she'd spoken to Matt Lawton.

'He's such a fine man,' Mrs Fitzgerald commented. 'It's a shame you both are unmarried. You should come back and visit during the matchmaking festival.'

Between her best friend Dayla and her two daughters, she had enough matchmakers in her life. 'I think I'd rather come back for the horse races on the beach in Glenbeigh, or the Puck Fair.'

'The races are absolutely grand, and you'd enjoy Puck,' she agreed. 'It does get crowded in Killorglin during the fair, though, and it can get a little wild. They have to bring Gardai in from all over because of the crowds.'

'Will you have a vacancy for me if I show up?'

The skin around her eyes crinkled as she smiled. 'Always.'

'All set,' Reese said, closing the door behind him. Lauren noticed his face was flushed.

After thanking their host for the great meal, they gathered up all the bags containing the gifts they'd bought at the farm: Aran sweaters for Erin and Lindsey, wool socks for Dayla. Reese had bought two new hats for himself, while Lauren had splurged on a gorgeous cape she was sure she'd only ever wear once a year when she pulled it out of the closet and twirled around in front of her bedroom mirror in it.

Excusing themselves, they walked back to the guest-house.

'Are you OK?' Lauren asked as Reese used his key to unlock the door. His color had returned but he still seemed a little off since the phone call.

'What? Me? Yeah, just a little tired, I guess.' He shouldered it open, dropping his shopping bags inside. Without another word he walked to his room, with Lauren following to hers. She deposited her purchases on the dresser and promptly went to bed, even though it was barely past dinnertime.

We're both exhausted. Her last thought before sleep overcame her was *We'll talk in the morning. Whatever is wrong can wait.*

FIFTY

THE SLAMMING OF a door woke Lauren out of a sound sleep. The waning afternoon sunlight that warmed the room had been replaced with a murky twilight. Glancing at the digital alarm clock on the nightstand, she groaned inwardly. It was eight o'clock. She wouldn't fall asleep until the wee hours of the morning now.

The stillness of the house seemed to hit her all at once. She smoothed her shirt over her jeans and grabbed her windbreaker from the back of the chair. 'Reese?' she called, stepping out into the hallway. His door was open, light on, but the room was empty.

Lauren felt her eyebrows draw together. She made her way into the kitchen to see the screen door closed but the back door open. From outside she could hear the sounds of the night critters waking up, different from home but still familiar somehow. She pulled her jacket over her head and walked outside.

The lights were on up in Mrs Fitzgerald's house, smoke curled from the chimney and the now familiar scent of burning peat filled her nose. She pictured the couple sitting in front of the fire, sipping their evening tea. Lauren knew Reese wasn't there.

She followed the fading light down the garden path to the gravel road toward the rocky beach, hugging her arms to her chest against the wind that had kicked up. As soon as she cleared the tall grass, she saw a silhouette against the retreating surf. Even from a distance she'd know Reese anywhere.

She stepped carefully onto the rocky beach. She wasn't trying to mask her approach. Round rocks slid and brittle branches snapped under her feet. Reese must have heard her coming, but he didn't turn around. He just stood staring off into the sea, both of his hands stuffed into the front pockets of his jeans.

Stepping up next to him so that they were shoulder to shoulder, but not touching, Lauren said, 'I heard you leave.'

He nodded once, looking up and down the deserted beach. 'I wanted to watch the sunset.' When she didn't respond he went on, 'It sure is pretty here.'

'It is.'

They let the comfort of familiarity surround them in silence for a few minutes. Lauren's short dark hair tossed in the wind, while Reese's Irish hat miraculously stayed perched on his scarred head.

'Do you get the feeling we should be holding hands right now?' Reese asked, eyes on the water.

In that moment, standing shoulder to shoulder, watching the sun dip into the bay, Lauren felt like they were the only two people on the planet.

'Have you ever felt like holding my hand?' she asked, staring straight ahead at the pinks and oranges of the sunset, not unlike the colors of the painting they'd risked their lives over. The painting that had cost two other people theirs.

The receding tide left bits of seaweed, driftwood and shells scattered in front of them. A few stray gulls circled lazily in the sky overhead.

'Every minute since the day I met you.'

A long pause stretched out between them, neither knowing what the right thing to say next was. There are only a few moments in a person's life when they can actually feel the dynamics of a relationship shift in a monumental way. When they recognize that a definitive line has been crossed and there's no way to go back. A tightness filled Lauren's chest. It seemed like they were teetering on some kind of ledge. Or cliff.

'So what happens now?' she asked.

Turning to look at his face, she saw the apples of his caramel-colored cheeks were flushed pink from the wind. His green eyes were rimmed in red.

'Charlotte is pregnant.'

And just like that, all of her fragile hopes, her pushed-aside daydreams, were dashed against the rocks like waves crashing into the shore.

'That's a good thing, right?' she finally ventured, realizing she'd been holding her breath. 'You always said you wanted to be a dad.'

'It is a good thing.' His voice was a whisper that was barely audible. 'It's a great thing.' He looked away from her, back to the water. 'It's funny how one phone call can change your entire life.'

Lauren swallowed hard, searching for the right thing to say. 'I like Charlotte a lot. She's going to make a great mom and you're going to make a fantastic father. You'll have someone to play catch with besides Watson.'

'She has a fiancé,' he said, like she hadn't spoken at all. 'They got back together right after we stopped doing…' he fumbled for words, 'whatever it was we were doing.' Lauren remembered Reese telling her it was over between them before it had even really begun, because Charlotte wasn't over her ex. She tried to remember how long ago that conversation had been. Months.

'When is the baby due?'

He let out a stuttering breath. 'Lauren, she's eight months along. She only told me because the fiancé made her. She wants him to adopt the baby. And she wants me to sign off on it.'

Eight months. The baby would be here any minute. Reese's baby. 'What did you say to that?'

'I said no, of course.'

She threw out a half-hearted joke. 'So I won't have much time to get you a baby gift when we get home.'

'Don't,' he said, his voice cracking. 'Please don't. Not now. This is not how I wanted to find out I was going to be a father. Because I do want to be a dad. Not part-time. All the time. And not because some other guy is forcing the mother to do the right thing.'

'I've got news for you, Reese,' she said, catching his eyes with hers. 'You will be a dad all the time. You will be that baby's father forever. It may not have happened the way you wanted it to, but I promise you, that child will be the best thing you ever did.'

Now he let out a soft laugh that sounded more like a sob. 'I know I don't give you credit for anything unless it's unavoidable, but you've always been a hell of a mom. I know it's a lot to ask, but I'm really going to need your help. I have no idea what to do next.'

Remembering how afraid she'd been when she found out she was pregnant at eighteen, she felt a lump swelling in her throat. She'd been terrified to tell her parents, scared to tell her future ex-husband, afraid of what her friends and family would think. She knew the worry and anxiety Reese was going through and how alone he felt. And she knew that now was not the time to even consider any kind of romantic relationship with him. 'I'm here, Reese. I'll always be here for you. Just like you've always been there for me. We'll figure it out.'

She tried to decipher the look in his eyes as she slipped her hand into his. Love? Gratitude? Fear? A mix of all three? His hand was warm and dry as he squeezed it tight. 'Thank you.'

It wasn't the way she'd wanted it to happen or for the reason she'd imagined, but it was good.

They both turned back and caught the last instant before the sun slipped beneath the water.

FIFTY-ONE

THEY WALKED BACK to the guesthouse in silence, holding hands until they reached the door. When they let go, their fingers brushed for just an instant and Lauren felt the raw emotion of the last hour draining away. She knew once they went inside that they'd go to their separate bedrooms without speaking, and even though it was just past sundown, they wouldn't emerge until it was time for breakfast the next morning.

And that's exactly what happened.

What was there to say about the situation? Lauren thought as she stared at the ceiling from her bed. She listened for the sound of Reese's snoring but all she heard was the ticking of the clock. She pictured him lying in bed doing the same thing she was doing. *If this isn't a sign that we are not meant to be a couple, I don't know what is.*

She took comfort in the fact that he wanted her in his life, that he needed her. Romance and sex weren't everything. She'd learned that the hard way. *They were barely anything, if you really thought about it*, she told herself. She hadn't had a lover since her disastrous affair with her ex-husband had fallen apart two and a half years before. She'd come close, gone on plenty of dates, only to break things off before they got physical. Reese, on the other hand, had a string of physical relationships which he'd broken off before they'd gotten emotional. And now here they were, together but so far apart they might as well be on opposite sides of the planet, instead of across the hall from each other.

Lauren knew she'd continue to be there for Reese, no matter what. That wasn't even in dispute. She'd make sure his baby had its own room in her house and help him get it ready. She'd make sure his baby had a highchair and a playpen and teething rings and diaper cream. She'd teach him how to hold the baby and burp him or her. Hopefully, Charlotte would let him have a say in the naming process. Maybe there'd be a Shane Reese junior.

A smile dusted her lips. She'd had her babies, raised them by herself and now they were off, out in the world. Getting the chance to be along for this ride with Reese was beyond special. She was about to share with him the things she'd had to do all alone. Having her daughters was by far the best thing she'd ever done in her life. She used to imagine having someone she loved by her side who loved her daughters too, watching them reach all their milestones. That would have been better than any rose-petal-strewn sheets or diamond rings.

She knew when she and Reese woke up in the morning, they wouldn't talk about what had almost happened between them. They wouldn't discuss it again until they got home, and probably not even then. They'd go back to Buffalo, bury their feelings for each other and get on with their lives. They'd hash together a plan for the baby, talking it out, brainstorming, until they came up with solutions and answers, because together that's how they got stuff done. She'd do everything she could to pass her physical and he'd help her. She'd go back to work and they'd dig into the Henderson case. He'd call her Big Bird and she'd remind him to not chew like a cow.

It wasn't perfect, but it was how partners did things.

FIFTY-TWO

'I'M SO GLAD you decided to meet with me, my dear.' Always the gentleman, Howard Whitney stood when Lauren walked in.

'I almost didn't,' she admitted, still hovering near the doorway of his private office at his lakeside estate. 'I don't know what we have to talk about.'

'Please,' he motioned to the chair in front of his desk. 'Have a seat.'

She knew she shouldn't be there. Her involvement in the case, with the painting, and with both him and his ex-wife, was over. She wanted to leave it that way. She and Reese had been home from Ireland for two weeks, and they'd been busy getting things ready for Reese's baby. The impending arrival had eclipsed everything else in their lives. Still, she was curious. She'd gotten the call from him that morning, while she and Reese were trying to figure out the instructions on how to put the bassinet together. She'd known the call would come eventually; she had actually thought it would come much sooner.

'Don't answer it,' Reese warned. 'Don't get sucked into more drama.'

Of course she'd answered it, and here she was, at Whitney's estate, in a room that looked like it was straight out of a 1960s James Bond movie. Stuffed trophy animals were mounted all over the walls. Pictures of him standing over the poor animals he'd traveled across the world to slaughter covered the spaces in between. A giant lion's head was positioned directly over his desk. Just looking at the poor magnificent beast turned her stomach. To top it off, Howard sat behind a huge mahogany desk, an unlit cigar clamped between his fingers. The only things missing were a white suit, straw hat and a string tie. She was just waiting for someone to stick their head in the door and call him *Boss*.

He picked up on her distaste, seemed to revel in it. *He and his ex-wife like to live like walking clichés*, she noted, wondering if they were ever genuine about anything, except maybe their mutual greed.

'I think I'll stand.' She'd noticed that the seat was covered in a leopard-skin fabric. At least she hoped it was fabric.

'Whatever makes you comfortable,' he said, fingers caressing the intricate carving at the end of the armrest on his elaborate chair. 'Can I get you anything? A drink, perhaps?'

She shook her head. 'How about we talk about why you asked me here?'

'Right to the point. I do like you, Miss Riley.' He gave her a smile of straight white veneers. 'I wanted to thank you in person for the good work you did in Ireland.'

'I wasn't working for you,' she reminded him. But she knew that wasn't strictly true. Shamus Gorham had reported Jimmy's death immediately to him, and Lauren was sure it was Howard Whitney who'd put Shamus up to calling his ex-wife. How else would Shamus have gotten Sharon's number? He'd orchestrated everything from the very beginning. Howard Whitney had played every single one of them.

'Don't I know it.' He leaned forward, palms splayed flat on the desk. 'You could have run off with the painting. You could have taken Shamus Gorham up on his offer. And yet you still turned my Picasso over to the authorities, knowing my ex-wife wasn't going to give you another dime.'

You knew that about me five minutes after I left your house. You made sure I was the type to not take the painting. What would you have had Gorham do to me once I got to Ireland if I was? she wondered. 'It's called integrity. After Jimmy Breen's death was declared a murder, it wasn't about your wall decoration for me anymore. No piece of art is worth a man's life.'

'That's a point I'd love to debate you on some other time,' he said.

She smirked at the offer. 'I think I'm busy that day.'

'You wouldn't have come here today if you weren't curious. That's what gets people like you and me in trouble, isn't it? Our curiosity.'

'That may be true,' she agreed, 'but I'm nothing like you.'

He pointed his cigar at her, smile never faltering. 'Don't be so sure about that.' He stood up and came around the front of his desk, arms out in a sort of surrendering gesture. 'I'm not the enemy here. I was brutally assaulted and robbed by my ex-wife. And yet you paint me with the same brush as her.'

'No pun intended, right?'

'I understand where your judgments are coming from. You see two people who once loved each other engaged in a decades-long battle over what's essentially nothing. To you. For people like my ex-wife and myself, we find art eternal. It transcends any one owner. People will be admiring and marveling over that painting for generations to come. I probably won't live to see the matter get settled, so I wanted you to know I've already willed the painting to the granddaughter you met on your last visit here. She appreciates art as much as I do. Maybe more.'

While it gave her some pleasure to know that Kelsey, who had impressed her as kind and intelligent when they met, might be the recipient of the painting, Lauren wasn't in the mood for Whitney's lectures on the timelessness of art. 'I apologize if I seem callous to you. I am sorry you were victimized. I'm glad the painting isn't hidden away and lost forever, but I don't want your money. I just want to convince the police department I'm healthy and get back to work.'

'You won't take the reward money,' he said, not acknowledging her apologies, 'so I found another way to thank you.'

For some reason, the way he said that made her chest tighten. 'That's not necessary.'

He went on, 'When you go back for your follow-up physical, you'll pass. I've seen to it.'

Lauren's mind flipped to her struggling for breath in the back of Scannell's patrol car and Reese's hand on her shoulder blades, trying to calm her. 'I'll either pass or fail, there's nothing you can do unless you want to give me a lung.'

He held up his cigar. 'I don't think you'd want one of mine. Besides, it's been taken care of. You'll get your job back and the district attorney and mayor will keep their hands out of it.'

She crossed her arms over her chest to hide its quickening rise and fall. She didn't want to let him know he was getting to her. 'They finally have a legitimate chance to get rid of me, why wouldn't they take it?'

'Favors, my dear. People owe me favors.'

'I don't want to be one of the people who owe you favors,' she stressed.

'I should think this will make us even.' He sat back down in his chair, putting the unlit cigar in a heavy glass ashtray. Folding his hands neatly in front of him, he said, 'You'll pass your physical this year. Next year, I cannot say. That's up to you.'

One thing Lauren had learned on the job was that there was no such thing as *no strings attached*. If he was just being altruistic, Howard Whitney would have called in his favors and she would never have known about it. She would have gone to her follow-up and miraculously passed. She knew that sometime in the future, could be a year, could be two, he'd want something from her, and just as easily as he'd made her pass, he could make her fail again. And he wanted her to know it.

'I don't know what to say to that.'

'For once, she has no witty comeback.' He was reveling in the position he'd put her in. 'The local FBI office is going to have a press conference later today. I was invited to attend. They can't release the painting to me, but they are going to thank the Irish national police for recovering it.' She'd heard about the press conference on the radio as she was driving to his estate. They'd made no mention of her and Reese's involvement.

As if he'd read her mind, he added, 'I imagine all the intrigue with Jimmy and my ex-wife and you will come out during the civil proceedings.'

'Another round of court battles for you and Sharon. How fun.'

He chuckled at that last comment. 'Would you like to be my special guest today? See the Picasso up close?'

The last thing she wanted to do was to be anywhere near that cursed piece of canvas. Lauren felt herself inching toward the door. 'If you'll excuse me, I have some errands to run. Thank you for enlightening me on your behind-the-scenes work on my behalf.'

He waved it off. 'It's the least I can do for you.'

Or the most, you manipulative prick, she thought as she put her hand on the doorknob. 'I'd better go now. Have a great day, Mr Whitney.'

'It was lovely to see you and thanks again for all you did.' He didn't get up from his seat. 'We'll talk soon, I'm sure of it.'

Unfortunately, Lauren was sure of it too.

FIFTY-THREE

LAUREN STEPPED OUT onto the wide expanse of Howard Whitney's front porch. The breeze from the lake ruffled her hair, but there was no salt smell, no fishing boats bobbing offshore, just sail boats trying to catch the wind on a gray, cloudy day.

She'd taken Sharon Whitney's case because she'd been tired of the emotional drain of investigating unsolved homicides. In her head, she knew there had been some arrogance on her part, the thought that *this was just a painting, how hard could it be?* Two homicides later, all she wanted to do was concentrate on Reese and his forthcoming baby. In a way she was glad she was on leave, she really was tired of death and murders. She wanted to concentrate on new life.

She got into her Ford Escape and headed back toward the city. She had one more stop to make.

The painters had finished the spare room the day before in a gorgeous shade of pastel green. Reese had met with Charlotte and her fiancé the day after they'd gotten home. He was convinced she was having a baby girl. Lauren had seen Charlotte just yesterday, when she stopped over to look at the room they were converting into the nursery, and thought from the way she was carrying that she was having a boy. Lauren had blown up like a balloon with both her pregnancies. Charlotte had a perfectly round little bump that she cradled as she inspected the changing table. She and her fiancé seemed happy and agreeable, as they poked around the baby's room and glanced at each other in approval. Lauren hoped for Reese's and the baby's sake that they could continue to maintain the amicable relationship. In her gut, though, she knew that was easier said than done. Charlotte and Reese were basically strangers.

Lauren's own daughters would be done with exams in a week and would both be home to help plan the shower and get things ready. Reese hadn't wanted a baby shower, but Lindsey and Erin insisted, and he could never say no to them. Lauren had helped him put items on his registry the night before, explaining that even though the baby wouldn't need a lot of the things right away, you had no idea when you would need them so it was better to have them ready. Watching him pick out a stuffed elephant, she could see the spark of excitement in his face.

She made her way back to North Buffalo, to the mansions on Nottingham Terrace, so different from the humble cottages of County Kerry. Pulling into Sharon Whitney's circular drive, Lauren hoped her ex-client was home. She hadn't bothered to call and check.

She rang the bell and waited, no longer having the urge to touch the fancy door. She heard footsteps coming toward her and a tall man in his early sixties with receding but neatly combed gray hair opened the door. He wore a navy blue blazer over a collared shirt and gray pants. For some reason the outfit reminded Lauren of an airline steward. 'May I help you?'

'I need to talk to Sharon Whitney.'

'I'm afraid she's indisposed at the moment. If you leave your name and number with me—'

Lauren stepped forward, causing him to almost stumble back as he got out of her way. 'I'm Lauren Riley. She'll want to talk with me. I'll wait here until she's done being indisposed.'

'Miss, I'm afraid I'm going to have to ask you to leave.' There was real panic in his voice, as if in all his years working as Mrs Whitney's assistant, or whatever he was, he'd never had anyone defy his requests.

'I think I'm OK right here.' She crossed her arms over her chest. 'Why don't you go and get her. Tell her I'm here and I have something for her.'

He looked toward the sitting room and back at Lauren, still unsure of how to proceed. As he opened his mouth to say something, Sharon Whitney's voice filled the foyer. 'It's all right, Peter. I can take it from here. Can you go check on my dinner reservations for tonight and make sure they added two more people to the guest list?' She appeared in the doorway off to the right, where she hung in the frame, as if she was leery of getting too close to Lauren. 'Please.'

He looked from his employer to Lauren and back again before nodding. 'Very good, Mrs Whitney. Call for me if you need anything.'

He thinks I'm going to physically attack her, Lauren mused at the ridiculousness of it. *She thinks so too.*

'What can I do for you, Miss Riley?' she asked, leaning against the door frame. That was as close as she was going to get. As if to try to appear unbothered and in control, she mirrored Lauren's posture, folding her arms over her cream-colored boat neck sweater.

'I wanted to make sure you got this back.' Lauren reached into her jacket pocket and pulled out the original check Sharon Whitney had given her. She held it up, so Sharon could see it, then tore it to shreds and let the pieces fall to the floor.

'Did that make you feel better?' Sharon asked, not budging from her spot.

'Not really. What would make me feel better would be to see you in jail.'

That laugh like the tinkling of bells came out. 'My lawyers assure me that's not going to happen, despite your little tape recording.'

'I've always believed justice gets served in a variety of ways,' Lauren countered. 'Your greed and spite indirectly cost two men their lives. I know now you hired me and sent me off so quickly because Jimmy was in the process of arranging to get that painting back to you when he was murdered. It was almost in your hands.' Lauren pinched two fingers together, leaving an inch of space between them. 'You were this close. And now you'll never get your hands on it, ever.'

'You think that's a win for you?'

Lauren shrugged. 'I know at least it's not one for you. Those people in Keelnamara didn't deserve the anguish you set in motion by hiring Jimmy to steal that painting. You tried to use him to kill your ex-husband and got double-crossed. You tried to use me when Jimmy got killed for it. Poor Robber Shea got sucked into something he didn't fully understand and got slaughtered.' Lauren suppressed the image of Robber taped to that office chair soaked in his own blood. 'I'd like to think karma will step in at some point and you'll get what you deserve.'

'Not everyone gets what they deserve.' Sharon Whitney smiled and picked a piece of lint off her pale pink skirt, fluttering her fingers so it fell to the ground with the ripped-up pieces of the check. 'Certainly you haven't.'

More threats, Lauren thought, catching the icy cold amused look in the woman's eyes. She reached behind her and grabbed the doorknob. 'I wouldn't be so smug if I were you. You still have to pay the insurance company back the one and a half million dollars they paid out, and I have it on good authority the IRS is looking into your finances and tax records.' The smile on Sharon's face vanished immediately. 'You've been involved in some shady art dealings that sure do look like money laundering. Oh, and I wouldn't try and use your credit card today, I'm pretty certain all your accounts have been frozen.'

Sharon Whitney took a step forward, eyes wide and mouth opening to say something, but Lauren cut her off. 'It's not even close to what you deserve, but it's a damn good start.'

Lauren strode out of the mansion into the driveway and turned her face up to the sky as she walked to her car. It was still cloudy and overcast. *Victims become villains and villains turn out to be victims sometimes*, the thought echoed through her head.

Hopping into her car, she headed for home, where Reese was waiting with a crib mobile he'd ordered online that needed to be assembled.

So much for being tough homicide detectives. A smile crept across her face as she cruised along the city streets. Then a pain in her side flared up and she gripped the steering wheel a little harder. The pain was getting worse, not better, even with physical therapy. *And so much for being through with Sharon and Howard Whitney*.

She's going to be too busy losing every cent she has trying to get that painting back to worry about me. The pain was throbbing now. Lauren was clutching her ribs, bent over the wheel. *Mr Whitney is the one I have to watch out for. There's something else he wants, he's just biding his time until he springs it on me.*

I can't worry about that now, she told herself as her own gated neighborhood came into view. The late May sunshine broke through the clouds, dividing the overcast sky. *That'll be a story for another day.*

* * * * *

ACKNOWLEDGMENTS

WRITING A BOOK is a lonely process, but then comes the tricky part—taking that lump of a manuscript and shaping it into the finished book. I would not have been able to write this story without the help of Stephen, Caitriona and Maoliosa Scales. Thank you for all the FaceTime chats, text messages, and emails. You helped me bring my little Irish townland to life on the pages.

I owe a huge debt of gratitude to John Galvin, an extraordinary writer who happens to be a retired Garda. Thank you for all your help, your pages of notes, and for putting up with email after email of questions. Because of the nature of writing fiction, any mistakes in Irish police procedure are definitely mine and not his.

A very special thank you goes to Robert Wittman. Your input was invaluable. You took the time to answer every question, let me run every scenario by you and patiently explained the nuances of investigating art theft. Your generosity is amazing, and I am truly grateful to you. If my book is one tenth as interesting as your real life, I've succeeded. Once again, any mistakes in art theft investigation in this book are mine, not his.

Thank you to my agent Bob Mecoy and my editors at Severn House—Carl Smith and Natasha Bell. I know I can drive you crazy with my flurry of emails. I'm still getting the hang of this writer thing. Until I do, thanks for your patience with me.

To my first readers—Joyce Maguda, Pat Carrington, and Michael Breen—I don't know where I'd be without you guys. Thank you!

The support I've received from the Western New York community has been overwhelming. From libraries, to book clubs, to bookstores and local groups, everyone has cheered me on. I am truly blessed to live here.

There aren't enough words to thank my husband Dan, or my children, Mary and Natalie. At the end of the day, you three are all that matter.

Thank you, God. Every day is a gift.